SHADES OF GREENE

Graham Greene was born in 1904 and educated at Berkhamsted School, where his father was headmaster. On graduating from Balliol College, Oxford University, where he published a book of verse, he worked for three years as a subeditor on *The Times* (London). He established his reputation with his fourth novel, *Stamboul Train*, which he classed as an 'entertainment,' in order to distinguish it from more serious work. In 1935 he made a journey across Liberia, described in *Journey without Maps*, and on his return was appointed film critic of the *Spectator*. In 1926 he had been received into the Roman Catholic Church, and he was commissioned to visit Mexico in 1938 and report on the religious persecution there. As a result he wrote *The Lawless Roads* and, later, *The Power and the Glory*.

Brighton Rock was published in 1938, and in 1940 he became literary editor of the *Spectator*. The next year he undertook work for the British Foreign Office and was sent to Sierra Leone in 1941–3. One of his major postwar novels, *The Heart of the Matter*, is set in West Africa and is considered by many to be his finest book. This was followed by *The End of the Affair*, *The Quiet American* (a story set in Vietnam), *Our Man in Havana*, and *A Burnt-Out Case*. *The Comedians* and twelve other novels have been filmed, plus two of his short stories, and *The Third Man* was written as a film treatment. In 1967 he published a collection of short stories under the title *May We Borrow Your Husband?*

In all Graham Greene has written some thirty novels, 'entertainments,' plays, children's books, travel books, and collections of essays and short stories. He was made a Companion of Honour in 1966. Among his latest publications are his long-awaited autobiography, *A Sort of Life* (1971), *The Honorary Consul* (1973), *Lord Rochester's Monkey* (1974), and *An Impossible Woman: The Memories of Dottoressa Moor of Capri* (edited; 1975).

Shades of Greene

The televised stories of
GRAHAM GREENE

PENGUIN BOOKS

Penguin Books Ltd, Harmondsworth,
Middlesex, England
Penguin Books, 625 Madison Avenue,
New York, New York 10022, U.S.A.
Penguin Books Australia Ltd, Ringwood,
Victoria, Australia
Penguin Books Canada Limited, 2801 John Street,
Markham, Ontario, Canada L3R 1B4
Penguin Books (N.Z.) Ltd, 182–190 Wairau Road,
Auckland 10, New Zealand

First published in Great Britain by
The Bodley Head and William Heinemann 1975
First published in the United States of America by
Penguin Books 1977

ISBN 0 14 00.4023 4

Printed in the United States of America by
Offset Paperback Mfrs., Inc., Dallas, Pennsylvania
Set in Monotype Plantin

'When Greek Meets Greek,' 'Special Duties,' 'The Destructors,'
'Alas, Poor Maling,' 'A Chance for Mr Lever,' 'A Little Place off the
Edgware Road,' 'The Blue Film,' 'A Drive in the Country,' and
'The Case for the Defence' first appeared in *Twenty-one Stories*,
published in Great Britain by William Heinemann (1954) and in the
United States of America by The Viking Press (1962). 'Cheap in
August,' 'The Invisible Japanese Gentlemen,' 'Mortmain,' 'The
Root of All Evil,' 'Chagrin in Three Parts,' 'Two Gentle People,'
and 'The Over-night Bag' first appeared in *May We Borrow Your
Husband?*, published in Great Britain by The Bodley Head (1967)
and in the United States of America by The Viking Press (1967).
'Dream of a Strange Land' and 'Under the Garden' first appeared
in *A Sense of Reality*, published in Great Britain by The Bodley
Head (1963) and in the United States of America by The Viking
Press (1963). All three volumes are collected together as *The Collected
Stories*, published in Great Britain jointly by The Bodley Head and
William Heinemann (1972) and in the United States of America by
The Viking Press (1973).

CONTENTS

SHADES OF GREENE

When Greek Meets Greek

CAST

MR FENNICK, Paul Scofield
LORD DRIVER, Roy Kinnear
ELISABETH, Annette Robertson
PRISKETT, Derek Smith
FREDERICK, Terence Budd
LANDLADY, Stella Tanner
REVEREND SIMON MILAN,
　　　　　Frank Thornton
SCOUT, Jack Woolgar
POLICEMAN, Jerold Wells
and
John Rapley
John Marquand
Andrew Laurence
Michael Guest
Charles West

Dramatised by Clive Exton
Directed by Alan Cooke

When Greek Meets Greek

[1]

When the chemist had shut his shop for the night he went through a door at the back of the hall that served both him and the flats above, and then up two flights and a half of stairs carrying an offering of a little box of pills. The box was stamped with his name and address: Priskett, 14, New End Street, Oxford. He was a middle-aged man with a thin moustache and scared evasive eyes: he wore his long white coat even when he was off duty as if it had the power of protecting him like a King's uniform from his enemies. So long as he wore it he was free from summary trial and execution.

On the top landing was a window: outside Oxford spread through the spring evening: the peevish noise of innumerable bicycles, the gasworks, the prison, and the grey spires, beyond the bakers and confectioners, like paper frills. A door was marked with a visiting-card Mr Nicholas Fennick, B.A.: the chemist rang three short times.

The man who opened the door was sixty years old at least, with snow-white hair and a pink babyish skin. He wore a mulberry velvet dinner jacket, and his glasses swung on the end of a wide black ribbon. He said with a kind of boisterousness, 'Ah, Priskett, step in, Priskett. I had just sported my oak for a moment . . .'

'I brought you some more of my pills.'

'Invaluable, Priskett. If only you had taken a degree – the Society of Apothecaries would have been enough – I would have appointed you resident medical officer of St Ambrose's.'

'How's the college doing?'

'Give me your company for a moment in the common-room, and you shall know all.'

Mr Fennick led the way down a little dark passage cluttered with mackintoshes: Mr Priskett, feeling his way uneasily from mackintosh to mackintosh, kicked in front of him a pair of girl's shoes. 'One day,' Mr Fennick said, 'we must build . . .' and he made a broad confident gesture with his glasses that seemed to press back the walls of the common-room: a small round table covered with a landlady's cloth, three or four shiny chairs and a glass-fronted bookcase containing a copy of *Every Man His own Lawyer*. 'My niece Elisabeth,' Mr Fennick said, 'my medical adviser.' A very young girl with a lean pretty face nodded perfunctorily from behind a typewriter. 'I am going to train Elisabeth,' Mr Fennick said, 'to act as bursar. The strain of being both bursar and president of the college is upsetting my stomach. The pills . . . thank you.'

Mr Priskett said humbly, 'And what do you think of the college, Miss Fennick?'

'My name's Cross,' the girl said. 'I think it's a good idea. I'm surprised my uncle thought of it.'

'In a way it was – partly – my idea.'

'I'm more surprised still,' the girl said firmly.

Mr Priskett, folding his hands in front of his white coat as though he were pleading before a tribunal, went on: 'You see, I said to your uncle that with all these colleges being taken over by the military and the tutors having nothing to do they ought to start teaching by correspondence.'

'A glass of audit ale, Priskett?' Mr Fennick suggested. He took a bottle of brown ale out of a cupboard and poured out two gaseous glasses.

'Of course,' Mr Priskett pleaded, 'I hadn't thought of all this – the common-room, I mean, and St Ambrose's.'

'My niece,' Mr Fennick said, 'knows very little of the set-up.' He began to move restlessly around the room touching things with his hand. He was rather like an aged bird of prey inspecting the grim components of its nest.

The girl said briskly, 'As I see it, Uncle is running a swindle called St Ambrose's College, Oxford.'

'Not a swindle, my dear. The advertisement was very carefully worded.' He knew it by heart: every phrase had been carefully checked with his copy of *Every Man His Own Lawyer* open on the table. He repeated it now in a voice full and husky with bottled brown ale. 'War conditions prevent you going to Oxford. St Ambrose's – Tom Brown's old college – has made an important break with tradition. For the period of the war only it will be possible to receive tuition by post wherever you may be, whether defending the Empire on the cold rocks of Iceland or on the burning sands of Libya, in the main street of an American town or a cottage in Devonshire . . .'

'You've overdone it,' the girl said. 'You always do. That hasn't got a cultured ring. It won't catch anybody but suckers.'

'There are plenty of suckers,' Mr Fennick said.

'Go on.'

'Well, I'll skip that bit. "Degree-diplomas will be granted at the end of three terms instead of the usual three years."' He explained, 'That gives a quick turnover. One can't wait for money these days. "Gain a real Oxford education at Tom Brown's old college. For full particulars of tuition fees, battels, etc., write to the Bursar.""'

'And do you mean to say the University can't stop that?'

'Anybody,' Mr Fennick said with a kind of pride, 'can start a college anywhere. I've never said it was part of the University.'

'But battels – battels mean board and lodgings.'

'In this case,' Mr Fennick said, 'it's quite a nominal fee – to keep your name in perpetuity on the books of the old firm – I mean the college.'

'And the tuition . . .'

'Priskett here is the science tutor. I take history and classics. I thought that you, my dear, might tackle – economics?'

'I don't know anything about them.'

'The examinations, of course, have to be rather simple – within the capacity of the tutors. (There is an excellent public library here.) And another thing – the fees are returnable if the diploma-degree is not granted.'

'You mean . . .'

'Nobody will ever fail,' Mr Priskett brought breathlessly out with scared excitement.

'And you are really getting results?'

'I waited, my dear, until I could see the distinct possibility of at least six hundred a year for the three of us before I wired you. And today – beyond all my expectations – I have received a letter from Lord Driver. He is entering his son at St Ambrose's.'

'But how can he come here?'

'In his absence, my dear, on his country's service. The Drivers have always been a military family. I looked them up in Debrett.'

'What do you think of it?' Mr Priskett asked with anxiety and triumph.

'I think it's rich. Have you arranged a boat-race?'

'There, Priskett,' Mr Fennick said proudly, raising his glass of audit ale, 'I told you she was a girl of the old stock.'

[2]

Directly he heard his landlady's feet upon the stairs the elderly man with the grey shaven head began to lay his wet tea-leaves round the base of the aspidistra. When she opened the door he was dabbing the tea-leaves in tenderly with his fingers. 'A lovely plant, my dear.'

But she wasn't going to be softened at once: he could tell that: she waved a letter at him. 'Listen,' she said, 'what's this Lord Driver business?'

'My name, my dear: a good Christian name like Lord George Sanger had.'

'Then why don't they put Mr Lord Driver on the letter?'

'Ignorance, just ignorance.'

'I don't want any hanky-panky from my house. It's always been honest.'

'Perhaps they didn't know if I was an esquire or just a plain mister, so they left it blank.'

'It's sent from St Ambrose's College, Oxford: people like that ought to know.'

'It comes, my dear, of having such a good address. W.1. And all the gentry live in Mewses.' He made a half-hearted snatch at the letter, but the landlady held it out of reach.

'What are the likes of you writing to Oxford College about?'

'My dear,' he said with strained dignity, 'I may have been a little unfortunate: it may even be that I have spent a few years in chokey, but I have the rights of a free man.'

'And a son in quod.'

'Not in quod, my dear. Borstal is quite another institution. It is – a kind of college.'

'Like St Ambrose's.'

'Perhaps not quite of the same rank.'

He was too much for her: he was usually in the end too much for her. Before his first stay at the Scrubs he had held a number of positions as manservant and even butler: the way he raised his eyebrows he had learned from Lord Charles Manville: he wore his clothes like an eccentric peer, and you might say that he had even learned the best way to pilfer from old Lord Bellen who had a penchant for silver spoons.

'And now, my dear, if you'd just let me have my letter?' He put his hand tentatively forward: he was as daunted by her as she was by him: they sparred endlessly and lost to each other; interminably the battle was never won – they were always afraid. This time it was his victory. She slammed the door. Suddenly, ferociously, when the door had closed, he made a little vulgar noise at the aspidistra. Then he put on his glasses and began to read.

His son had been accepted for St Ambrose's, Oxford. The great fact stared up at him above the sprawling decorative signature of the President. Never had he been more thankful for the coincidence of his name. 'It will be my great pleasure,' the President wrote, 'to pay personal attention to your son's career at St Ambrose's. In these days it is an honour to welcome a member of a great military family like yours.' Driver felt an odd mixture of amusement and of genuine pride. He'd put one over on them, but his breast swelled within his waistcoat at the idea that now he had a son at Oxford.

But there were two snags – minor snags when he considered how far he'd got already. It was apparently an old Oxford custom that fees should be paid in advance, and then there were the examinations. His son couldn't do them himself: Borstal would not allow it, and he wouldn't be out for another six months. Besides the whole beauty of the idea was that he should receive the gift of an Oxford degree as a kind of welcome home. Like a chess player who is always several moves ahead he was already seeing his way around these difficulties.

The fees he felt sure in his case were only a matter of bluff: a peer could always get credit, and if there was any trouble after the degree had been awarded, he could just tell them to sue and be damned. No Oxford college would like to admit that it had been imposed on by an old lag. But the examinations? A funny little knowing smile twitched the corners of his mouth: a memory of the Scrubs five years ago and the man they called Daddy, the Reverend Simon Milan. He was a short time prisoner – they were all short time prisoners at the Scrubs: no sentence of over three years was ever served there. He remembered the tall lean aristocratic parson with his iron-grey hair and his narrow face like a lawyer's which had gone somehow soft inside with too much love. A prison, when you came to think of it, contained as much knowledge as a University: there were doctors, financiers, clergy. He knew where he could find Mr Milan: he was employed in a boarding-house near Euston Square, and for a few drinks he would do most things – he would certainly make out some fine examination papers. 'I can just hear him now,' Driver reminded himself ecstatically, 'talking Latin to the warders.'

[3]

It was autumn in Oxford: people coughed in the long queues for sweets and cakes, and the mists from the river seeped into the cinemas past the commissionaires on the look-out for people without gas-masks. A few under-graduates picked their way through the evacuated swarm; they always looked in a hurry: so much had to be got through in so little time before the army claimed them. There were lots of pickings for racketeers, Elisabeth Cross thought, but not much of a chance for a girl to find a husband: the oldest Oxford racket had been elbowed out by the black markets in Woodbines, toffees, toma-toes.

There had been a few days last spring when she had treated St Ambrose's as a joke, but when she saw the money actually coming in, the whole thing seemed less amusing. Then for some weeks she was acutely unhappy – until she realized that of all the war-time rackets this was the most harmless. They were not reducing supplies like the Ministry of Food, or destroying confidence like the Ministry of Information: her uncle paid income-tax, and they even to some extent educated people. The suckers, when they took their diploma-degrees, would know several things they hadn't known before.

But that didn't help a girl to find a husband.

She came moodily out of the matinée, carrying a bunch

of papers she should have been correcting. There was only one 'student' who showed any intelligence at all, and that was Lord Driver's son. The papers were forwarded from 'somewhere in England' via London by his father; she had nearly found herself caught out several times on points of history, and her uncle she knew was straining his rusty Latin to the limit.

When she got home she knew that there was something in the air: Mr Priskett was sitting in his white coat on the edge of a chair and her uncle was finishing a stale bottle of beer. When something went wrong he never opened a new bottle: he believed in happy drinking. They watched her in silence. Mr Priskett's silence was gloomy, her uncle's preoccupied. Something had to be got round – it couldn't be the university authorities: they had stopped bothering him long ago – a lawyer's letter, an irascible interview, and their attempt to maintain 'a monopoly of local education' – as Mr Fennick put it – had ceased.

'Good evening,' Elisabeth said. Mr Priskett looked at Mr Fennick and Mr Fennick frowned.

'Has Mr Priskett run out of pills?'

Mr Priskett winced.

'I've been thinking,' Elisabeth said, 'that as we are now in the third term of the academic year, I should like a rise in salary.'

Mr Priskett drew in his breath sharply, keeping his eyes on Mr Fennick.

'I should like another three pounds a week.'

Mr Fennick rose from his table; he glared ferociously into the top of his dark ale, his frown beetled. The chemist scraped his chair a little backward. And then Mr Fennick spoke.

'We are such stuff as dreams are made on,' he said and hiccupped slightly.

'Kidneys,' Elisabeth said.

'Rounded by a sleep. And these our cloud-capped towers . . .'

'You are misquoting.'

'Vanished into air, into thin air.'

'You've been correcting the English papers.'

'Unless you allow me to think, to think rapidly and deeply, there won't be any more examination papers,' Mr Fennick said.

'Trouble?'

'I've always been a Republican at heart. I don't see why we want a hereditary peerage.'

'*À la lanterne*,' Elisabeth said.

'This man Lord Driver: why should a mere accident of birth . . . ?'

'He refuses to pay?'

'It isn't that. A man like that expects credit: it's right that he should have credit. But he's written to say that he's coming down tomorrow to see his boy's college. The old fat-headed sentimental fool,' Mr Fennick said.

'I knew you'd be in trouble sooner or later.'

'That's the sort of damn fool comfortless thing a girl would say.'

'It just needs brain.'

Mr Fennick picked up a brass ash-tray – and then put it down again carefully.

'It's quite simple as soon as you begin to think.'

'Think?'

Mr Priskett scraped a chair-leg.

'I'll meet him at the station with a taxi, and take him to – say Balliol. Lead him straight through into the inner quad, and there you'll be, just looking as if you'd come out of the Master's lodging.'

'He'll know it's Balliol.'

'He won't. Anybody who knew Oxford couldn't be stupid enough to send his son to St Ambrose's.'

'Of course it's true. These military families are a bit crass.'

'You'll be in an enormous hurry. Convocation or something. Whip him round the Hall, the Chapel, the Library, and hand him back to me outside the Master's. I'll take him out to lunch and see him into his train. It's simple.'

Mr Fennick said broodingly, 'Sometimes I think you're a terrible girl, terrible. Is there nothing you wouldn't think up?'

'I believe,' Elisabeth said, 'that if you're going to play your own game in a world like this, you've got to play it properly. Of course,' she said, 'if you are going to play a different game, you go to a nunnery or to the wall and like it. But I've only got one game to play.'

[4]

It really went off very smoothly. Driver found Elisabeth at the barrier: she didn't find him because she was expecting something different. Something about him worried her; it wasn't his clothes or the monocle he never seemed to use – it was something subtler than that. It was almost as though he were afraid of her, he was so ready to fall in with her plans. 'I don't want to be any trouble, my dear, any trouble at all. I know how busy the President must be.' When she explained that they would be lunching together in town, he even seemed relieved. 'It's just the bricks of the dear old place,' he said. 'You mustn't mind my being a sentimentalist, my dear.'

'Were you at Oxford?'

'No, no. The Drivers, I'm afraid, have neglected the things of the mind.'

'Well, I suppose a soldier needs brains?'

He took a sharp look at her, and then answered in quite a different sort of voice, 'We believed so in the Lancers.' Then he strolled beside her to the taxi, twirling his monocle, and all the way up from the station he was silent, taking little quiet sideways peeks at her, appraising, approving.

'So this is St Ambrose's,' he said in a hearty voice just before the porter's lodge and she pushed him quickly by, through the first quad, towards the Master's house, where on the doorstep with a B.A. gown over his arm stood Mr Fennick permanently posed like a piece of garden statuary. 'My uncle, the President,' Elisabeth said.

'A charming girl, your niece,' Driver said as soon as they were alone together. He had really only meant to make conversation, but as soon as he had spoken the old two crooked minds began to move in harmony.

'She's very home-loving,' Mr Fennick said. 'Our famous elms,' he went on, waving his hand skywards. 'St Ambrose's rooks.'

'Crooks?' Driver exclaimed.

'Rooks. In the elms. One of our great modern poets wrote about them. "St Ambrose elms, oh St Ambrose elms", and about "St Ambrose rooks calling in wind and rain".'

'Pretty. Very pretty.'

'Nicely turned, I think.'

'I meant your niece.'

21

'Ah, yes. This way to the Hall. Up these steps. So often trodden, you know, by Tom Brown.'

'Who was Tom Brown?'

'The great Tom Brown – one of Rugby's famous sons.' He added thoughtfully, 'She'll make a fine wife – and mother.'

'Young men are beginning to realize that the flighty ones are not what they want for a lifetime.'

They stopped by mutual consent on the top step: they nosed towards each other like two old blind sharks who each believes that what stirs the water close to him is tasty meat.

'Whoever wins her,' Mr Fennick said, 'can feel proud. She'll make a fine hostess. . . .'

'I and my son,' Driver said, 'have talked seriously about marriage. He takes rather an old-fashioned view. He'll make a good husband . . .'

They walked into the hall, and Mr Fennick led the way round the portraits. 'Our founder,' he said, pointing at a full-bottomed wig. He chose it deliberately: he felt it smacked a little of himself. Before Swinburne's portrait he hesitated: then pride in St Ambrose's conquered caution. 'The great poet Swinburne,' he said. 'We sent him down.'

'Expelled him?'

'Yes. Bad morals.'

'I'm glad you are strict about those.'

'Ah, your son is in safe hands at St Amb's.'

'It makes me very happy,' Driver said. He began to scrutinize the portrait of a 19th-century divine. 'Fine brushwork,' he said. 'Now religion – I believe in religion. Basis of the family.' He said with a burst of confidence, 'You know our young people ought to meet.'

Mr Fennick gleamed happily. 'I agree.'

'If he passes. . . .'

'Oh, he'll certainly pass,' Mr Fennick said.

'He'll be on leave in a week or two. Why shouldn't he take his degree in person?'

'Well, there'd be difficulties.'

'Isn't it the custom?'

'Not for postal graduates. The Vice-Chancellor likes to make a small distinction . . . but Lord Driver, in the case of so distinguished an alumnus, I suggest that I should be deputed to present the degree to your son in London.'

'I'd like him to see his college.'

'And so he shall in happier days. So much of the college is shut now. I would like him to visit it for the first time when its glory is restored. Allow me and my niece to call on you.'

'We are living very quietly.'

'Not serious financial trouble, I hope?'

'Oh, no, no.'

'I'm so glad. And now let us rejoin the dear girl.'

[5]

It always seemed to be more convenient to meet at railway stations. The coincidence didn't strike Mr Fennick who had fortified himself for the journey with a good deal of audit ale, but it struck Elisabeth. The college lately had not been fulfilling expectations, and that was partly due to the laziness of Mr Fennick: from his conversation lately it almost seemed as though he had begun to regard the college as only a step to something else – what she couldn't quite make out. He was always talking about

23

Lord Driver and his son Frederick and the responsibilities of the peerage. His Republican tendencies had quite lapsed. 'That dear boy,' was the way he referred to Frederick, and he marked him 100% for Classics. 'It's not often Latin and Greek go with military genius,' he said. 'A remarkable boy.'

'He's not so hot on economics,' Elisabeth said.

'We mustn't demand too much book-learning from a soldier.'

At Paddington Lord Driver waved anxiously to them through the crowd; he wore a very new suit – one shudders to think how many coupons had been gambled away for the occasion. A little behind him was a very young man with a sullen mouth and a scar on his cheek. Mr Fennick bustled forward; he wore a black raincoat over his shoulder like a cape and carrying his hat in his hand he disclosed his white hair venerably among the porters.

'My son – Frederick,' Lord Driver said. The boy sullenly took off his hat and put it on again quickly: they wore their hair in the army very short.

'St Ambrose's welcomes her new graduate,' Mr Fennick said.

Frederick grunted.

The presentation of the degree was made in a private room at Mount Royal. Lord Driver explained that his house had been bombed – a time bomb, he added, a rather necessary explanation since there had been no raids recently. Mr Fennick was satisfied if Lord Driver was. He had brought up a B.A. gown, a mortar-board and a Bible in his suitcase, and he made quite an imposing little ceremony between the book-table, the sofa and the radiator, reading out a Latin oration and tapping

Frederick lightly on the head with the Bible. The degree-diploma had been expensively printed in two colours by an Anglo-Catholic firm. Elisabeth was the only uneasy person there. Could the world, she wondered, really contain two such suckers? What was this painful feeling growing up in her that perhaps it contained four?

After a little light lunch with bottled brown beer – 'almost as good, if I may say so, as our audit ale,' Mr Fennick beamed – the President and Lord Driver made elaborate moves to drive the two young people together. 'We've got to talk a little business,' Mr Fennick said, and Lord Driver hinted, 'You've not been to the movies for a year, Frederick.' They were driven out together into bombed shabby Oxford Street while the old men rang cheerfully down for whisky.

'What's the idea?' Elisabeth said.

He was good-looking; she liked his scar and his sullenness; there was almost too much intelligence and purpose in his eyes. Once he took off his hat and scratched his head: Elisabeth again noticed his short hair. He certainly didn't look a military type. And his suit, like his father's, looked new and ready-made. Hadn't he had any clothes to wear when he came on leave?

'I suppose,' she said, 'they are planning a wedding.'

His eyes lit gleefully up. 'I wouldn't mind,' he said.

'You'd have to get leave from your C.O., wouldn't you?'

'C.O.?' he asked in astonishment, flinching a little like a boy who has been caught out, who hasn't been prepared beforehand with that question. She watched him carefully, remembering all the things that had seemed to her odd since the beginning.

'So you haven't been to the movies for a year,' she said.

'I've been on service.'

'Not even an Ensa show?'

'Oh, I don't count those.'

'It must be awfully like being in prison.'

He grinned weakly, walking faster all the time, so that she might easily have been pursuing him through the Hyde Park gates.

'Come clean,' she said. 'Your father's not Lord Driver.'

'Oh yes, he is.'

'Any more than my uncle's President of a College.'

'What?' He began to laugh – it was an agreeable laugh, a laugh you couldn't trust but a laugh which made you laugh back and agree that in a crazy world like this all sorts of things didn't matter a hang. 'I'm just out of Borstal,' he said. 'What's yours?'

'Oh, I haven't been in prison yet.'

He said, 'You'll never believe me, but all that ceremony – it looked phoney to me. Of course Dad swallowed it.'

'And my uncle swallowed you. . . . I couldn't quite.'

'Well, the wedding's off. In a way I'm sorry.'

'I'm still free.'

'Well,' he said, 'we might discuss it,' and there in the pale Autumn sunlight of the Park they did discuss it – from all sorts of angles. There were bigger frauds all round them: officials of the Ministries passed carrying little portfolios; controllers of this and that purred by in motor-cars, and men with the big blank faces of advertisement hoardings strode purposefully in khaki with scarlet tabs down Park Lane from the Dorchester. Their fraud was a small one by the world's standard, and a harmless one: the boy from Borstal and the girl from nowhere at all – from the draper's counter and the semi-detached villa. 'He's got a few hundred stowed away, I'm sure of that,' said Fred. 'He'd make a settlement if he thought he could get the President's niece.'

'I wouldn't be surprised if Uncle had five hundred. He'd put it all down for Lord Driver's son.'

'We'd take over this college business. With a bit of capital we could really make it go. It's just chicken-feed now.'

They fell in love for no reason at all, in the park, on a bench to save twopences, planning their fraud on the old frauds they knew they could outdo. Then they went back and Elisabeth declared herself before she'd got properly inside the door. 'Frederick and I want to get married.' She almost felt sorry for the old fools as their faces lit up, suddenly, simultaneously, because everything had been so easy, and then darkened with caution as they squinted at each other. 'This is very surprising,' Lord Driver said, and the President said, 'My goodness, young people work fast.'

All night the two old men planned their settlements, and the two young ones sat happily back in a corner, watching them fence, with the secret knowledge that the world is always open to the young.

Cheap in August

CAST

MARY, Virginia McKenna
HENRY, Leo McKern
CHARLIE, Paul Maxwell
MYRA BACKUS, Helen Horton
PROFESSOR'S WIFE, Betty McDowall
DEAN'S WIFE, Mary Barclay
ST LOUIS WOMEN,
       Bessie Love
       Tucker McGuire
       Pat Starr
MR FRANKLIN, David Cargill
BARMAN, Trevor Thomas
WAITER, Allister Bain
RECEPTIONIST, Wayne Browne

Dramatised by Philip Mackie
Directed by Alvin Rakoff

Cheap in August

[1]

It was cheap in August: the essential sun, the coral reefs, the bamboo bar and the calypsos – they were all of them at cut prices, like the slightly soiled slips in a bargain-sale. Groups arrived periodically from Philadelphia in the manner of school-treats and departed with less *bruit*, after an exact exhausting week, when the picnic was over. Perhaps for twenty-four hours the swimming-pool and the bar were almost deserted, and then another school-treat would arrive, this time from St Louis. Everyone knew everyone else; they had bussed together to an air-port, they had flown together, together they had faced an alien customs; they would separate during the day and greet each other noisily and happily after dark, exchang-ing impressions of 'shooting the rapids', the botanic gardens, the Spanish fort. 'We are doing that tomorrow.'

Mary Watson wrote to her husband in Europe, 'I had to get away for a bit and it's so cheap in August.' They had been married ten years and they had only been separated three times. He wrote to her every day and the letters arrived twice a week in little bundles. She arranged them like newspapers by the date and read them in the correct order. They were tender and precise; what with his research, with preparing lectures and writing letters, he had little time to *see* Europe – he insisted on calling it 'your Europe' as though to assure her that he had not for-gotten the sacrifice which she must have made by marry-ing an American professor from New England, but sometimes little criticisms of 'her Europe' escaped him: the food was too rich, cigarettes too expensive, wine too often served and milk very difficult to obtain at lunchtime – which might indicate that, after all, she ought not to exaggerate her sacrifice. Perhaps it would have been a good thing if James Thomson, who was his special study at the moment, had written *The Seasons* in America – an American fall, she had to admit, was more beautiful than an English autumn.

Mary Watson wrote to him every other day, but sometimes a postcard only, and she was apt to forget if she had repeated the postcard. She wrote in the shade of the bamboo bar where she could see everyone who passed on the way to the swimming-pool. She wrote truthfully, 'It's so cheap in August; the hotel is not half full, and the heat and the humidity are very tiring. But, of course, it's a change.' She had no wish to appear extravagant; the salary, which to her European eyes had seemed astronomically large for a professor of literature, had long dwindled to its proper proportions, relative to the price of steaks and salads – she must justify with a little enthusiasm the money she was spending in his absence. So she wrote also about the flowers in the botanic gardens – she had ventured that far on one occasion – and with less truth of the beneficial changes wrought by the sun and the lazy life on her friend Margaret who from 'her England' had written and demanded her company: a Margaret, she admitted frankly to herself, who was not visible to any eye but the eye of faith. But then Charlie had complete faith. Even good qualities become with the erosion of time a reproach. After ten years of being happily married, she thought, one undervalues security and tranquillity.

She read Charlie's letters with great attention. She

31

longed to find in them one ambiguity, one evasion, one time-gap which he had ill-explained. Even an unusually strong expression of love would have pleased her, for its strength might have been there to counterweigh a sense of guilt. But she couldn't deceive herself that there was any sense of guilt in Charlie's facile flowing informative script. She calculated that if he had been one of the poets he was now so closely studying, he would have completed already a standard-sized epic during his first two months in 'her Europe', and the letters, after all, were only a spare-time occupation. They filled up the vacant hours, and certainly they could have left no room for any other occupation. 'It is ten o'clock at night, it is raining outside and the temperature is rather cool for August, not above fifty-six degrees. When I have said good-night to you, my dear one, I shall go happily to bed with the thought of you. I have a long day tomorrow at the museum and dinner in the evening with the Henry Wilkinsons who are passing through on their way from Athens – you remember the Henry Wilkinsons, don't you?' (Didn't she just?) She had wondered whether, when Charlie returned, she might perhaps detect some small unfamiliar note in his love-making which would indicate that a stranger had passed that way. Now she disbelieved in the possibility, and anyway the evidence would arrive too late – it was no good to her now that she might be justified later. She wanted her justification immediately, a justification not alas! for any act that she had committed but only for an intention, for the intention of betraying Charlie, of having, like so many of her friends, a holiday affair (the idea had come to her immediately the dean's wife had said, 'It's so cheap in Jamaica in August').

The trouble was that, after three weeks of calypsos in

the humid evenings, the rum punches (for which she could no longer disguise from herself a repugnance), the warm Martinis, the interminable red snappers, and tomatoes with everything, there had been no affair, not even the hint of one. She had discovered with disappointment the essential morality of a holiday resort in the cheap season; there were no opportunities for infidelity, only for writing postcards – with great brilliant blue skies and seas – to Charlie. Once a woman from St Louis had taken too obvious pity on her, when she sat alone in the bar writing postcards, and invited her to join their party which was about to visit the botanic gardens – 'We are an awfully jolly bunch,' she had said with a big turnip smile. Mary exaggerated her English accent to repel her better and said that she didn't much care for flowers. It had shocked the woman as deeply as if she had said she did not care for television. From the motion of the heads at the other end of the bar, the agitated clinking of the Coca-Cola glasses, she could tell that her words were being repeated from one to another. Afterwards, until the jolly bunch had taken the airport limousine on the way back to St Louis, she was aware of averted heads. She was English, she had taken a superior attitude to flowers, and as she preferred even warm Martinis to Coca-Cola, she was probably in their eyes an alcoholic.

It was a feature common to most of these jolly bunches that they contained no male attachment, and perhaps that was why the attempt to look attractive was completely abandoned. Huge buttocks were exposed in their full horror in tight large-patterned Bermuda shorts. Heads were bound in scarves to cover rollers which were not removed even by lunch-time – they stuck out like small mole-hills. Daily she watched the bums lurch by like hippos on the way to the water. Only in the evening would the women change from the monstrous shorts into monstrous cotton frocks, covered with mauve or scarlet flowers, in order to take dinner on the terrace where formality was demanded in the book of rules, and the few men who appeared were forced to wear jackets and ties though the thermometer stood at close on eighty degrees after sunset. The market in femininity being such, how could one hope to see any male foragers? Only old and broken husbands were sometimes to be seen towed towards an Issa store advertising free-port prices.

She had been encouraged during the first week by the sight of three men with crew-cuts who went past the bar towards the swimming-pool wearing male bikinis. They were far too young for her, but in her present mood she would have welcomed altruistically the sight of another's romance. Romance is said to be contagious, and if in the candle-lit evenings the 'informal' coffee tavern had contained a few young amorous couples, who could say what men of maturer years might not eventually arrive to catch the infection? But her hopes dwindled. The young men came and went without a glance at the Bermuda shorts or the pinned hair. Why should they stay? They were certainly more beautiful than any girl there and they knew it.

By nine o'clock most evenings Mary Watson was on her way to bed. A few evenings of calypsos, of quaint false impromptus and the hideous jangle of rattles, had been enough. Outside the closed windows of the hotel annexe the boxes of the air-conditioners made a continuous rumble in the starred and palmy night like over-fed hotel guests. Her room was full of dried air which bore no more resemblance to fresh air than the dried figs to the newly picked fruit. When she looked in the glass to brush her hair she often regretted her lack of charity to the jolly bunch from St Louis. It was true she did not wear Bermuda shorts nor coil her hair in rollers, but her hair was streaky nonetheless with heat and the mirror reflected more plainly than it seemed to do at home her thirty-nine years. If she had not paid in advance for a four-weeks *pension* on her individual round-trip tour, with tickets exchangeable for a variety of excursions, she would have turned tail and returned to the campus. Next year, she thought, when I am forty, I must feel grateful that I have preserved the love of a good man.

She was a woman given to self-analysis, and perhaps because it is a great deal easier to direct questions to a particular face rather than to a void (one has the right to expect some kind of a response even from eyes one sees many times a day in a compact), she posed the questions to herself with a belligerent direct stare into the looking-glass. She was an honest woman, and for that reason the questions were all the cruder. She would say to herself, I have slept with no one other than Charlie (she wouldn't admit as sexual experiences the small exciting half-way points that she had reached before marriage); why am I now seeking to find a strange body, which will probably give me less pleasure than the body I already know? It had been more than a month before Charlie brought her real pleasure. Pleasure, she had learnt, grew with habit, so that if it were not really pleasure that she now looked for, what was it? The answer could only be the unfamiliar. She had friends, even on the respectable campus, who had admitted to her, in the frank admirable American way, their adventures. These had usually been in Europe – a

35

momentary marital absence had given opportunity for a momentary excitement, and then with what a sigh of relief they had found themselves safely at home. All the same they felt afterwards that they had enlarged their experience; they understood something that their husbands did not really understand – the real character of a Frenchman, an Italian, even – there were such cases – of an Englishman.

Mary Watson was painfully aware, as an Englishwoman, that her experience was confined to one American. They all, on the campus, believed her to be European, but all she knew was confined to one man and he was a citizen of Boston who had no curiosity for the great Western regions. In a sense she was more American by choice than he was by birth. Perhaps she was less European even than the wife of the Professor of Romance Languages, who had confided to her that once – overwhelmingly – in Antibes . . . it had happened only once because the sabbatical year was over . . . her husband was up in Paris checking manuscripts before they flew home . . .

Had she herself, Mary Watson sometimes wondered, been just such a European adventure which Charlie mistakenly had domesticated ? (She couldn't pretend to be a tigress in a cage, but they kept smaller creatures in cages, white mice, love-birds.) And, to be fair, Charlie too was her adventure, her American adventure, the kind of man whom at twenty-seven she had not before encountered in frowsy London. Henry James had described the type, and at that moment in her history she had been reading a great deal of Henry James: 'A man of intellect whose body was not much to him and its senses and appetites not importunate.' All the same for a while she had made the appetites importunate.

That was her private conquest of the American continent, and when the Professor's wife had spoken of the dancer of Antibes (no, that was a Roman inscription – the man had been a *marchand de vin*) she had thought, The lover I know and admire is American and I am proud of it. But afterwards came the thought: American or New England ? Yet to know a country must one know every region sexually ?

It was absurd at thirty-nine not to be content. She had her man. The book on James Thomson would be published by the University Press, and Charlie had the intention afterwards of making a revolutionary break from the romantic poetry of the eighteenth century into a study of the American image in European literature – it was to be called *The Double Reflection*: the effect of Fenimore Cooper on the European scene: the image of America presented by Mrs Trollope – the details were not yet worked out. The study might possibly end with the first arrival of Dylan Thomas on the shores of America – at the Cunard quay or at Idlewild ? That was a point for later research. She examined herself again closely in the glass – the new decade of the forties stared frankly back at her – an Englander who had become a New Englander. After all she hadn't travelled very far – Kent to Connecticut. This was not just the physical restlessness of middle age, she argued; it was the universal desire to see a little bit further, before one surrendered to old age and the blank certitude of death.

[2]

Next day she picked up her courage and went as far as the swimming-pool. A strong wind blew and whipped up

37

the waves in the almost land-girt harbour – the hurricane season would soon be here. All the world creaked around her: the wooden struts of the shabby harbour, the jalousies of the small hopeless houses which looked as though they had been knocked together from a make-it-yourself kit, the branches of the palms – a long, weary, worn-out creaking. Even the water of the swimming-pool imitated in miniature the waves of the harbour.

She was glad that she was alone in the swimming-pool, at least for all practical purposes alone, for the old man splashing water over himself, like an elephant, in the shallow end hardly counted. He was a solitary elephant and not one of the hippo band. They would have called her with merry cries to join them – and it's difficult to be stand-offish in a swimming-pool which is common to all as a table is not. They might even in their resentment have ducked her – pretending like schoolchildren that it was all a merry game; there was nothing she put beyond those thick thighs, whether they were encased in bikinis or Bermuda shorts. As she floated in the pool her ears were alert for their approach. At the first sound she would get well away from the water, but today they were probably making an excursion to Tower Isle on the other side of the island, or had they done that yesterday ? Only the old man watched her, pouring water over his head to keep away sunstroke. She was safely alone, which was the next best thing to the adventure she had come here to find. All the same, as she sat on the rim of the pool, and let the sun and wind dry her, she realized the extent of her solitude. She had spoken to no one but black waiters and Syrian receptionists for more than two weeks. Soon, she thought, I shall even begin to miss Charlie – it would be an ignoble finish to what she had intended to be an adventure.

A voice from the water said to her, 'My name's Hickslaughter – Henry Hickslaughter.' She couldn't have sworn to the name in court, but that was how it had sounded at the time and he never repeated it. She looked down at a polished mahogany crown surrounded by white hair; perhaps he resembled Neptune more than an elephant. Neptune was always outsize, and as he had pulled himself a little out of the water to speak, she could see the rolls of fat folding over the blue bathing-slip, with tough hair lying like weeds along the ditches. She replied with amusement, 'My name is Watson. Mary Watson.'

'You're English?'

'My husband's American,' she said in extenuation.

'I haven't seen him around, have I?'

'He's in England,' she said with a small sigh, for the geographical and national situation seemed too complicated for casual explanation.

'You like it here?' he asked and lifting a hand-cup of water he distributed it over his bald head.

'So so.'

'Got the time on you?'

She looked in her bag and told him, 'Eleven fifteen.'

'I've had my half hour,' he said and trod heavily away towards the ladder at the shallow end.

An hour later, staring at her lukewarm Martini with its great green unappetizing olive, she saw him looming down at her from the other end of the bamboo bar. He wore an ordinary shirt open at the neck and a brown leather belt; his type of shoes in her childhood had been known as co-respondent, but one seldom saw them today. She wondered what Charlie would think of her pick-up;

39

unquestionably she had landed him, rather as an angler struggling with a heavy catch finds that he has hooked nothing better than an old boot. She was no angler; she didn't know whether a boot would put an ordinary hook out of action altogether, but she knew that *her* hook could be irremediably damaged. No one would approach her if she were in his company. She drained the Martini in one gulp and even attacked the olive so as to have no excuse to linger in the bar.

'Would you do me the honour,' Mr Hickslaughter asked, 'of having a drink with me?' His manner was completely changed; on dry land he seemed unsure of himself and spoke with an old-fashioned propriety.

'I'm afraid I've only just finished one. I have to be off.' Inside the gross form she thought she saw a tousled child with disappointed eyes. 'I'm having lunch early today.' She got up and added rather stupidly, for the bar was quite empty, 'You can have my table.'

'I don't need a drink that much,' he said solemnly. 'I was just after company.' She knew that he was watching her as she moved to the adjoining coffee tavern, and she thought with guilt, at least I've got the old boot off the hook. She refused the shrimp cocktail with tomato ketchup and fell back as was usual with her on a grape-fruit, with grilled trout to follow. 'Please no tomato with the trout,' she implored, but the black waiter obviously didn't understand her. While she waited she began with amusement to picture a scene between Charlie and Mr Hickslaughter, who happened for the purpose of her story to be crossing the campus. 'This is Henry Hickslaughter, Charlie. We used to go bathing together when I was in Jamaica.' Charlie, who always wore English clothes, was very tall, very thin, very concave. It was a satisfaction to know that he would never lose his figure – his nerves would see to that and his extreme sensibility. He hated anything gross; there was no grossness in *The Seasons*, not even in the lines on spring.

She heard slow footsteps coming up behind her and panicked. 'May I share your table?' Mr Hickslaughter asked. He had recovered his terrestrial politeness, but only so far as speech was concerned, for he sat firmly down without waiting for her reply. The chair was too small for him; his thighs overlapped like a double mattress on a single bed. He began to study the menu.

'They copy American food; it's worse than the reality,' Mary Watson said.

'You don't like American food?'

'Tomatoes even with the trout!'

'Tomatoes? Oh, you mean tomatoes,' he said, correcting her accent. 'I'm very fond of tomatoes myself.'

'And fresh pineapple in the salad.'

'There's a lot of vitamins in fresh pineapple.' Almost as if he wished to emphasize their disagreement, he ordered shrimp cocktail, grilled trout and a sweet salad. Of course, when her trout arrived, the tomatoes were there. 'You can have mine if you want to,' she said and he accepted with pleasure. 'You are very kind. You are really very kind.' He held out his plate like Oliver Twist.

She began to feel oddly at ease with the old man. She would have been less at ease, she was certain, with a possible adventure: she would have been wondering about her effect on him, while now she could be sure that she gave him pleasure – with the tomatoes. He was perhaps less the old anonymous boot than an old shoe comfortable to wear. And curiously enough, in spite of his first approach and in spite of his correcting her over the pronunciation of tomatoes, it was not really an old American shoe of which she was reminded. Charlie wore English clothes over his English figure, he studied English eighteenth-century literature, his book would be published in England by the Cambridge University Press who would buy sheets, but she had the impression that he was far more fashioned as an American shoe than Hickslaughter. Even Charlie, whose manners were perfect, if they had met for the first time today at the swimming-pool, would have interrogated her more closely. Interrogation had always seemed to her a principal part of American social life – an inheritance perhaps from the Indian smoke-fires: 'Where are you from? Do you know the so and so's? Have you been to the botanic gardens?' It came over her that Mr Hickslaughter, if that were really his name, was perhaps an American reject – not necessarily more flawed than the pottery rejects of famous firms you find in bargain-basements.

She found herself questioning *him*, with circumlocutions, while he savoured the tomatoes. 'I was born in London. I couldn't have been born much more than six hundred miles from there without drowning, could I? But you belong to a continent thousands of miles wide and long. Where were you born?' (She remembered a character in a Western movie directed by John Ford who asked, 'Where do you hail from, stranger?' The question was more frankly put than hers.)

He said, 'St Louis.'

'Oh, then there are lots of your people here – you are not alone.' She felt a slight disappointment that he might belong to the jolly bunch.

'I'm alone,' he said. 'Room 63.' It was in her own corridor on the third floor of the annexe. He spoke firmly as though he were imparting information for future use. 'Five doors down from you.'

'Oh.'

'I saw you come out your first day.'

'I never noticed you.'

'I keep to myself unless I see someone I like.'

'Didn't you see anyone you liked from St Louis?'

'I'm not all that fond of St Louis, and St Louis can do without me. I'm not a favourite son.'

'Do you come here often?'

'In August. It's cheap in August.' He kept on surprising her. First there was his lack of local patriotism, and now his frankness about money or rather about the lack of it, a frankness that could almost be classed as an un-American activity.

'Yes.'

'I have to go where it's reasonable,' he said, as though he were exposing his bad hand to a partner at gin.

'You've retired?'

'Well – I've been retired.' He added, 'You ought to take salad . . . It's good for you.'

'I feel quite well without it.'

'You could do with more weight.' He added appraisingly, 'A couple of pounds.' She was tempted to tell him that he could do with less. They had both seen each other exposed.

'Were you in business?' She was being driven to interrogate. He hadn't asked her a personal question since his first at the pool.

'In a way,' he said. She had a sense that he was supremely uninterested in his own doings; she was

43

certainly discovering an America which she had not known existed.

She said, 'Well, if you'll excuse me . . .'

'Aren't you taking any dessert?'

'No, I'm a light luncher.'

'It's all included in the price. You ought to eat some fruit.' He was looking at her under his white eyebrows with an air of disappointment which touched her.

'I don't care much for fruit and I want a nap. I always have a nap in the afternoon.'

Perhaps, after all, she thought, as she moved away through the formal dining-room, he is disappointed only because I'm not taking full advantage of the cheap rate.

She passed his room going to her own: the door was open and a big white-haired mammy was making the bed. The room was exactly like her own; the same pair of double beds, the same wardrobe, the same dressing-table in the same position, the same heavy breathing of the air-conditioner. In her own room she looked in vain for the thermos of iced water; then she rang the bell and waited for several minutes. You couldn't expect good service in August. She went down the passage; Mr Hickslaughter's door was still open and she went in to find the maid. The door of the bathroom was open too and a wet cloth lay on the tiles.

How bare the bedroom was. At least she had taken the trouble to add a few flowers, a photograph and half a dozen books on a bedside table which gave her room a lived-in air. Beside his bed there was only a literary digest lying open and face down; she turned it over to see what he was reading – as she might have expected it was something to do with calories and proteins. He had begun writing a letter at his dressing-table and with the simple unscrupulousness of an intellectual she began to read it with her ears cocked for any sound in the passage.

'Dear Joe,' she read, 'the draft was two weeks late last month and I was in real difficulties. I had to borrow from a Syrian who runs a tourist junk-shop in Curaçao and pay him interest. You owe me a hundred dollars for the interest. It's your own fault. Mum never gave us lessons on how to live with an empty stomach. Please add it to the next draft and be sure to do that, you wouldn't want me coming back to collect. I'll be here till the end of August. It's cheap in August, and a man gets tired of nothing but Dutch, Dutch, Dutch. Give my love to Sis.'

The letter broke off unfinished. Anyway she would have had no opportunity to read more because someone was approaching down the passage. She went to the door in time to see Mr Hickslaughter on the threshold. He said, 'You looking for me?'

'I was looking for the maid. She was in here a minute ago.'

'Come in and sit down.'

He looked through the bathroom door and then at the room in general. Perhaps it was only an uneasy conscience which made her think that his eyes strayed a moment to the unfinished letter.

'She's forgotten my iced water.'

'You can have mine if it's filled.' He shook his thermos and handed it to her.

'Thanks a lot.'

'When you've had your sleep . . .' he began and looked away from her. Was he looking at the letter?

'Yes?'

'We might have a drink.'

She was, in a sense, trapped. She said, 'Yes.'

'Give me a ring when you wake up.'

'Yes.' She said nervously, 'Have a good sleep yourself.'

'Oh, I don't sleep.' He didn't wait for her to leave the room before turning away, swinging that great elephantine backside of his towards her. She had walked into a trap baited with a flask of iced water, and in her room she drank the water gingerly as though it might have a flavour different from hers.

[3]

She found it difficult to sleep: the old fat man had become an individual since she had read his letter. She couldn't help comparing his style with Charlie's. 'When I have said good-night to you, my dear one, I shall go happily to bed with the thought of you.' In Mr Hickslaughter's there was an ambiguity, a hint of menace. Was it possible that the old man could be dangerous?

At half past five she rang up room 63. It was not the kind of adventure she had planned, but it was an adventure nonetheless. 'I'm awake,' she said.

'You coming for a drink?' he asked.

'I'll meet you in the bar.'

'Not the bar,' he said. 'Not at the prices they charge for bourbon. I've got all we need here.' She felt as though she were being brought back to the scene of a crime, and she needed a little courage to knock on the door.

He had everything prepared: a bottle of Old Walker, a bucket of ice, two bottles of soda. Like books, drinks can make a room inhabited. She saw him as a man fighting in his own fashion against the sense of solitude.

'Siddown,' he said, 'make yourself comfortable,' like a character in a movie. He began to pour out two highballs.

46

She said, 'I've got an awful sense of guilt. I did come in here for iced water, but I was curious too. I read your letter.'

'I knew someone had touched it,' he said.

'I'm sorry.'

'Who cares? It was only to my brother.'

'I had no business . . .'

'Look,' he said, 'if I came into your room and found a letter open I'd read it, wouldn't I? Only your letter would be more interesting.'

'Why?'

'I don't write love letters. Never did and I'm too old now.' He sat down on a bed – she had the only easy chair. His belly hung in heavy folds under his sports-shirt, and his flies were a little open. Why was it always fat men who left them unbuttoned? He said, 'This is good bourbon,' taking a drain of it. 'What does your husband do?' he asked – it was his first personal question since the pool and it took her by surprise.

'He writes about literature. Eighteenth-century poetry,' she added, rather inanely under the circumstances.

'Oh.'

'What did you do? I mean when you worked.'

'This and that.'

'And now?'

'I watch what goes on. Sometimes I talk to someone like you. Well, no, I don't suppose I've ever talked to anyone like you before.' It might have seemed a compliment if he had not added, 'A professor's wife.'

'And you read the *Digest*?'

'Ye-eh. They make books too long – I haven't the

47

patience. Eighteenth-century poetry. So they wrote poetry back in those days, did they?'

She said, 'Yes,' not sure whether or not he was mocking her.

'There was a poem I liked at school. The only one that ever stuck in my head. By Longfellow, I think. You ever read Longfellow?'

'Not really. They don't read him much in school any longer.'

'Something about "Spanish sailors with bearded lips and something and mystery of the ships and the something of the sea". It hasn't stuck all that well, but I suppose I learned it sixty years ago and even more. Those were the days.'

'The 1900s?'

'No, no. I meant pirates, Kidd and Bluebeard and those fellows. This was their stamping ground, wasn't it? The Caribbean. It makes you kind of sick to see those women going around in their shorts here.' His tongue had been tingled into activity by the bourbon.

It occurred to her that she had never really been curious about another human being; she had been in love with Charlie, but he hadn't aroused her curiosity except sexually, and she had satisfied that only too quickly. She asked him, 'Do you love your sister?'

'Yes, of course, why? How do you know I've got a sister?'

'And Joe?'

'You certainly read my letter. Oh, he's O.K.'

'O.K.?'

'Well, you know how it is with brothers. I'm the eldest in my family. There was one that died. My sister's twenty years younger than I am. Joe's got the means. He looks after her.'

'You haven't got the means?'

'I had the means. I wasn't good at managing them though. We aren't here to talk about myself.'

'I'm curious. That's why I read your letter.'

'You? Curious about me?'

'It could be, couldn't it?'

She had confused him, and now that she had the upper hand, she felt that she was out of the trap; she was free, she could come and go as she pleased, and if she chose to stay a little longer, it was her own choice.

'Have another bourbon?' he said. 'But you're English. Maybe you'd prefer Scotch?'

'Better not mix.'

'No.' He poured her another glass. He said, 'I was wondering – sometimes I want to get away from this joint for a little. What about having dinner down the road?'

'It would be stupid,' she said. 'We've both paid our *pension* here, haven't we? And it would be the same dinner in the end. Red snapper. Tomatoes.'

'I don't know what you have against tomatoes.' But he did not deny the good sense of her economic reasoning: he was the first unsuccessful American she had ever had a drink with. One must have seen them in the street ... But even the young men who came to the house were not yet unsuccessful. The Professor of Romance Languages had perhaps hoped to be head of a university – success is relative, but it remains success.

He poured out another glass. She said, 'I'm drinking all your bourbon.'

'It's in a good cause.'

She was a little drunk by now and things – which only *seemed* relevant – came to her mind. She said, 'That thing of Longfellow's. It went on – something about "the thoughts of youth are long, long thoughts". I must have read it somewhere. That was the refrain, wasn't it?'

'Maybe. I don't remember.'

'Did you want to be a pirate when you were a boy?'

He gave an almost happy grin. He said, 'I succeeded. That's what Joe called me once – "pirate".'

'But you haven't any buried treasure?'

He said, 'He knows me well enough not to send me a hundred dollars. But if he feels scared enough that I'll come back – he might send fifty. And the interest was only twenty-five. He's not mean, but he's stupid.'

'How?'

'He ought to know I wouldn't go back. I wouldn't do one thing to hurt Sis.'

'Would it be any good if I asked you to have dinner with me?'

'No. It wouldn't be right.' In some ways he was obviously very conservative. 'It's as you said – you don't want to go throwing money about.' When the bottle of Old Walker was half empty, he said, 'You'd better have some food even if it is red snapper and tomatoes.'

'Is your name really Hickslaughter?'

'Something like that.'

They went downstairs, following rather carefully in each other's footsteps like ducks. In the formal restaurant open to all the heat of the evening, the men sat and sweated in their jackets and ties. They passed, the two of them, through the bamboo bar into the coffee tavern, which was lit by candles that increased the heat. Two young men with crew-cuts sat at the next table – they weren't the same young men she had seen before, but they came out of the same series. One of them said, 'I'm not denying that he has a certain style, but even if you *adore* Tennessee Williams . . .'

'Why did he call you a pirate?'

'It was just one of those things.'

When it came to the decision there seemed nothing to choose except red snapper and tomatoes, and again she offered him her tomatoes; perhaps he had grown to expect it and already she was chained by custom. He was an old man, he had made no pass which she could reasonably reject – how could a man of his age make a pass to a woman of hers? – and yet all the same she had a sense that she had landed on a conveyor belt. . . . The future was not in her hands, and she was a little scared. She would have been more frightened if it had not been for her unusual consumption of bourbon.

'It was good bourbon,' she commented for something to say, and immediately regretted it. It gave him an opening.

'We'll have another glass before bed.'

'I think I've drunk enough.'

'A good bourbon won't hurt you. You'll sleep well.'

'I always sleep well.' It was a lie – the kind of unimportant lie one tells a husband or a lover in order to keep some privacy. The young man who had been talking about Tennessee Williams rose from his table. He was very tall and thin and he wore a skin-tight black sweater; his small elegant buttocks were outlined in skin-tight trousers. It was easy to imagine him a degree more naked. Would he have looked at her, she wondered, with interest if she had not been sitting there in the company of a fat old man so horribly clothed? It was unlikely; his body was not designed for a woman's caress.

'I don't.'

'You don't what?'

'I don't sleep well.' The unexpected self-disclosure after all his reticences came as a shock. It was as though he had put out one of his square brick-like hands and pulled her to him. He had been aloof, he had evaded her personal questions, he had lulled her into a sense of security, but now every time she opened her mouth, she seemed doomed to commit an error, to invite him nearer. Even her harmless remark about the bourbon. . . . She said stupidly, 'Perhaps it's the change of climate.'

'What change of climate?'

'Between here and . . . and . . .'

'Curaçao? I guess there's no great difference. I don't sleep there either.'

'I've got some very good pills . . .' she said rashly.

'I thought you said you slept well.'

'Oh, there are always times. It's sometimes just a question of digestion.'

'Yes, digestion. You're right there. A bourbon will be good for that. If you've finished dinner . . .'

She looked across the coffee tavern to the bamboo bar, where the young man stood *déhanché*, holding a glass of crème-de-menthe between his face and his companion's like an exotically coloured monocle.

Mr Hickslaughter said in a shocked voice, 'You don't care for that type, do you?'

'They're often good conversationalists.'

'Oh, conversation. . . . If that's what you want.' It was as though she had expressed an un-American liking for snails or frogs' legs.

'Shall we have our bourbon in the bar? It's a little cooler tonight.'

'And pay and listen to their chatter? No, we'll go upstairs.'

He swung back again in the direction of old-fashioned courtesy and came behind her to pull her chair – even Charlie was not so polite, but was it politeness or the determination to block her way of escape to the bar?

They entered the lift together. The black attendant had a radio turned on, and from the small brown box came the voice of a preacher talking about the Blood of the Lamb. Perhaps it was a Sunday, and that would explain the temporary void around them – between one jolly bunch and another. They stepped out into the empty corridor like undesirables marooned. The boy followed them out and sat down upon a chair beside the elevator to wait for another signal, while the voice continued to talk about the Blood of the Lamb. What was she afraid of? Mr Hickslaughter began to unlock his door. He was much older than her father would have been if he had been still alive; he could be her grandfather – the excuse, 'What will the boy think?' was inadmissible – it was even shocking, for his manner had never ceased to be correct. He might be old, but what right had she to think of him as 'dirty'?

'Damn the hotel key . . .' he said. 'It won't open.'

She turned the handle for him. 'The door wasn't locked.'

'I can sure do with a bourbon after those nancies . . .'

But now she had her excuse ready on the lips. 'I've had one too many already, I'm afraid. I've got to sleep it off.' She put her hand on his arm. 'Thank you so much . . . It was a lovely evening.' She was aware how insulting her

53

English accent sounded as she walked quickly down the corridor leaving it behind her like a mocking presence, mocking all the things she liked best in him: his ambiguous character, his memory of Longfellow, his having to make ends meet.

She looked back when she reached her room: he was standing in the passage as though he couldn't make up his mind to go in. She was reminded of an old man whom she had passed one day on the campus leaning on his broom among the unswept autumn leaves.

[4]

In her room she picked up a book and tried to read. It was Thomson's *Seasons*. She had carried it with her, so that she could understand any reference to his work that Charlie might make in a letter. This was the first time she had opened it, and she was not held:

> And now the mounting Sun dispels the Fog:
> The rigid Hoar-Frost melts before his Beam;
> And hung on every Spray, on every Blade
> Of Grass, the myriad Dew-Drops twinkle round.

If she could be so cowardly, she thought, with a harmless old man like that, how could she have faced the real decisiveness of an adventure? One was not, at her age, 'swept off the feet'. Charlie had been proved just as sadly right to trust her as she was right to trust Charlie. Now with the difference in time he would be leaving the Museum, or rather, if this were a Sunday as the Blood of the Lamb seemed to indicate, he would probably have just quit writing in his hotel room. After a successful day's work he always resembled an advertisement for a new shaving-cream: a kind of glow. . . . She found it irritating, like living with a halo. Even his voice had a different timbre and he would call her 'old girl' and pat her bottom patronizingly. She preferred him when he was touchy with failure: only temporary failure, of course, the failure of an idea which hadn't worked out, the touchiness of a child's disappointment at a party which has not come up to his expectations, not the failure of the old man – the rusted framework of a ship transfixed once and for all upon the rock where it had struck.

She felt ignoble. What earthly risk could the old man represent to justify refusing him half an hour's companionship? He could no more assault her than the boat could detach itself from the rock and steam out to sea for the Fortunate Islands. She pictured him sitting alone with his half-empty bottle of bourbon seeking unconsciousness. Or was he perhaps finishing the crude blackmailing letter to his brother? What a story she would make of it one day, she thought with self-disgust as she took off her dress, her evening with a blackmailer and 'pirate'.

There was one thing she could do for him: she could give him her bottle of pills. She put on her dressing-gown and retrod the corridor, room by room, until she arrived at 63. His voice told her to come in. She opened the door and in the light of the bedside lamp saw him sitting on the edge of the bed wearing a crumpled pair of cotton pyjamas with broad mauve stripes. She began, 'I've brought you . . .' and then she saw to her amazement that he had been crying. His eyes were red and the evening darkness of his cheeks sparkled with points like dew. She had only once before seen a man cry – Charlie, when the University Press had decided against his first volume of literary essays.

'I thought you were the maid,' he said. 'I rang for her.'

'What did you want?'

'I thought she might take a glass of bourbon,' he said.

'Did you want so much . . . ? I'll take a glass.' The bottle was still on the dressing-table where they had left it and the two glasses – she identified hers by the smear of lipstick. 'Here you are,' she said, 'drink it up. It will make you sleep.'

He said, 'I'm not an alcoholic.'

'Of course you aren't.'

She sat on the bed beside him and took his left hand in hers. It was cracked and dry and she wanted to clean back the cuticle until she remembered that was something she did for Charlie.

'I wanted company,' he said.

'I'm here.'

'You'd better turn off the bell-light or the maid will come.'

'She'll never know what she missed in the way of Old Walker.'

When she returned from the door he was lying back against the pillows in an odd twisted position, and she thought again of the ship broken-backed upon the rocks. She tried to pick up his feet to lay them on the bed, but they were like heavy stones at the bottom of a quarry.

'Lie down,' she said, 'you'll never be sleepy that way. What do you do for company in Curaçao?'

'I manage,' he said.

'You've finished the bourbon. Let me put out the lights.'

'Its no good pretending to you,' he said.

56

'Pretending?'

'I'm afraid of the dark.'

She thought, I'll smile later when I think of who it was I feared. She said, 'Do the old pirates you fought come back to haunt you?'

'I've done some bad things,' he said, 'in my time.'

'Haven't we all?'

'Nothing extraditable,' he explained as though that were an extenuation.

'If you take one of my pills . . .'

'You won't go – not yet?'

'No, no. I'll stay till you're sleepy.'

'I've been wanting to talk to you for days.'

'I'm glad you did.'

'Would you believe it – I hadn't got the nerve.' If she had shut her eyes it might have been a very young man speaking. 'I don't know your sort.'

'Don't you have my sort in Curaçao?'

'No.'

'You haven't taken the pill yet.'

'I'm afraid of not waking up.'

'Have you so much to do tomorrow?'

'I mean ever.' He put out his hand and touched her knee, searchingly, without sensuality, as if he needed support from the bone. 'I'll tell you what's wrong. You're a stranger, so I can tell you. I'm afraid of dying, with nobody around, in the dark.'

'Are you ill?'

'I wouldn't know. I don't see doctors. I don't like doctors.'

'But why should you think . . .?'

'I'm over seventy. The Bible age. It could happen any day now.'

'You'll live to a hundred,' she said with an odd conviction.

'Then I'll have to live with my fear the hell of a long time.'

'Was that why you were crying?'

'No. I thought you were going to stay awhile, and then suddenly you went. I guess I was disappointed.'

'Are you never alone in Curaçao?'

'I pay not to be alone.'

'As you'd have paid the maid?'

'Ye-eh. Sort of.'

It was as though she were discovering for the first time the interior of the enormous continent on which she had elected to live. America had been Charlie, it had been New England; through books and movies she had been aware of the wonders of nature like some great cineramic film with Lowell Thomas cheapening the Painted Desert and the Grand Canyon with his clichés. There had been no mystery anywhere from Miami to Niagara Falls, from Cape Cod to the Pacific Palisades; tomatoes were served on every plate and Coca-Cola in every glass. Nobody anywhere admitted failure or fear; they were like sins 'hushed up' – worse perhaps than sins, for sins have glamour – they were bad taste. But here, stretched on the bed, dressed in striped pyjamas which Brooks Brothers would have disowned, failure and fear talked to her without shame, and in an American accent. It was as though she were living in the remote future, after God knew what catastrophe.

She said, 'I wasn't for sale? There was only the Old Walker to tempt *me*.'

He raised his antique Neptune head a little way from the pillow and said, 'I'm not afraid of death. Not sudden death. Believe me, I've looked for it here and there. It's the certain-sure business, closing in on you, like tax-inspectors . . .'

She said, 'Sleep now.'

'I can't.'

'Yes, you can.'

'If you'd stay with me awhile . . .'

'I'll stay with you. Relax.' She lay down on the bed beside him on the outside of the sheet. In a few minutes he was deeply asleep and she turned off the light. He grunted several times and spoke only once, when he said, 'You've got me wrong,' and after that he became for a little while like a dead man in his immobility and his silence, so that during that period she fell asleep. When she woke she was aware from his breathing that he was awake too. He was lying away from her so that their bodies wouldn't touch. She put out her hand and felt no repulsion at all at his excitement. It was as though she had spent many nights beside him in the one bed, and when he made love to her, silently and abruptly in the darkness, she gave a sigh of satisfaction. There was no guilt; she would be going back in a few days, resigned and tender, to Charlie and Charlie's loving skill, and she wept a little, but not seriously, at the temporary nature of this meeting.

'What's wrong?' he asked.

'Nothing. Nothing. I wish I could stay.'

'Stay a little longer. Stay till it's light.' That would not be very long. Already they could distinguish the grey masses of the furniture standing around them like Caribbean tombs.

'Oh yes, I'll stay till it's light. That wasn't what I meant.' His body began to slip out of her, and it was as though he were carrying away her unknown child, away in the direction of Curaçao, and she tried to hold him back, the fat old frightened man whom she almost loved.

He said, 'I never had this in mind.'

'I know. Don't say it. I understand.'

'I guess after all we've got a lot in common,' he said, and she agreed in order to quieten him. He was fast asleep by the time the light came back, so she got off the bed without waking him and went to her room. She locked the door and began with resolution to pack her bag: it was time for her to leave, it was time for term to start again. She wondered afterwards, when she thought of him, what it was they could have had in common, except the fact, of course, that for both of them Jamaica was cheap in August.

The Invisible
Japanese Gentlemen

CAST

THE AUTHOR, Denholm Elliott
THE MAN, Royce Mills
THE GIRL, Celia Bannerman

Dramatised by John Mortimer
Directed by Alastair Reid

The Invisible
Japanese Gentlemen

There were eight Japanese gentlemen having a fish dinner at Bentley's. They spoke to each other rarely in their incomprehensible tongue, but always with a courteous smile and often with a small bow. All but one of them wore glasses. Sometimes the pretty girl who sat in the window beyond gave them a passing glance, but her own problem seemed too serious for her to pay real attention to anyone in the world except herself and her companion.

She had thin blonde hair and her face was pretty and *petite* in a Regency way, oval like a miniature, though she had a harsh way of speaking – perhaps the accent of the school, Roedean or Cheltenham Ladies' College, which she had not long ago left. She wore a man's signet-ring on her engagement finger, and as I sat down at my table, with the Japanese gentlemen between us, she said, 'So you see we could marry next week.'

'Yes?'

Her companion appeared a little distraught. He refilled their glasses with Chablis and said, 'Of course, but Mother . . .' I missed some of the conversation then, because the eldest Japanese gentleman leant across the table, with a smile and a little bow, and uttered a whole paragraph like the mutter from an aviary, while everyone bent towards him and smiled and listened, and I couldn't help attending to him myself.

The girl's fiancé resembled her physically. I could see

them as two miniatures hanging side by side on white wood panels. He should have been a young officer in Nelson's navy in the days when a certain weakness and sensitivity were no bar to promotion.

She said, 'They are giving me an advance of five hundred pounds, and they've sold the paperback rights already.' The hard commercial declaration came as a shock to me; it was a shock too that she was one of my own profession. She couldn't have been more than twenty. She deserved better of life.

He said, 'But my uncle . . .'

'You know you don't get on with him. This way we shall be quite independent.'

'*You* will be independent,' he said grudgingly.

'The wine-trade wouldn't really suit you, would it? I spoke to my publisher about you and there's a very good chance . . . if you began with some reading . . .'

'But I don't know a thing about books.'

'I would help you at the start.'

'My mother says that writing is a good crutch . . .'

'Five hundred pounds and half the paperback rights is a pretty solid crutch,' she said.

'This Chablis is good, isn't it?'

'I daresay.'

I began to change my opinion of him – he had not the Nelson touch. He was doomed to defeat. She came alongside and raked him fore and aft. 'Do you know what Mr Dwight said?'

'Who's Dwight?'

'Darling, you don't listen, do you? My publisher. He said he hadn't read a first novel in the last ten years which showed such powers of observation.'

'That's wonderful,' he said sadly, 'wonderful.'

'Only he wants me to change the title.'

'Yes?'

'He doesn't like *The Ever-Rolling Stream*. He wants to call it *The Chelsea Set*.'

'What did you say?'

'I agreed. I do think that with a first novel one should try to keep one's publisher happy. Especially when, really, he's going to pay for our marriage, isn't he?'

'I see what you mean.' Absent-mindedly he stirred his Chablis with a fork – perhaps before the engagement he had always bought champagne. The Japanese gentlemen had finished their fish and with very little English but with elaborate courtesy they were ordering from the middle-aged waitress a fresh fruit salad. The girl looked at them, and then she looked at me, but I think she saw only the future. I wanted very much to warn her against any future based on a first novel called *The Chelsea Set*. I was on the side of his mother. It was a humiliating thought, but I was probably about her mother's age.

I wanted to say to her, Are you certain your publisher is telling you the truth? Publishers are human. They may sometimes exaggerate the virtues of the young and the pretty. Will *The Chelsea Set* be read in five years? Are you prepared for the years of effort, 'the long defeat of doing nothing well'? As the years pass writing will not become any easier, the daily effort will grow harder to endure, those 'powers of observation' will become enfeebled; you will be judged, when you reach your forties, by performance and not by promise.

'My next novel is going to be about St Tropez.'

'I didn't know you'd ever been there.'

'I haven't. A fresh eye's terribly important. I thought we might settle down there for six months.'

'There wouldn't be much left of the advance by that time.'

'The advance is only an advance. I get fifteen per cent after five thousand copies and twenty per cent after ten. And of course another advance will be due, darling, when the next book's finished. A bigger one if *The Chelsea Set* sells well.'

'Suppose it doesn't.'

'Mr Dwight says it will. He ought to know.'

'My uncle would start me at twelve hundred.'

'But, darling, how could you come then to St Tropez?'

'Perhaps we'd do better to marry when you come back.'

She said harshly, 'I mightn't come back if *The Chelsea Set* sells enough.'

'Oh.'

She looked at me and the party of Japanese gentlemen. She finished her wine. She said, 'Is this a quarrel?'

'No.'

'I've got the title for the next book – *The Azure Blue.*'

'I thought azure *was* blue.'

She looked at him with disappointment. 'You don't really want to be married to a novelist, do you?'

'You aren't one yet.'

'I was born one – Mr Dwight says. My powers of observation . . .'

'Yes. You told me that, but, dear, couldn't you observe a bit nearer home? Here in London.'

'I've done that in *The Chelsea Set*. I don't want to repeat myself.'

The bill had been lying beside them for some time now. He took out his wallet to pay, but she snatched the paper out of his reach. She said, 'This is my celebration.'

'What of?'

'*The Chelsea Set*, of course. Darling, you're awfully decorative, but sometimes – well, you simply don't connect.'

'I'd rather . . . if you don't mind . . .'

'No, darling, this is on me. And Mr Dwight, of course.'

He submitted just as two of the Japanese gentlemen gave tongue simultaneously, then stopped abruptly and bowed to each other, as though they were blocked in a doorway.

I had thought the two young people matching miniatures, but what a contrast in fact there was. The same type of prettiness could contain weakness and strength. Her Regency counterpart, I suppose, would have borne a dozen children without the aid of anaesthetics, while he would have fallen an easy victim to the first dark eyes in Naples. Would there one day be a dozen books on her shelf? They have to be born without an anaesthetic too. I found myself hoping that *The Chelsea Set* would prove to be a disaster and that eventually she would take up photographic modelling while he established himself solidly in the wine-trade in St James's. I didn't like to think of her as the Mrs Humphrey Ward of her generation – not that I would live so long. Old age saves us from the realization of a great many fears. I wondered to which publishing firm Dwight belonged. I could imagine the blurb he would have already written about her abrasive powers of observation. There would be a photo, if he was wise, on the back of the jacket, for reviewers, as well as publishers, are human, and she didn't look like Mrs Humphrey Ward.

I could hear them talking while they found their coats

at the back of the restaurant. He said, 'I wonder what all those Japanese are doing here?'

'Japanese?' she said. 'What Japanese, darling? Sometimes you are so evasive I think you don't want to marry me at all.'

Special Duties

CAST

MR FERRARO, John Gielgud
FATHER DEWES, Daniel O'Herlihy
MRS FERRARO, Judy Campbell
MISS SANDERSON, Ann Beach
HOPKINSON, Aubrey Morris
LANDLADY, Rita Webb
CHAUFFEUR, Colin Rix
POLICEMAN, Robert Gary
and
Lynne White
Cherie Lunghi
Susan Shaper
Angela Ellis

Dramatised by John Mortimer
Directed by Alastair Reid

Special Duties

William Ferraro, of Ferraro & Smith, lived in a great house in Montagu Square. One wing was occupied by his wife who believed herself to be an invalid and obeyed strictly the dictate that one should live every day as if it were one's last. For this reason her wing for the last ten years had invariably housed some Jesuit or Dominican priest with a taste for good wine and whisky and an emergency bell in his bedroom. Mr Ferraro looked after his salvation in more independent fashion. He retained the firm grasp on practical affairs that had enabled his grandfather, who had been a fellow exile with Mazzini, to found the great business of Ferraro & Smith in a foreign land. God has made man in his image, and it was not unreasonable for Mr Ferraro to return the compliment and to regard God as the director of some supreme business which yet depended for certain of its operations on Ferraro & Smith. The strength of a chain is in its weakest link, and Mr Ferraro did not forget his responsibility.

Before leaving for his office at 9.30 Mr Ferraro as a matter of courtesy would telephone to his wife in the other wing. 'Father Dewes speaking,' a voice would say.

'How is my wife?'

'She passed a good night.'

The conversation seldom varied. There had been a time when Father Dewes' predecessor made an attempt to bring Mr and Mrs Ferraro into a closer relationship, but he had desisted when he realized how hopeless his aim was, and how on the few occasions when Mr Ferraro dined with them in the other wing an inferior claret was served at table and no whisky was drunk before dinner.

Mr Ferraro, having telephoned from his bedroom where he took his breakfast, would walk, rather as God walked in the Garden, through his library lined with the correct classics and his drawing-room, on the walls of which hung one of the most expensive art collections in private hands. Where one man would treasure a single Degas, Renoir, Cézanne, Mr Ferraro bought wholesale – he had six Renoirs, four Degas, five Cézannes. He never tired of their presence, they represented a substantial saving in death-duties.

On this particular Monday morning it was also May the first. The sense of spring had come punctually to London and the sparrows were noisy in the dust. Mr Ferraro too was punctual, but unlike the seasons he was as reliable as Greenwich time. With his confidential secretary – a man called Hopkinson – he went through the schedule for the day. It was not very onerous, for Mr Ferraro had the rare quality of being able to delegate responsibility. He did this the more readily because he was accustomed to make unexpected checks, and woe betide the employee who failed him. Even his doctor had to submit to a sudden counter-check from a rival consultant. 'I think,' he said to Hopkinson, 'this afternoon I will drop in to Christie's and see how Maverick is getting on.' (Maverick was employed as his agent in the purchase of pictures.) What better could be done on a fine May afternoon than check on Maverick? He added, 'Send in Miss Saunders,' and drew forward a personal file which even Hopkinson was not allowed to handle.

Miss Saunders moused in. She gave the impression of moving close to the ground. She was about thirty years old with indeterminate hair and eyes of a startling clear blue which gave her otherwise anonymous face a resemblance to a holy statue. She was described in the firm's books as 'assistant confidential secretary' and her duties were 'special' ones. Even her qualifications were special: she had been head girl at the Convent of Saint Latitudinaria, Woking, where she had won in three successive years the special prize for piety – a little triptych of Our Lady with a background of blue silk, bound in Florentine leather and supplied by Burns Oates & Washbourne. She also had a long record of unpaid service as a Child of Mary.

'Miss Saunders,' Mr Ferraro said, 'I find no account here of the indulgences to be gained in June.'

'I have it here, sir. I was late home last night as the plenary indulgence at St Etheldreda's entailed the Stations of the Cross.'

She laid a typed list on Mr Ferraro's desk: in the first column the date, in the second the church or place of pilgrimage where the indulgence was to be gained, and in the third column in red ink the number of days saved from the temporal punishments of Purgatory. Mr Ferraro read it carefully.

'I get the impression, Miss Saunders,' he said, 'that you are spending too much time on the lower brackets. Sixty days here, fifty days there. Are you sure you are not wasting your time on these? One indulgence of 300 days will compensate for many such. I noticed just now that your estimate for May is lower than your April figures, and your estimate for June is nearly down to the March level. Five plenary indulgences and 1,565 days – a very good April work. I don't want you to slacken off.'

'April is a very good month for indulgences, sir. There is Easter. In May we can depend only on the fact

72

that it is Our Lady's month. June is not very fruitful, except at Corpus Christi. You will notice a little Polish church in Cambridgeshire . . .'

'As long as you remember, Miss Saunders, that none of us is getting younger. I put a great deal of trust in you, Miss Saunders. If I were less occupied here, I could attend to some of these indulgences myself. You pay great attention, I hope, to the conditions.'

'Of course I do, Mr Ferraro.'

'You are always careful to be in a State of Grace?'

Miss Saunders lowered her eyes. 'That is not very difficult in my case, Mr Ferraro.'

'What is your programme today?'

'You have it there, Mr Ferraro.'

'Of course. St Praxted's, Canon Wood. That is rather a long way to go. You have to spend the whole afternoon on a mere sixty days' indulgence?'

'It was all I could find for today. Of course there are always the plenary indulgences at the Cathedral. But I know how you feel about not repeating during the same month.'

'My only point of superstition,' Mr Ferraro said. 'It has no basis, of course, in the teaching of the Church.'

'You wouldn't like an occasional repetition for a member of your family, Mr Ferraro, your wife . . . ?'

'We are taught, Miss Saunders, to pay first attention to our own souls. My wife should be looking after her own indulgences – she has an excellent Jesuit adviser – I employ you to look after mine.'

'You have no objection to Canon Wood?'

'If it is really the best you can do. So long as it does not involve overtime.'

73

'Oh no, Mr Ferraro. A decade of the Rosary, that's all.'

After an early lunch – a simple one in a City chop-house which concluded with some Stilton and a glass of excellent port – Mr Ferraro visited Christie's. Maverick was satisfactorily on the spot and Mr Ferraro did not bother to wait for the Bonnard and the Monet which his agent had advised him to buy. The day remained warm and sunny, but there were confused sounds from the direction of Trafalgar Square which reminded Mr Ferraro that it was Labour Day. There was something inappropriate to the sun and the early flowers under the park trees in these processions of men without ties carrying dreary banners covered with bad lettering. A desire came to Mr Ferraro to take a real holiday, and he nearly told his chauffeur to drive to Richmond Park. But he always preferred, if it were possible, to combine business with pleasure, and it occurred to him that if he drove out now to Canon Wood, Miss Saunders should be arriving about the same time, after her lunch interval, to start the afternoon's work.

Canon Wood was one of those new suburbs built around an old estate. The estate was a public park, the house, formerly famous as the home of a minor Minister who served under Lord North at the time of the American rebellion, was now a local museum, and a street had been built on the little windy hill-top once a hundred acre field: a Charrington coal agency, the window dressed with one large nugget in a metal basket, a Home & Colonial Stores, an Odeon cinema, a large Anglican church. Mr Ferraro told his driver to ask the way to the Roman Catholic church.

'There isn't one here,' the policeman said.

'St Praxted's?'

'There's no such place,' the policeman said.

Mr Ferraro, like a Biblical character, felt a loosening of the bowels.

'St Praxted's, Canon Wood.'

'Doesn't exist, sir,' the policeman said. Mr Ferraro drove slowly back towards the City. This was the first time he had checked on Miss Saunders – three prizes for piety had won his trust. Now on his homeward way he remembered that Hitler had been educated by the Jesuits, and yet hopelessly he hoped.

In his office he unlocked the drawer and took out the special file. Could he have mistaken Canonbury for Canon Wood? But he had not been mistaken, and suddenly a terrible doubt came to him how often in the last three years Miss Saunders had betrayed her trust. (It was after a severe attack of pneumonia three years ago that he had engaged her – the idea had come to him during the long insomnias of convalescence.) Was it possible that not one of these indulgences had been gained? He couldn't believe that. Surely a few of that vast total of 36,892 days must still be valid. But only Miss Saunders could tell him how many. And what had she been doing with her office time – those long hours of pilgrimage? She had once taken a whole week-end at Walsingham.

He rang for Mr Hopkinson, who could not help remarking on the whiteness of his employer's face. 'Are you feeling quite well, Mr Ferraro?'

'I have had a severe shock. Can you tell me where Miss Saunders lives?'

'She lives with an invalid mother near Westbourne Grove.'

'The exact address, please.'

Mr Ferraro drove into the dreary waste of Bayswater: great family houses had been converted into private hotels or fortunately bombed into car parks. In the terraces behind dubious girls leant against the railings, and a street band blew harshly round a corner. Mr Ferraro found the house, but he could not bring himself to ring the bell. He sat crouched in his Daimler waiting for something to happen. Was it the intensity of his gaze that brought Miss Saunders to an upper window, a coincidence, or retribution? Mr Ferraro thought at first that it was the warmth of the day that had caused her to be so inefficiently clothed, as she slid the window a little wider open. But then an arm circled her waist, a young man's face looked down into the street, a hand pulled a curtain across with the familiarity of habit. It became obvious to Mr Ferraro that not even the conditions for an indulgence had been properly fulfilled.

If a friend could have seen Mr Ferraro that evening mounting the steps of Montagu Square, he would have been surprised at the way he had aged. It was almost as though he had assumed during the long afternoon those 36,892 days he had thought to have saved during the last three years from Purgatory. The curtains were drawn, the lights were on, and no doubt Father Dewes was pouring out the first of his evening whiskies in the other wing. Mr Ferraro did not ring the bell, but let himself quietly in. The thick carpet swallowed his footsteps like quicksand. He switched on no lights: only a red-shaded lamp in each room had been lit ready for his use and now guided his steps. The pictures in the drawing-room reminded him of death-duties: a great Degas bottom like an atomic explosion mushroomed above a bath: Mr Ferraro passed on into the library: the leather-bound classics reminded him of dead authors. He sat down in a chair and a slight pain in his chest reminded him of his double pneumonia. He was three years nearer death than when Miss Saunders was appointed first. After a long while Mr Ferraro knotted his fingers together in the shape some people use for prayer. With Mr Ferraro it was an indication of decision. The worst was over: time lengthened again ahead of him. He thought: 'Tomorrow I will set about getting a really reliable secretary.'

The Destructors

CAST

MR THOMAS, George Hilsdon
TREVOR, Nicholas Drake
BLACKIE, Phil Daniels
THE GANG,
      John Fowler

      David Nunn

      Christopher Burke

      Tony London

      Raymond Boal

      Paul Andrew

      John Williams

      Mark Burdis

      Gabriel Kelly

      Paul Pender
LORRY DRIVER, Chris Webb
MR BURTON, Michael Byrne
MRS BURTON, Mary Miller
NIGHTWATCHMAN, Fred Radley

Dramatised by John Mortimer
Directed by Michael Apted

The Destructors

[1]

It was on the eve of August Bank Holiday that the latest recruit became the leader of the Wormsley Common Gang. No one was surprised except Mike, but Mike at the age of nine was surprised by everything. 'If you don't shut your mouth,' somebody once said to him, 'you'll get a frog down it.' After that Mike kept his teeth tightly clamped except when the surprise was too great.

The new recruit had been with the gang since the beginning of the summer holidays, and there were possibilities about his brooding silence that all recognized. He never wasted a word even to tell his name until that was required of him by the rules. When he said 'Trevor' it was a statement of fact, not as it would have been with the others a statement of shame or defiance. Nor did anyone laugh except Mike, who finding himself without support and meeting the dark gaze of the newcomer opened his mouth and was quiet again. There was every reason why T., as he was afterwards referred to, should have been an object of mockery – there was his name (and they substituted the initial because otherwise they had no excuse not to laugh at it), the fact that his father, a former architect and present clerk, had 'come down in the world' and that his mother considered herself better than the neighbours. What but an odd quality of danger, of the unpredictable, established him in the gang without any ignoble ceremony of initiation?

The gang met every morning in an impromptu

car-park, the site of the last bomb of the first blitz. The leader, who was known as Blackie, claimed to have heard it fall, and no one was precise enough in his dates to point out that he would have been one year old and fast asleep on the down platform of Wormsley Common Underground Station. On one side of the car-park leant the first occupied house, No. 3, of the shattered Northwood Terrace – literally leant, for it had suffered from the blast of the bomb and the side walls were supported on wooden struts. A smaller bomb and some incendiaries had fallen beyond, so that the house stuck up like a jagged tooth and carried on the further wall relics of its neighbour, a dado, the remains of a fireplace. T., whose words were almost confined to voting 'Yes' or 'No' to the plan of operations proposed each day by Blackie, once startled the whole gang by saying broodingly, 'Wren built that house, father says.'

'Who's Wren?'

'The man who built St Paul's.'

'Who cares?' Blackie said. 'It's only Old Misery's.'

Old Misery – whose real name was Thomas – had once been a builder and decorator. He lived alone in the crippled house, doing for himself: once a week you could see him coming back across the common with bread and vegetables, and once as the boys played in the car-park he put his head over the smashed wall of his garden and looked at them.

'Been to the lav,' one of the boys said, for it was common knowledge that since the bombs fell something had gone wrong with the pipes of the house and Old Misery was too mean to spend money on the property. He could do the redecorating himself at cost price, but **he had never** learnt plumbing. The lav was a wooden shed at the bottom of the narrow garden with a star-shaped hole in the door: it had escaped the blast which had smashed the house next door and sucked out the window-frames of No. 3.

The next time the gang became aware of Mr Thomas was more surprising. Blackie, Mike and a thin yellow boy, who for some reason was called by his surname Summers, met him on the common coming back from the market. Mr Thomas stopped them. He said glumly, 'You belong to the lot that play in the car-park?'

Mike was about to answer when Blackie stopped him. As the leader he had responsibilities. 'Suppose we are?' he said ambiguously.

'I got some chocolates,' Mr Thomas said. 'Don't like 'em myself. Here you are. Not enough to go round, I don't suppose. There never is,' he added with sombre conviction. He handed over three packets of Smarties.

The gang was puzzled and perturbed by this action and tried to explain it away. 'Bet someone dropped them and he picked 'em up,' somebody suggested.

'Pinched 'em and then got in a bleeding funk,' another thought aloud.

'It's a bribe,' Summers said. 'He wants us to stop bouncing balls on his wall.'

'We'll show him we don't take bribes,' Blackie said, and they sacrificed the whole morning to the game of bouncing that only Mike was young enough to enjoy. There was no sign from Mr Thomas.

Next day T. astonished them all. He was late at the rendezvous, and the voting for that day's exploit took place without him. At Blackie's suggestion the gang was to disperse in pairs, take buses at random and see how many free rides could be snatched from unwary conductors (the operation was to be carried out in pairs to avoid cheating). They were drawing lots for their companions when T. arrived.

'Where you been, T.?' Blackie asked. 'You can't vote now. You know the rules.'

'I've been *there*,' T. said. He looked at the ground, as though he had thoughts to hide.

'Where?'

'At Old Misery's.' Mike's mouth opened and then hurriedly closed again with a click. He had remembered the frog.

'At Old Misery's?' Blackie said. There was nothing in the rules against it, but he had a sensation that T. was treading on dangerous ground. He asked hopefully, 'Did you break in?'

'No. I rang the bell.'

'And what did you say?'

'I said I wanted to see his house.'

'What did he do?'

'He showed it me.'

'Pinch anything?'

'No.'

'What did you do it for then?'

The gang had gathered round: it was as though an impromptu court were about to form and try some case of deviation. T. said, 'It's a beautiful house,' and still watching the ground, meeting no one's eyes, he licked his lips first one way, then the other.

'What do you mean, a beautiful house?' Blackie asked with scorn.

'It's got a staircase two hundred years old like a corkscrew. Nothing holds it up.'

'What do you mean, nothing holds it up. Does it float?'

'It's to do with opposite forces, Old Misery said.'

'What else?'

'There's panelling.'

'Like in the Blue Boar?'

'Two hundred years old.'

'Is Old Misery two hundred years old?'

Mike laughed suddenly and then was quiet again. The meeting was in a serious mood. For the first time since T. had strolled into the car-park on the first day of the holidays his position was in danger. It only needed a single use of his real name and the gang would be at his heels.

'What did you do it for?' Blackie asked. He was just, he had no jealousy, he was anxious to retain T. in the gang if he could. It was the word 'beautiful' that worried him – that belonged to a class world that you could still see parodied at the Wormsley Common Empire by a man wearing a top hat and a monocle, with a haw-haw accent. He was tempted to say, 'My dear Trevor, old chap,' and unleash his hell hounds. 'If you'd broken in,' he said sadly – that indeed would have been an exploit worthy of the gang.

'This was better,' T. said. 'I found out things.' He continued to stare at his feet, not meeting anybody's eye, as though he were absorbed in some dream he was unwilling – or ashamed – to share.

'What things?'

'Old Misery's going to be away all tomorrow and Bank Holiday.'

Blackie said with relief, 'You mean we could break in?'

'And pinch things?' somebody asked.

Blackie said, 'Nobody's going to pinch things. Breaking in – that's good enough, isn't it? We don't want any court stuff.'

'I don't want to pinch anything,' T. said. 'I've got a better idea.'

'What is it?'

T. raised eyes, as grey and disturbed as the drab August day. 'We'll pull it down,' he said. 'We'll destroy it.'

Blackie gave a single hoot of laughter and then, like Mike, fell quiet, daunted by the serious implacable gaze. 'What'd the police be doing all the time?' he said.

'They'd never know. We'd do it from inside. I've found a way in.' He said with a sort of intensity, 'We'd be like worms, don't you see, in an apple. When we came out again there'd be nothing there, no staircase, no panels, nothing but just walls, and then we'd make the walls fall down – somehow.'

'We'd go to jug,' Blackie said.

'Who's to prove? and anyway we wouldn't have pinched anything.' He added without the smallest flicker of glee, 'There wouldn't be anything to pinch after we'd finished.'

'I've never heard of going to prison for breaking things,' Summers said.

'There wouldn't be time,' Blackie said. 'I've seen housebreakers at work.'

'There are twelve of us,' T. said. 'We'd organize.'

'None of us know how . . .'

'I know,' T. said. He looked across at Blackie. 'Have you got a better plan?'

'Today,' Mike said tactlessly, 'we're pinching free rides . . .'

'Free rides,' T. said. 'Kid stuff. You can stand down, Blackie, if you'd rather . . .'

'The gang's got to vote.'

'Put it up then.'

Blackie said uneasily, 'It's proposed that tomorrow and Monday we destroy Old Misery's house.'

'Here, here,' said a fat boy called Joe.

'Who's in favour?'

T. said, 'It's carried.'

'How do we start?' Summers asked.

'He'll tell you,' Blackie said. It was the end of his leadership. He went away to the back of the car-park and began to kick a stone, dribbling it this way and that. There was only one old Morris in the park, for few cars were left there except lorries: without an attendant there was no safety. He took a flying kick at the car and scraped a little paint off the rear mudguard. Beyond, paying no more attention to him than to a stranger, the gang had gathered round T.; Blackie was dimly aware of the fickleness of favour. He thought of going home, of never returning, of letting them all discover the hollowness of T.'s leadership, but suppose after all what T. proposed was possible – nothing like it had ever been done before. The fame of the Wormsley Common car-park gang would surely reach around London. There would be headlines in the papers. Even the grown-up gangs who ran the betting at the all-in wrestling and the barrow-boys would hear with respect of how Old Misery's house had been destroyed. Driven by the pure, simple and altruistic ambition of fame for the gang, Blackie came back to where T. stood in the shadow of old Misery's wall.

T. was giving his orders with decision: it was as though this plan had been with him all his life, pondered through the seasons, now in his fifteenth year crystallized with the pain of puberty. 'You,' he said to Mike, 'bring some big nails, the biggest you can find, and a hammer. Anybody who can better bring a hammer and a screwdriver. We'll need plenty of them. Chisels too. We can't have too many chisels. Can anybody bring a saw?'

'I can,' Mike said.

'Not a child's saw,' T. said. 'A real saw.'

Blackie realized he had raised his hand like any ordinary member of the gang.

'Right, you bring one, Blackie. But now there's a difficulty. We want a hacksaw.'

'What's a hacksaw?' someone asked.

'You can get 'em at Woolworth's,' Summers said.

The fat boy called Joe said gloomily, 'I knew it would end in a collection.'

'I'll get one myself,' T. said. 'I don't want your money. But I can't buy a sledge-hammer.'

Blackie said, 'They are working on No. 15. I know where they'll leave their stuff for Bank Holiday.'

'Then that's all,' T. said. 'We meet here at nine sharp.'

'I've got to go to church,' Mike said.

'Come over the wall and whistle. We'll let you in.'

[2]

On Sunday morning all were punctual except Blackie, even Mike. Mike had a stroke of luck. His mother felt ill, his father was tired after Saturday night, and he was told to go to church alone with many warnings of what would happen if he strayed. Blackie had difficulty in smuggling out the saw, and then in finding the sledge-hammer at the back of No. 15. He approached the house from a lane at the rear of the garden, for fear of the policeman's beat along the main road. The tired evergreens kept off a stormy sun: another wet Bank Holiday was being prepared over the Atlantic, beginning in swirls of dust under the trees. Blackie climbed the wall into Misery's garden.

There was no sign of anybody anywhere. The lav stood like a tomb in a neglected graveyard. The curtains were drawn. The house slept. Blackie lumbered nearer with the saw and the sledge-hammer. Perhaps after all nobody had turned up: the plan had been a wild invention: they had woken wiser. But when he came close to the back door he could hear a confusion of sound hardly louder than a hive in swarm: a clickety-clack, a bang bang, a scraping, a creaking, a sudden painful crack. He thought: it's true, and whistled.

They opened the back door to him and he came in. He had at once the impression of organization, very different from the old happy-go-lucky ways under his leadership. For a while he wandered up and down stairs looking for T. Nobody addressed him: he had a sense of great urgency, and already he could begin to see the plan. The interior of the house was being carefully demolished without touching the outer walls. Summers with hammer and chisel was ripping out the skirting-boards in the ground floor dining-room: he had already smashed the panels of the door. In the same room Joe was heaving up the parquet blocks, exposing the soft wood floor-boards over the cellar. Coils of wire came out of the damaged skirting and Mike sat happily on the floor clipping the wires.

On the curved stairs two of the gang were working

hard with an inadequate child's saw on the banisters –
when they saw Blackie's big saw they signalled for it
wordlessly. When he next saw them a quarter of the
banisters had been dropped into the hall. He found T. at
last in the bathroom – he sat moodily in the least cared-
for room in the house, listening to the sounds coming up
from below.

'You've really done it,' Blackie said with awe. 'What's
going to happen?'

'We've only just begun,' T. said. He looked at the
sledge-hammer and gave his instructions. 'You stay here
and break the bath and the wash-basin. Don't bother
about the pipes. They come later.'

Mike appeared at the door. 'I've finished the wires, T.,'
he said.

'Good. You've just got to go wandering round now.
The kitchen's in the basement. Smash all the china and
glass and bottles you can lay hold of. Don't turn on the
taps – we don't want a flood – yet. Then go into all the
rooms and turn out drawers. If they are locked get one of
the others to break them open. Tear up any papers you
find and smash all the ornaments. Better take a carving-
knife with you from the kitchen. The bedroom's opposite
here. Open the pillows and tear up the sheets. That's
enough for the moment. And you, Blackie, when you've
finished in here crack the plaster in the passage up with
your sledge-hammer.'

'What are you going to do?' Blackie asked.

'I'm looking for something special,' T. said.

It was nearly lunch-time before Blackie had finished
and went in search of T. Chaos had advanced. The kitchen was a shambles of broken glass and china. The
dining-room was stripped of parquet, the skirting was up,

the door had been taken off its hinges, and the destroyers had moved up a floor. Streaks of light came in through the closed shutters where they worked with the seriousness of creators – and destruction after all is a form of creation. A kind of imagination had seen this house as it had now become.

Mike said, 'I've got to go home for dinner.'

'Who else?' T. asked, but all the others on one excuse or another had brought provisions with them.

They squatted in the ruins of the room and swapped unwanted sandwiches. Half an hour for lunch and they were at work again. By the time Mike returned they were on the top floor, and by six the superficial damage was completed. The doors were all off, all the skirtings raised, the furniture pillaged and ripped and smashed – no one could have slept in the house except on a bed of broken plaster. T. gave his orders – eight o'clock next morning, and to escape notice they climbed singly over the garden wall, into the car-park. Only Blackie and T. were left: the light had nearly gone, and when they touched a switch, nothing worked – Mike had done his job thoroughly.

'Did you find anything special?' Blackie asked.

T. nodded. 'Come over here,' he said, 'and look.' Out of both pockets he drew bundles of pound notes. 'Old Misery's savings,' he said. 'Mike ripped out the mattress, but he missed them.'

'What are you going to do? Share them?'

'We aren't thieves,' T. said. 'Nobody's going to steal anything from this house. I kept these for you and me – a celebration.' He knelt down on the floor and counted them out – there were seventy in all. 'We'll burn them,' he said, 'one by one,' and taking it in turns they held a note upwards and lit the top corner, so that the flame burnt slowly towards their fingers. The grey ash floated above them and fell on their heads like age. 'I'd like to see Old Misery's face when we are through,' T. said.

'You hate him a lot?' Blackie asked.

'Of course I don't hate him,' T. said. 'There'd be no fun if I hated him.' The last burning note illuminated his brooding face. 'All this hate and love,' he said, 'it's soft, it's hooey. There's only things, Blackie,' and he looked round the room crowded with the unfamiliar shadows of half things, broken things, former things. 'I'll race you home, Blackie,' he said.

[3]

Next morning the serious destruction started. Two were missing – Mike and another boy whose parents were off to Southend and Brighton in spite of the slow warm drops that had begun to fall and the rumble of thunder in the estuary like the first guns of the old blitz. 'We've got to hurry,' T. said.

Summers was restive. 'Haven't we done enough?' he asked. 'I've been given a bob for slot machines. This is like work.'

'We've hardly started,' T. said. 'Why, there's all the floors left, and the stairs. We haven't taken out a single window. You voted like the others. We are going to *destroy* this house. There won't be anything left when we've finished.'

They began again on the first floor picking up the top floor-boards next the outer wall, leaving the joists exposed. Then they sawed through the joists and retreated into the hall, as what was left of the floor heeled and sank. They had learnt with practice, and the second floor collapsed more easily. By the evening an odd exhilaration seized them as they looked down the great hollow of the house. They ran risks and made mistakes: when they thought of the windows it was too late to reach them. 'Cor,' Joe said, and dropped a penny down into the dry rubble-filled well. It cracked and span amongst the broken glass.

'Why did we start this?' Summers asked with astonishment; T. was already on the ground, digging at the rubble, clearing a space along the outer wall. 'Turn on the taps,' he said. 'It's too dark for anyone to see now, and in the morning it won't matter.' The water overtook them on the stairs and fell through the floorless rooms.

It was then they heard Mike's whistle at the back. 'Something's wrong,' Blackie said. They could hear his urgent breathing as they unlocked the door.

'The bogies?' Summers asked.

'Old Misery,' Mike said. 'He's on his way.' He put his head between his knees and retched. 'Ran all the way,' he said with pride.

'But why?' T. said. 'He told me . . .' He protested with the fury of the child he had never been, 'It isn't fair.'

'He was down at Southend,' Mike said, 'and he was on the train coming back. Said it was too cold and wet.' He paused and gazed at the water. 'My, you've had a storm here. Is the roof leaking?'

'How long will he be?'

'Five minutes. I gave Ma the slip and ran.'

'We better clear,' Summers said. 'We've done enough, anyway.'

'Oh no, we haven't. Anybody could do this –' 'this' was the shattered hollowed house with nothing left but the walls. Yet walls could be preserved. Façades were valuable. They could build inside again more beautifully than before. This could again be a home. He said angrily, 'We've got to finish. Don't move. Let me think.'

'There's no time,' a boy said.

'There's got to be a way,' T. said. 'We couldn't have got this far . . .'

'We've done a lot,' Blackie said.

'No. No, we haven't. Somebody watch the front.'

'We can't do any more.'

'He may come in at the back.'

'Watch the back too.' T. began to plead. 'Just give me a minute and I'll fix it. I swear I'll fix it.' But his authority had gone with his ambiguity. He was only one of the gang. 'Please,' he said.

'Please,' Summers mimicked him, and then suddenly struck home with the fatal name. 'Run along home, Trevor.'

T. stood with his back to the rubble like a boxer knocked groggy against the ropes. He had no words as his dreams shook and slid. Then Blackie acted before the gang had time to laugh, pushing Summers backward. 'I'll watch the front, T.,' he said, and cautiously he opened the shutters of the hall. The grey wet common stretched ahead, and the lamps gleamed in the puddles. 'Someone's coming, T. No, it's not him. What's your plan, T.?'

'Tell Mike to go out to the lav and hide close beside it. When he hears me whistle he's got to count ten and start to shout.'

'Shout what?'

'Oh, "Help", anything.'

'You hear, Mike,' Blackie said. He was the leader

93

again. He took a quick look between the shutters. 'He's coming, T.'

'Quick, Mike. The lav. Stay here, Blackie, all of you, till I yell.'

'Where are you going, T.?'

'Don't worry. I'll see to this. I said I would, didn't I?'

Old Misery came limping off the common. He had mud on his shoes and he stopped to scrape them on the pavement's edge. He didn't want to soil his house, which stood jagged and dark between the bomb-sites, saved so narrowly, as he believed, from destruction. Even the fanlight had been left unbroken by the bomb's blast. Somewhere somebody whistled. Old Misery looked sharply round. He didn't trust whistles. A child was shouting: it seemed to come from his own garden. Then a boy ran into the road from the car-park. 'Mr Thomas,' he called, 'Mr Thomas.'

'What is it?'

'I'm terribly sorry, Mr Thomas. One of us got taken short, and we thought you wouldn't mind, and now he can't get out.'

'What do you mean, boy?'

'He's got stuck in your lav.'

'He'd no business. . . . Haven't I seen you before?'

'You showed me your house.'

'So I did. So I did. That doesn't give you the right to . . .'

'Do hurry, Mr Thomas. He'll suffocate.'

'Nonsense. He can't suffocate. Wait till I put my bag in.'

'I'll carry your bag.'

'Oh no, you don't. I carry my own.'

'This way, Mr Thomas.'

'I can't get in the garden that way. I've got to go through the house.'

'But you *can* get in the garden this way, Mr Thomas. We often do.'

'You often do?' He followed the boy with a scandalized fascination. 'When? What right . . . ?'

'Do you see . . . ? the wall's low.'

'I'm not going to climb walls into my own garden. It's absurd.'

'This is how we do it. One foot here, one foot there, and over.' The boy's face peered down, an arm shot out, and Mr Thomas found his bag taken and deposited on the other side of the wall.

'Give me back my bag,' Mr Thomas said. From the loo a boy yelled and yelled. 'I'll call the police.'

'Your bag's all right, Mr Thomas. Look. One foot there. On your right. Now just above. To your left.' Mr Thomas climbed over his own garden wall. 'Here's your bag, Mr Thomas.'

'I'll have the wall built up,' Mr Thomas said, 'I'll not have you boys coming over here, using my loo.' He stumbled on the path, but the boy caught his elbow and supported him. 'Thank you, thank you, my boy,' he murmured automatically. Somebody shouted again through the dark. 'I'm coming, I'm coming,' Mr Thomas called. He said to the boy beside him, 'I'm not unreasonable. Been a boy myself. As long as things are done regular. I don't mind you playing round the place Saturday mornings. Sometimes I like company. Only it's got to be regular. One of you asks leave and I say Yes. Sometimes I'll say No. Won't feel like it. And you come in at the front door and out at the back. No garden walls.'

'Do get him out, Mr Thomas.'

'He won't come to any harm in my loo,' Mr Thomas said, stumbling slowly down the garden. 'Oh, my rheumatics,' he said. 'Always get 'em on Bank Holiday. I've got to go careful. There's loose stones here. Give me your hand. Do you know what my horoscope said yesterday? "Abstain from any dealings in first half of week. Danger of serious crash." That might be on this path,' Mr Thomas said. 'They speak in parables and double meanings.' He paused at the door of the loo. 'What's the matter in there?' he called. There was no reply.

'Perhaps he's fainted,' the boy said.

'Not in my loo. Here, you, come out,' Mr Thomas said, and giving a great jerk at the door he nearly fell on his back when it swung easily open. A hand first supported him and then pushed him hard. His head hit the opposite wall and he sat heavily down. His bag hit his feet. A hand whipped the key out of the lock and the door slammed. 'Let me out,' he called, and heard the key turn in the lock. 'A serious crash,' he thought, and felt dithery and confused and old.

A voice spoke to him softly through the star-shaped hole in the door. 'Don't worry, Mr Thomas,' it said, 'we won't hurt you, not if you stay quiet.'

Mr Thomas put his head between his hands and pondered. He had noticed that there was only one lorry in the car-park, and he felt certain that the driver would not come for it before the morning. Nobody could hear him from the road in front, and the lane at the back was seldom used. Anyone who passed there would be hurrying home and would not pause for what they would certainly take to be drunken cries. And if he did call 'Help', who, on a lonely Bank Holiday evening, would have the courage to investigate? Mr Thomas sat on the loo and pondered with the wisdom of age.

After a while it seemed to him that there were sounds in the silence – they were faint and came from the direction of his house. He stood up and peered through the ventilation-hole – between the cracks in one of the shutters he saw a light, not the light of a lamp, but the wavering light that a candle might give. Then he thought he heard the sound of hammering and scraping and chipping. He thought of burglars – perhaps they had employed the boy as a scout, but why should burglars engage in what sounded more and more like a stealthy form of carpentry? Mr Thomas let out an experimental yell, but nobody answered. The noise could not even have reached his enemies.

[4]

Mike had gone home to bed, but the rest stayed. The question of leadership no longer concerned the gang. With nails, chisels, screwdrivers, anything that was sharp and penetrating, they moved around the inner walls worrying at the mortar between the bricks. They started too high, and it was Blackie who hit on the damp course and realized the work could be halved if they weakened the joints immediately above. It was a long, tiring, unamusing job, but at last it was finished. The gutted house stood there balanced on a few inches of mortar between the damp course and the bricks.

There remained the most dangerous task of all, out in the open at the edge of the bomb-site. Summers was sent to watch the road for passers-by, and Mr Thomas, sitting on the loo, heard clearly now the sound of sawing. It no longer came from his house, and that a little reassured him. He felt less concerned. Perhaps the other noises too had no significance.

A voice spoke to him through the hole. 'Mr Thomas.'

'Let me out,' Mr Thomas said sternly.

'Here's a blanket,' the voice said, and a long grey sausage was worked through the hole and fell in swathes over Mr Thomas's head.

'There's nothing personal,' the voice said. 'We want you to be comfortable tonight.'

'Tonight,' Mr Thomas repeated incredulously.

'Catch,' the voice said. 'Penny buns – we've buttered them, and sausage-rolls. We don't want you to starve, Mr Thomas.'

Mr Thomas pleaded desperately. 'A joke's a joke, boy. Let me out and I won't say a thing. I've got rheumatics. I got to sleep comfortable.'

'You wouldn't be comfortable, not in your house, you wouldn't. Not now.'

'What do you mean, boy?' But the footsteps receded. There was only the silence of night: no sound of sawing. Mr Thomas tried one more yell, but he was daunted and rebuked by the silence – a long way off an owl hooted and made away again on its muffled flight through the sound-less world.

At seven next morning the driver came to fetch his lorry. He climbed into the seat and tried to start the engine. He was vaguely aware of a voice shouting, but it didn't concern him. At last the engine responded and he backed the lorry until it touched the great wooden shore that supported Mr Thomas's house. That way he could drive right out and down the street without reversing. The lorry moved forward, was momentarily checked as

98

though something were pulling it from behind, and then went on to the sound of a long rumbling crash. The driver was astonished to see bricks bouncing ahead of him, while stones hit the roof of his cab. He put on his brakes. When he climbed out the whole landscape had suddenly altered. There was no house beside the car-park, only a hill of rubble. He went round and examined the back of his lorry for damage, and found a rope tied there that was still twisted at the other end round part of a wooden strut.

The driver again became aware of somebody shouting. It came from the wooden erection which was the nearest thing to a house in that desolation of broken brick. The driver climbed the smashed wall and unlocked the door. Mr Thomas came out of the loo. He was wearing a grey blanket to which flakes of pastry adhered. He gave a sobbing cry. 'My house,' he said. 'Where's my house?'

'Search me,' the driver said. His eye lit on the remains of a bath and what had once been a dresser and he began to laugh. There wasn't anything left anywhere.

'How dare you laugh,' Mr Thomas said. 'It was my house. My house.'

'I'm sorry,' the driver said, making heroic efforts, but when he remembered the sudden check to his lorry, the crash of bricks falling, he became convulsed again. One moment the house had stood there with such dignity between the bomb-sites like a man in a top hat, and then, bang, crash, there wasn't anything left – not anything. He said, 'I'm sorry. I can't help it, Mr Thomas. There's nothing personal, but you got to admit it's funny.'

Alas, Poor Maling

CAST

1ST FIRE-WATCHER, George Tovey
2ND FIRE-WATCHER, Basil Henson
MALING, John Bird
PASSENGER, John Baskomb
PIANIST, Margot Field
DOCTOR, James Bree
SIR JOSHUA, John Boxer
WESBY HYTHE, Clifford Parrish
DEXTER, Rayner Newmark

Dramatised by Graham Greene
Directed by Graham Evans

Alas, Poor Maling

Poor inoffensive ineffectual Maling! I don't want you to smile at Maling and his borborygmi, as the doctors always smiled when he consulted them, as they must have smiled even after the sad climax of September 3rd, 1940, when his borborygmi held up for twenty-four fatal hours the amalgamation of the Simcox and Hythe Newsprint Companies. Simcox's interests had always been dearer to Maling than life: hard-driven, conscientious, happy in his work, he wanted no position higher than their secretary, and those twenty-four hours happened – for reasons it is unwise to go into here, for they involve intricacies in British income tax law – to be fatal to the company's existence. After that day he dropped altogether out of sight, and I shall always believe he crept away to die of a broken heart in some provincial printing works. Alas, poor Maling!

It was the doctors who called his complaint borborygmi: in England we usually call it just 'tummy rumbles'. I believe it's quite a harmless kind of indigestion, but in Maling's case it took a rather odd form. His stomach, he used to complain, blinking sadly downwards through his semi-circular reading glasses, had 'an ear'. It used to pick up notes in an extraordinary way and give them out again after meals. I shall never forget one embarrassing tea at the Piccadilly Hotel in honour of a party of provincial printers: it was the year before the war, and Maling had been attending the Symphony Concerts at Queen's Hall (he never went again). In the distance a dance orchestra had been playing 'The Lambeth Walk' (how tired one got of that tune in 1938 with its waggery and false bonhomie and its 'ois'). Suddenly in the happy silence between dances, as the printers sat back from a ruin of toasted tea-cakes, there emerged – faint as though from a distant part of the hotel, sad and plangent – the opening bars of a Brahms Concerto. A Scottish printer, who had an ear for good music, exclaimed with dour relish, 'My goodness, how that mon can play.' Then the music stopped abruptly, and an odd suspicion made me look at Maling. He was red as beetroot. Nobody noticed because the dance orchestra began again to the Scotsman's disgust with 'Boomps-a-Daisy', and I think I was the only one who detected a curious faint undertone of 'The Lambeth Walk' apparently coming from the chair where Maling sat.

It was after ten, when the printers had piled into taxis and driven away to Euston, that Maling told me about his stomach. 'It's quite unaccountable,' he said, 'like a parrot. It seems to pick up things at random.' He added with tears in his voice, 'I can't enjoy food any more. I never know what's going to happen afterwards. This afternoon wasn't the worst. Sometimes it's quite loud.' He brooded forlornly. 'When I was a boy I liked listening to German bands . . .'

'Haven't you seen a doctor?'

'They don't understand. They say it's just indigestion and nothing to worry about. Nothing to worry about! But then when I've been seeing a doctor it's always lain quiet.' I noticed that he spoke of his stomach as if it were a detested animal. He gazed bleakly at his knuckles and said, 'Now I've become afraid of any new noise. I never know. It doesn't take any notice of some, but others seem . . . well, to fascinate it. At a first hearing. Last year when they took up Piccadilly it was the road drills. I used to get them all over again after dinner.'

I said rather stupidly, 'I suppose you've tried the usual salts,' and I remember – it was my last sight of him – his expression of despair as though he had ceased to expect comprehension from any living soul.

It was my last sight of him because the war pitched me out of the printing trade into all sorts of odd occupations, and it was only at second-hand that I heard the account of the strange board meeting which broke poor Maling's heart.

What the papers called the blitz-and-pieces krieg against Britain had been going on for about a week: in London we were just settling down to air-raid alarms at the rate of five or six a day, but the 3rd of September, the anniversary of the war, had so far been relatively peaceful. There was a general feeling, however, that Hitler might celebrate the anniversary with a big attack. It was therefore in an atmosphere of some tension that Simcox and Hythe had their joint meeting.

It took place in the traditional grubby little room above the Simcox offices in Fetter Lane: the round table dating from the original Joshua Simcox, the steel engraving of a printing works dated 1875, and an irrelevant copy of a Bible which had always been the only book in the big glass bookcase except for a volume of type faces. Old Sir Joshua Simcox was in the chair: you can picture his snow-white hair and the pale pork-like Nonconformist features. Wesby Hythe was there, and half a dozen other directors with narrow canny faces and neat black coats: they all looked a little strained. If the new income-tax regulations were to be evaded, they had to work quickly. As for Maling he crouched over his pad, nervously ready to advise anybody on anything.

There was one interruption during the reading of the minutes. Wesby Hythe, who was an invalid, complained that a typewriter in the next room was getting on his nerves. Maling blushed and went out: I think he must have swallowed a tablet because the typewriter stopped. Hythe was impatient. 'Hurry up,' he said, 'hurry up. We haven't all night.' But that was exactly what they had.

After the minutes had been read Sir Joshua began explaining elaborately in a Yorkshire accent that their motives were entirely patriotic: they hadn't any intention of evading tax: they just wanted to contribute to the war effort, drive, economy. . . . He said, 'The proof of the pudden' . . .' and at that moment the air-raid sirens started. As I have said a mass attack was expected: it wasn't the time for delay: a dead man couldn't evade income tax. The directors gathered up their papers and bolted for the basement.

All except Maling. You see, he knew the truth. I think it had been the reference to pudding which had roused the sleeping animal. Of course he should have confessed, but think for a moment: would you have had the courage, after watching those elderly men with white slips to their waistcoats pelt with a horrifying lack of dignity to safety? I know I should have done exactly what Maling did, have followed Sir Joshua down to the basement in the desperate hope that for once the stomach would do the right thing and make amends. But it didn't. The joint boards of Simcox and Hythe stayed in the basement for 12 hours, and Maling stayed with them, saying nothing. You see, for some unaccountable reason of taste, poor Maling's stomach had picked up the note of the Warning only too effectively, but it had somehow never taken to the All Clear.

Mortmain

CAST

PHILIP, Ronald Hines
JULIA, Susan Penhaligon
JOSEPHINE, Eleanor Bron
PUBLISHER, John Westbrook
USHER, John Owens
GUEST WITH BEARD, Paul Williamson
LADY GUEST, Jennie Goossens

Dramatised by John Mortimer
Directed by Graham Evans

Mortmain

How wonderfully secure and peaceful a genuine marriage seemed to Carter, when he attained it at the age of forty-two. He even enjoyed every moment of the church service, except when he saw Josephine wiping away a tear as he conducted Julia down the aisle. It was typical of this new frank relationship that Josephine was there at all. He had no secrets from Julia; they had often talked together of his ten tormented years with Josephine, of her extravagant jealousy, of her well-timed hysterics. 'It was her insecurity,' Julia argued with understanding, and she was quite convinced that in a little while it would be possible to form a friendship with Josephine.

'I doubt it, darling.'

'Why? I can't help being fond of anyone who loved you.'

'It was a rather cruel love.'

'Perhaps at the end when she knew she was losing you, but darling, there *were* happy years.'

'Yes.' But he wanted to forget that he had ever loved anyone before Julia.

Her generosity sometimes staggered him. On the seventh day of their honeymoon, when they were drinking retsina in a little restaurant on the beach by Sunium, he accidentally took a letter from Josephine out of his pocket. It had arrived the day before and he had concealed it, for fear of hurting Julia. It was typical of Josephine that she could not leave him alone for the brief period of the honeymoon. Even her handwriting was now abhorrent to him – very neat, very small, in black ink the

108

colour of her hair. Julia was platinum-fair. How had he ever thought that black hair was beautiful? Or been impatient to read letters in black ink?

'What's the letter, darling? I didn't know there had been a post.'

'It's from Josephine. It came yesterday.'

'But you haven't even opened it!' she exclaimed without a word of reproach.

'I don't want to think about her.'

'But, darling, she may be ill.'

'Not she.'

'Or in distress.'

'She earns more with her fashion-designs than I do with my stories.'

'Darling, let's be kind. We can afford to be. We are so happy.'

So he opened the letter. It was affectionate and uncomplaining and he read it with distaste.

Dear Philip, I didn't want to be a death's head at the reception, so I had no chance to say goodbye and wish you both the greatest possible happiness. I thought Julia looked terribly beautiful and so very, very young. You must look after her carefully. I know how well you can do that, Philip dear. When I saw her, I couldn't help wondering why you took such a long time to make up your mind to leave me. Silly Philip. It's much less painful to act quickly.

I don't suppose you are interested to hear about my activities now, but just in case you are worrying a little about me – you know what an old worrier you are – I want you to know that I'm working *very* hard at a whole series for – guess, the French *Vogue*. They are paying me a fortune in francs, and I simply have no time for unhappy thoughts. I've been back once – I hope you don't mind – to our apartment (slip of the tongue) because I'd lost a key sketch. I found it at the back of our communal drawer – the ideas-bank, do you remember? I thought I'd taken all my stuff away, but there it was between the leaves of the story you started that heavenly summer, and never finished, at Napoule. Now I'm rambling on when all I really wanted to say was: Be happy both of you. Love, Josephine.

Carter handed the letter to Julia and said, 'It could have been worse.'

'But would she like me to read it?'

'Oh, it's meant for both of us.' Again he thought how wonderful it was to have no secrets. There had been so many secrets during the last ten years, even innocent secrets, for fear of misunderstanding, of Josephine's rage or silence. Now he had no fear of anything at all: he could have trusted even a guilty secret to Julia's sympathy and comprehension. He said, 'I was a fool not to show you the letter yesterday. I'll never do anything like that again.' He tried to recall Spenser's line – '. . . port after stormie seas'.

When Julia had finished reading the letter she said, 'I think she's a wonderful woman. How very, very sweet of her to write like that. You know I was – only now and then of course – just a little worried about her. After all *I* wouldn't like to lose you after ten years.'

When they were in the taxi going back to Athens she said, 'Were you very happy at Napoule?'

'Yes, I suppose so. I don't remember, it wasn't like this.'

With the antennae of a lover he could feel her moving away from him, though their shoulders still touched. The sun was bright on the road from Sunium, the warm sleepy loving siesta lay ahead, and yet . . . 'Is anything the matter, darling?' he asked.

'Not really. . . . It's only . . . do you think one day you'll say the same about Athens as about Napoule? "I don't remember, it wasn't like this." '

'What a dear fool you are,' he said and kissed her. After that they played a little in the taxi going back to Athens, and when the streets began to unroll she sat up and combed her hair. 'You aren't really a cold man, are you?' she asked and he knew that all was right again. It was Josephine's fault that – momentarily – there had been a small division.

When they got out of bed to have dinner, she said, 'We must write to Josephine.'

'Oh no!'

'Darling, I know how you feel, but really it was a wonderful letter.'

'A picture-postcard then.'

So they agreed on that.

Suddenly it was autumn when they arrived back in London – if not winter already, for there was ice in the rain falling on the tarmac, and they had quite forgotten how early the lights came on at home – passing Gillette and Lucozade and Smith's Crisps, and no view of the Parthenon anywhere. The BOAC posters seemed more than usually sad – 'BOAC takes you there and brings you back'.

'We'll put on all the electric fires as soon as we get in,' Carter said, 'and it will be warm in no time at all.' But when they opened the door of the apartment they found the fires were already alight. Little glows greeted them in the twilight from the depths of the living-room and the bed-room.

'Some fairy has done this,' Julia said.

'Not a fairy of any kind,' Carter said. He had already seen the envelope on the mantelpiece addressed in black ink to 'Mrs Carter'.

Dear Julia, you won't mind my calling you Julia, will you? I feel we have so much in common, having loved the same man. Today was so icy that I could not help thinking of how you two were returning from the sun and the warmth to a cold flat. (I know how cold the flat can be. I used to catch a chill every year when we came back from the south of France.) So I've done a very presumptuous thing. I've slipped in and put on the fires, but to show you that I'll never do such a thing again, I've hidden my key under the mat outside the front door. That's just in case your plane is held up in Rome or somewhere. I'll telephone the airport and if by some unlikely chance you haven't arrived, I'll come back and turn out the fires for safety (and economy! the rates are awful). Wishing you a very warm evening in your new home, love from Josephine.

P.S. I did notice that the coffee jar was empty, so I've left a packet of Blue Mountain in the kitchen. It's the only coffee Philip really cares for.

'Well,' Julia said laughing, 'she does think of everything.'

'I wish she'd just leave us alone,' Carter said.

'We wouldn't be warm like this, and we wouldn't have any coffee for breakfast.'

'I feel that she's lurking about the place and she'll walk

in at any moment. Just when I'm kissing you.' He kissed Julia with one careful eye on the door.

'You *are* a bit unfair, darling. After all, she's left her key under the mat.'

'She might have had a duplicate made.'

She closed his mouth with another kiss.

'Have you noticed how erotic an aeroplane makes you after a few hours?' Carter asked.

'Yes.'

'I suppose it's the vibration.'

'Let's do something about it, darling.'

'I'll just look under the mat first. To make sure she wasn't lying.'

He enjoyed marriage – so much that he blamed himself for not having married before, forgetting that in that case he would have been married to Josephine. He found Julia, who had no work of her own, almost miraculously available. There was no maid to mar their relationship with habits. As they were always together, at cocktail parties, in restaurants, at small dinner parties, they had only to meet each other's eyes . . . Julia soon earned the reputation of being delicate and easily tired, it occurred so often that they left a cocktail party after a quarter of an hour or abandoned a dinner after the coffee – 'Oh dear, I'm so sorry, such a vile headache, so stupid of me. Philip, *you* must stay . . .'

'Of course I'm not going to stay.'

Once they had a narrow escape from discovery on the stairs while they were laughing uncontrollably. Their host had followed them out to ask them to post a letter. Julia in the nick of time changed her laughter into what seemed to be a fit of hysterics. . . . Several weeks went by. It was a really successful marriage. . . . They liked –

between whiles – to discuss its success, each attributing the main merit to the other. 'When I think you might have married Josephine,' Julia said. 'Why didn't you marry Josephine?'

'I suppose at the back of our minds we knew it wasn't going to be permanent.'

'Are we going to be permanent?'

'If we aren't, nothing will ever be.'

It was early in November that the time-bombs began to go off. No doubt they had been planned to explode earlier, but Josephine had not taken into account the temporary change in his habits. Some weeks passed before he had occasion to open what they used to call the ideas-bank in the days of their closest companionship – the drawer in which he used to leave notes for stories, scraps of overheard dialogue and the like, and she would leave roughly sketched ideas for fashion advertisements.

Directly he opened the drawer he saw her letter. It was labelled heavily 'Top Secret' in black ink with a whimsically drawn exclamation mark in the form of a girl with big eyes (Josephine suffered in an elegant way from exophthalmic goitre) rising genie-like out of a bottle. He read the letter with extreme distaste:

Dear, you didn't expect to find me here, did you? But after ten years I can't not now and then say, Good-night or good-morning, how are you? Bless you. Lots of love (really and truly), Your Josephine.

The threat of 'now and then' was unmistakable. He slammed the drawer shut and said 'Damn' so loudly that Julia looked in. 'Whatever is it, darling?'

'Josephine again.'

She read the letter and said, 'You know, I can under-

stand the way she feels. Poor Josephine. Are you tearing
it up, darling?'

'What else do you expect me to do with it? Keep it for
a collected edition of her letters?'

'It just seems a bit unkind.'

'Me unkind to *her*? Julia, you've no idea of the sort
of life that we led those last years. I can show you scars:
when she was in a rage she would stub her cigarettes *anywhere*.'

'She felt she was losing you, darling, and she got desperate. They are my fault really, those scars, every one of
them.' He could see growing in her eyes that soft amused
speculative look which always led to the same thing.

Only two days passed before the next time-bomb went
off. When they got up Julia said, 'We really ought to
change the mattress. We both fall into a kind of hole in
the middle.'

'I hadn't noticed.'

'Lots of people change the mattress every week.'

'Yes. Josephine always did.'

They stripped the bed and began to roll the mattress.
Lying on the springs was a letter addressed to Julia.
Carter saw it first and tried to push it out of sight, but
Julia saw him.

'What's that?'

'Josephine, of course. There'll soon be too many letters
for one volume. We shall have to get them properly
edited at Yale like George Eliot's.'

'Darling, this is addressed to me. What were you
planning to do with it?'

'Destroy it in secret.'

'I thought we were going to have no secrets.'

'I had counted without Josephine.'

For the first time she hesitated before opening the letter. 'It's certainly a bit bizarre to put a letter here. Do you think it got there accidentally?'

'Rather difficult, I should think.'

She read the letter and then gave it to him. She said with relief, 'Oh, she explains why. It's quite natural really.' He read:

Dear Julia, how I hope you are basking in a really Greek sun. Don't tell Philip (Oh, but of course you wouldn't have secrets yet) but I never really cared for the south of France. Always that mistral, drying the skin. I'm glad to think you are not suffering there. We always planned to go to Greece when we could afford it, so I know Philip will be happy. I came in today to find a sketch and then remembered that the mattress hadn't been turned for at least a fortnight. We were rather distracted, you know, the last weeks we were together. Anyway I couldn't bear the thought of your coming back from the lotus islands and finding bumps in your bed the first night, so I've turned it for you. I'd advise you to turn it every week: otherwise a hole always develops in the middle. By the way I've put up the winter curtains and sent the summer ones to the cleaners at 153 Brompton Road. Love, Josephine.

'If you remember, she wrote to me that Napoule had been heavenly,' he said. 'The Yale editor will have to put in a cross-reference.'

'You *are* a bit cold-blooded,' Julia said. 'Darling, she's only trying to be helpful. After all I never knew about the curtains or the mattress.'

'I suppose you are going to write a long cosy letter in reply, full of household chat.'

'She's been waiting weeks for an answer. This is an *ancient* letter.'

'And I wonder how many more ancient letters there are waiting to pop out. By God, I'm going to search the flat through and through. From attic to basement.'

'We don't have either.'

'You know very well what I mean.'

'I only know you are getting fussed in an exaggerated way. You really behave as though you are frightened of Josephine.'

'Oh hell!'

Julia left the room abruptly and he tried to work. Later that day a squib went off – nothing serious, but it didn't help his mood. He wanted to find the dialling number for overseas telegrams and he discovered inserted in volume one of the directory a complete list in alphabetical order, typed on Josephine's machine on which O was always blurred, a complete list of the numbers he most often required. John Hughes, his oldest friend, came after Harrods; and there were the nearest taxi-rank, the chemist's, the butcher's, the bank, the dry-cleaner's, the greengrocer's, the fishmonger's, his publisher and agent, Elizabeth Arden's and local hairdressers' – marked in brackets ('For J. please note, quite reliable and very inexpensive') – it was the first time he noticed they had the same initials.

Julia, who saw him discover the list, said, 'The angel-woman. We'll pin it up over the telephone. It's really terribly complete.'

'After the crack in her last letter I'd have expected her to include Cartier's.'

'Darling, it wasn't a crack. It was a bare statement of

fact. If I hadn't a little money, we would have gone to the south of France too.'

'I suppose you think I married you to get to Greece.'

'Don't be an owl. You don't see Josephine clearly, that's all. You twist every kindness she does.'

'Kindness?'

'I expect it's the sense of guilt.'

After that he really began a search. He looked in cigarette-boxes, drawers, filing-cabinets, he went through all the pockets of the suits he had left behind, he opened the back of the television-cabinet, he lifted the lid of the lavatory-cistern, and even changed the roll of toilet-paper (it was quicker than unwinding the whole thing). Julia came to look at him, as he worked in the lavatory, without her usual sympathy. He tried the pelmets (who knew what they mightn't discover when next the curtains were sent for cleaning?), he took their dirty clothes out of the basket in case something had been overlooked at the bottom. He went on hands-and-knees through the kitchen to look under the gas-stove, and once, when he found a piece of paper wrapped around a pipe, he exclaimed in a kind of triumph, but it was nothing at all – a plumber's relic. The afternoon post rattled through the letter-box and Julia called to him from the hall – 'Oh, good, you never told me you took in the French *Vogue*.'

'I don't.'

'Sorry, there's a kind of Christmas card in another envelope. A subscription's been taken out for us by Miss Josephine Heckstall-Jones. I do call that sweet of her.'

'She's sold a series of drawings to them. I won't look at it.'

'Darling, you are being childish. Do you expect her to stop reading your books?'

118

'I only want to be left alone with you. Just for a few weeks. It's not so much to ask.'

'You're a bit of an egoist, darling.'

He felt quiet and tired that evening, but a little relieved in mind. His search had been very thorough. In the middle of dinner he had remembered the wedding-presents, still crated for lack of room, and insisted on making sure between the courses that they were still nailed down – he knew Josephine would never have used a screwdriver for fear of injuring her fingers, and she was terrified of hammers. The peace of a solitary evening at last descended on them: the delicious calm which they knew either of them could alter at any moment with a touch of the hand. Lovers cannot postpone as married people can. 'I am grown peaceful as old age tonight,' he quoted to her.

'Who wrote that?'

'Browning.'

'I don't know Browning. Read me some.'

He loved to read Browning aloud – he had a good voice for poetry, it was his small harmless Narcissism. 'Would you really like it?'

'Yes.'

'I used to read to Josephine,' he warned her.

'What do I care? We can't help doing *some* of the same things, can we, darling?'

'There is something I never read to Josephine. Even though I was in love with her, it wasn't suitable. We weren't – permanent.' He began:

How well I know what I mean to do
    When the long dark autumn-evenings come . . .

He was deeply moved by his own reading. He had never

loved Julia so much as at this moment. Here was home – nothing else had been other than a caravan.

> . . . I will speak now,
> No longer watch you as you sit
> Reading by firelight, that great brow
> And the spirit-small hand propping it,
> Mutely, my heart knows how.

He rather wished that Julia had really been reading, but then of course she wouldn't have been listening to him with such adorable attention.

> . . . If two lives join, there is oft a scar.
> They are one and one, with a shadowy third;
> One near one is too far.

He turned the page and there lay a sheet of paper (he would have discovered it at once, before reading, if she had put it in an envelope) with the black neat hand-writing.

Dearest Philip, only to say goodnight to you between the pages of your favourite book – and mine. We are so lucky to have ended in the way we have. With memories in common we shall for ever be a little in touch. Love, Josephine.

He flung the book and the paper on the floor. He said, 'The bitch. The bloody bitch.'

'I won't have you talk of her like that,' Julia said with surprising strength. She picked up the paper and read it.

'What's wrong with that?' she demanded. 'Do you hate memories? What's going to happen to our memories?'

'But don't you see the trick she's playing? Don't you understand? Are you an idiot, Julia?'

That night they lay in bed on opposite sides, not even touching with their feet. It was the first night since they had come home that they had not made love. Neither slept much. In the morning Carter found a letter in the most obvious place of all, which he had somehow neglected: between the leaves of the unused single-lined foolscap on which he always wrote his stories. It began, 'Darling, I'm sure you won't mind my using the old term . . .'

A Chance for Mr Lever

CAST

LEVER, Freddie Jones
BESTERMAN, John Wentworth
1ST HEAD BOY, Yemi Ajibade
1ST CHIEF, Sam Mansaray
EMILY, Vivienne Burgess
MAID, Rosalind Elliot
LUCAS, Shane Briant
ADAMSON, Christopher Benjamin
2ND CHIEF, Tommy Buson
BANK MANAGER, John Savident
SHOP ASSISTANT, James Cossins
2ND HEAD BOY, Ilarrio Bisi Pedro
DAVIDSON, John Golightly

Dramatised by Clive Exton
Directed by Peter Hammond

A Chance for Mr Lever

Mr Lever knocked his head against the ceiling and swore. Rice was stored above, and in the dark the rats began to move. Grains of rice fell between the slats on to his Revelation suitcase, his bald head, his cases of tinned food, the little square box in which he kept his medicines. His boy had already set up the camp-bed and mosquito-net, and outside in the warm damp dark his folding table and chair. The thatched pointed huts streamed away towards the forest and a woman went from hut to hut carrying fire. The glow lit her old face, her sagging breasts, her tattooed diseased body.

It was incredible to Mr Lever that five weeks ago he had been in London.

He couldn't stand upright; he went down on hands and knees in the dust and opened his suitcase. He took out his wife's photograph and stood it on the chop-box; he took out a writing-pad and an indelible pencil: the pencil had softened in the heat and left mauve stains on his pyjamas. Then, because the light of the hurricane lamp disclosed cockroaches the size of black-beetles flattened against the mud wall, he carefully closed the suitcase. Already in ten days he had learnt that they'd eat anything – socks, shirts, the laces out of your shoes.

Mr Lever went outside; moths beat against his lamp, but there were no mosquitoes; he hadn't seen or heard one since he landed. He sat in a circle of light carefully observed. The blacks squatted outside their huts and watched him; they were friendly, interested, amused, but their strict attention irritated Mr Lever. He could feel the small waves of interest washing round him, when he began to write, when he stopped writing, when he wiped his damp hands with a handkerchief. He couldn't touch his pocket without a craning of necks.

Dearest Emily, he wrote, *I've really started now. I'll send this letter back with a carrier when I've located Davidson. I'm very well. Of course everything's a bit strange. Look after yourself, my dear, and don't worry.*

'Massa buy chicken,' his cook said, appearing suddenly between the huts. A small stringy fowl struggled in his hands.

'Well,' Mr Lever said, 'I gave you a shilling, didn't I?'

'They no like,' the cook said. 'These low bush people.'

'Why don't they like? It's good money.'

'They want king's money,' the cook said, handing back the Victorian shilling. Mr Lever had to get up, go back into his hut, grope for his money-box, search through twenty pounds of small change: there was no peace.

He had learnt that very quickly. He had to economize (the whole trip was a gamble which scared him); he couldn't afford hammock carriers. He would arrive tired out after seven hours of walking at a village of which he didn't know the name and not for a minute could he sit quietly and rest. He must shake hands with the chief, he must see about a hut, accept presents of palm wine he was afraid to drink, buy rice and palm oil for the carriers, give them salts and aspirin, paint their sores with iodine. They never left him alone for five minutes on end until he went to bed. And then the rats began, rushing down the walls like water when he put out the light, gambolling among his cases.

I'm too old, Mr Lever told himself, I'm too old,

writing damply, indelibly, *I hope to find Davidson tomorrow. If I do, I may be back almost as soon as this letter. Don't economize on the stout and milk, dear, and call in the doctor if you feel bad. I've got a premonition this trip's going to turn out well. We'll take a holiday, you need a holiday*, and staring ahead past the huts and the black faces and the banana trees towards the forest from which he had come, into which he would sink again next day, he thought, Eastbourne, Eastbourne would do her a world of good; and he continued to write the only kind of lies he had ever told Emily, the lies which comforted. *I ought to draw at least three hundred in commission and expenses.* But it wasn't the sort of place where he'd been accustomed to sell heavy machinery; thirty years of it, up and down Europe and in the States, but never anything like this. He could hear his filter dripping in the hut, and somewhere somebody was playing something (he was so lost he hadn't got the simplest terms to his hands), something monotonous, melancholy, superficial, a twanging of palm fibres which seemed to convey that you weren't happy, but it didn't matter, everything would always be the same.

Look after yourself, Emily, he repeated. It was almost the only thing he found himself capable of writing to her; he couldn't describe the narrow, steep, lost paths, the snakes sizzling away like flames, the rats, the dust, the naked diseased bodies. He was unbearably tired of nakedness. *Don't forget* – It was like living with a lot of cows.

'The chief,' his boy whispered, and between the huts under a waving torch came an old stout man wearing a robe of native cloth and a battered bowler hat. Behind him his men carried six bowls of rice, a bowl of palm oil, two bowls of broken meat. 'Chop for the labourers,' the boy explained, and Mr Lever had to get up and smile and nod and try to convey without words that he was pleased, that the chop was excellent, that the chief would get a good dash in the morning. At first the smell had been almost too much for Mr Lever.

'Ask him,' he said to his boy, 'if he's seen a white man come through here lately. Ask him if a white man's been digging around here. Damn it,' Mr Lever burst out, the sweat breaking on the backs of his hands and on his bald head, 'ask him if he's seen Davidson?'

'Davidson?'

'Oh, hell,' Mr Lever said, 'you know what I mean. The white man I'm looking for.'

'White man?'

'What do you imagine I'm here for, eh? White man? Of course white man. I'm not here for my health.' A cow coughed, rubbed its horns against the hut and two goats broke through between the chief and him, up-setting the bowls of meat scraps; nobody cared, they picked the meat out of the dust and dung.

Mr Lever sat down and put his hands over his face, fat white well-cared-for hands with wrinkles of flesh over the rings. He felt too old for this.

'Chief say no white man been here long time.'

'How long?'

'Chief say not since he pay hut tax.'

'How long's that?'

'Long long time.'

'Ask him how far is it to Greh, tomorrow.'

'Chief say too far.'

'Nonsense,' Mr Lever said.

'Chief say too far. Better stay here. Fine town. No humbug.'

Mr Lever groaned. Every evening there was the same trouble. The next town was always too far. They would invent any excuse to delay him, to give themselves a rest.

'Ask the chief how many hours – ?'

'Plenty, plenty.' They had no idea of time.

'This fine chief. Fine chop. Labourers tired. No humbug.'

'We are going on,' Mr Lever said.

'This fine town. Chief say –'

He thought: if this wasn't the last chance, I'd give up. They nagged him so, and suddenly he longed for another white man (not Davidson, he daren't say anything to Davidson) to whom he could explain the desperation of his lot. It wasn't fair that a man, after thirty years' commercial travelling, should need to go from door to door asking for a job. He had been a good traveller, he had made money for many people, his references were excellent, but the world had moved on since his day. He wasn't streamlined; he certainly wasn't streamlined. He had been ten years retired when he lost his money in the depression.

Mr Lever walked up and down Victoria Street showing his references. Many of the men knew him, gave him cigars, laughed at him in a friendly way for wanting to take on a job at his age ('I can't somehow settle at home. The old warhorse you know . . .'), cracked a joke or two in the passage, went back that night to Maidenhead silent in the first-class carriage, shut in with age and ruin and how bad things were and poor devil his wife's probably sick.

It was in the rather shabby little office off Leadenhall Street that Mr Lever met his chance. It called itself an engineering firm, but there were only two rooms, a type-writer, a girl with gold teeth and Mr Lucas, a thin narrow man with a tic in one eyelid. All through the interview the eyelid flickered at Mr Lever. Mr Lever had never before fallen so low as this.

But Mr Lucas struck him as reasonably honest. He put 'all his cards on the table'. He hadn't got any money, but he had expectations; he had the handling of a patent. It was a new crusher. There was money in it. But you couldn't expect the big trusts to change over their machinery now. Things were too bad. You'd got to get in at the start, and that was where – why, that was where this chief, the bowls of chop, the nagging and the rats and the heat came in. They called themselves a republic, Mr Lucas said, he didn't know anything about that, they were not as black as they were painted, he supposed (ha, ha, nervously, ha, ha); anyway, this company had slipped agents over the border and grabbed a concession: gold and diamonds. He could tell Mr Lever in confidence that the trust was frightened of what they'd found. Now an enterprising man could just slip across (Mr Lucas liked the word slip, it made everything sound easy and secret) and introduce this new crusher to them: it would save them thousands when they started work, there'd be a fat commission, and afterwards, with that start . . . There was a fortune for them all.

'But can't you fix it up in Europe?'

Tic, tic, went Mr Lucas's eyelid. 'A lot of Belgians; they are leaving all decisions to the man on the spot. An Englishman called Davidson.'

'How about expenses?'

'That's the trouble,' Mr Lucas said. 'We are only beginning. What we want is a partner. We can't afford to send a man. But if you like a gamble . . .Twenty per cent commission.'

'Chief say excuse him.' The carriers squatted round the basins and scooped up the rice in their left hands. 'Of course. Of course,' Mr Lever said absent-mindedly. 'Very kind, I'm sure.'

He was back out of the dust and dark, away from the stink of goats and palm oil and whelping bitches, back among the rotarians and lunch at Stone's, 'the pint of old', and the trade papers; he was a good fellow again, finding his way back to Golders Green just a bit lit; his masonic emblem rattled on his watch-chain, and he bore with him from the tube station to his house in Finchley Road a sense of companionship, of broad stories and belches, a sense of bravery.

He needed all his bravery now; the last of his savings had gone into the trip. After thirty years he knew a good thing when he saw it, and he had no doubts about the new crusher. What he doubted was his ability to find Davidson. For one thing there weren't any maps; the way you travelled in the Republic was to write down a list of names and trust that someone in the villages you passed would understand and know the route. But they always said 'Too far'. Good fellowship wilted before the phrase.

'Quinine,' Mr Lever said. 'Where's my quinine?' His boy never remembered a thing; they just didn't care what happened to you; their smiles meant nothing, and Mr Lever, who knew better than anyone the value of a meaningless smile in business, resented their heartlessness, and turned towards the dilatory boy an expression of disappointment and dislike.

'Chief say white man in bush five hours away.'

'That's better,' Mr Lever said. 'It must be Davidson. He's digging for gold?'

'Ya. White man dig for gold in bush.'

'We'll be off early tomorrow,' Mr Lever said.

'Chief say better stop this town. Fever humbug white man.'

'Too bad,' Mr Lever said, and he thought with pleasure: my luck's changed. He'll want help. He won't refuse me a thing. A friend in need is a friend indeed, and his heart warmed towards Davidson, seeing himself arrive like an answer to prayer out of the forest, feeling quite biblical and vox humana. He thought: Prayer. I'll pray tonight, that's the kind of thing a fellow gives up, but it pays, there's something in it, remembering the long agonizing prayer on his knees, by the sideboard, under the decanters, when Emily went to hospital.

'Chief say white man dead.'

Mr Lever turned his back on them and went into his hut. His sleeve nearly overturned the hurricane lamp. He undressed quickly, stuffing his clothes into a suitcase away from the cockroaches. He wouldn't believe what he had been told; it wouldn't pay him to believe. If Davidson were dead, there was nothing he could do but return; he had spent more than he could afford; he would be a ruined man. He supposed that Emily might find a home with her brother, but he could hardly expect her brother – he began to cry, but you couldn't have told in the shadowy hut the difference between sweat and tears. He knelt down beside his camp-bed and mosquito-net and prayed on the dust of the earth floor. Up till now he had always been careful never to touch ground with his naked feet for fear of jiggers; there were jiggers everywhere, they only waited an opportunity to dig themselves in under the toe-nails, lay their eggs and multiply.

'O God,' Mr Lever prayed, 'don't let Davidson be dead; let him be just sick and glad to see me.' He couldn't bear the idea that he might not any longer be able to support Emily. 'O God, there's nothing I wouldn't do.' But that was an empty phrase; he had no real notion as yet of what he would do for Emily. They had been happy together for thirty-five years; he had never been more than momentarily unfaithful to her when he was lit after a rotarian dinner and egged on by the boys; whatever skirt he'd been with in his time, he had never for a moment imagined that he could be happy married to anyone else. It wasn't fair if, just when you were old and needed each other most, you lost your money and couldn't keep together.

But of course Davidson wasn't dead. What would he have died of? The blacks were friendly. People said the country was unhealthy, but he hadn't so much as heard a mosquito. Besides, you didn't die of malaria; you just lay between the blankets and took quinine and felt like death and sweated it out of you. There was dysentery, but Davidson was an old campaigner; you were safe if you boiled and filtered the water. The water was poison even to touch; it was unsafe to wet your feet because of guinea worm, but you didn't die of guinea worm.

Mr Lever lay in bed and his thoughts went round and round and he couldn't sleep. He thought: you don't die of a thing like guinea worm. It makes a sore on your foot, and if you put your foot in water you can see the eggs dropping out. You have to find the end of the worm, like a thread of cotton, and wind it round a match and wind it out of your leg without breaking; it stretches as high

132

as the knee. I'm too old for this country, Mr Lever thought.

Then his boy was beside him again. He whispered urgently to Mr Lever through the mosquito-net. 'Massa, the labourers say they go home.'

'Go home?' Mr Lever asked wearily; he had heard it so often before. 'Why do they want to go home? What is it now?' but he didn't really want to hear the latest squabble: that the Bande men were never sent to carry water because the headman was a Bande, that someone had stolen an empty treacle tin and sold it in the village for a penny, that someone wasn't made to carry a proper load, that the next day's journey was 'too far'. He said, 'Tell 'em they can go home. I'll pay them off in the morning. But they won't get any dash. They'd have got a good dash if they'd stayed.' He was certain it was just another try-on; he wasn't as green as all that.

'Yes, massa. They no want dash.'

'What's that?'

'They frightened fever humbug them like white man.'

'I'll get carriers in the village. They can go home.'

'Me too, massa.'

'Get out,' Mr Lever said; it was the last straw; 'get out and let me sleep.' The boy went at once, obedient even though a deserter, and Mr Lever thought: sleep, what a hope. He lifted the net and got out of bed (barefooted again: he didn't care a damn about the jiggers) and searched for his medicine box. It was locked, of course, and he had to open his suitcase and find the key in a trouser pocket. His nerves were more on edge than ever by the time he found the sleeping tablets and he took three of them. That made him sleep, heavily and dreamlessly, though when he woke he found that something had made him fling out his arms and open the net. If there had been a single mosquito in the place, he'd have been bitten, but of course there wasn't one.

He could tell at once that the trouble hadn't blown over. The village – he didn't know its name – was perched on a hilltop; east and west the forest flowed out beneath the little plateau; to the west it was a dark unfeatured mass like water, but in the east you could already discern the unevenness, the great grey cotton trees lifted above the palms. Mr Lever was always called before dawn, but no one had called him. A few of his carriers sat outside a hut sullenly talking; his boy was with them. Mr Lever went back inside and dressed; he thought all the time, I must be firm, but he was scared, scared of being deserted, scared of being made to return.

When he came outside again the village was awake: the women were going down the hill to fetch water, winding silently past the carriers, past the flat stones where the chiefs were buried, the little grove of trees where the rice birds, like green and yellow canaries, nested. Mr Lever sat down on his folding chair among the chickens and whelping bitches and cow dung and called his boy. He took 'a strong line'; but he didn't know what was going to happen. 'Tell the chief I want to speak to him,' he said.

There was some delay; the chief wasn't up yet, but presently he appeared in his blue and white robe, setting his bowler hat straight. 'Tell him,' Mr Lever said, 'I want carriers to take me to the white man and back. Two days.'

'Chief no agree,' the boy said.

Mr Lever said furiously, 'Damn it, if he doesn't agree, he won't get any dash from me, not a penny.' It occurred to him immediately afterwards how hopelessly dependent he was on these people's honesty. There in the hut for all to see was his money-box; they had only to take it. This wasn't a British or French colony; the blacks on the coast wouldn't bother, could do nothing if they did bother, because a stray Englishman had been robbed in the interior.

'Chief say how many?'

'It's only for two days,' Mr Lever said. 'I can do with six.'

'Chief say how much?'

'Sixpence a day and chop.'

'Chief no agree.'

'Ninepence a day then.'

'Chief say too far. A shilling.'

'All right, all right,' Mr Lever said, 'A shilling then. You others can go home if you want to. I'll pay you off now, but you won't get any dash, not a penny.'

He had never really expected to be left, and it gave him a sad feeling of loneliness to watch them move sullenly away (they were ashamed of themselves) down the hill to the west. They hadn't any loads, but they weren't singing; they drooped silently out of sight, his boy with them, and he was alone with his pile of boxes and the chief who couldn't talk a word of English. Mr Lever smiled tremulously.

It was ten o'clock before his new carriers were chosen; he could tell that none of them wanted to go, and they would have to walk through the heat of the middle day if they were to find Davidson before it was dark. He hoped the chief had explained properly where they were going; he couldn't tell; he was completely shut off from them, and when they started down the eastward slope, he might just as well have been alone.

They were immediately caught up in the forest. Forest conveys a sense of wildness and beauty, of an active natural force, but this Liberian forest was simply a dull green wilderness. You passed, on the path a foot or so wide, through an endless back garden of tangled weeds; it didn't seem to be growing round you, so much as dying. There was no life at all, except for a few large birds whose wings creaked overhead through the invisible sky like an unoiled door. There was no view, no way out for the eyes, no change of scene. It wasn't the heat that tired, so much as the boredom; you had to think of things to think about; but even Emily failed to fill the mind for more than three minutes at a time. It was a relief, a distraction, when the path was flooded and Mr Lever had to be carried on a man's back. At first he had disliked the strong bitter smell (it reminded him of a breakfast food he was made to eat as a child), but he soon got over that. Now he was unaware that they smelt at all; any more than he was aware that the great swallow-tailed butterflies, which clustered at the water's edge and rose in green clouds round his waist, were beautiful. His senses were dulled and registered very little except his boredom.

But they did register a distinct feeling of relief when his leading carrier pointed to a rectangular hole dug just off the path. Mr Lever understood. Davidson had come this way. He stopped and looked at it. It was like a grave dug for a small man, but it went down deeper than graves usually do. About twelve feet below there was black water, and a few wooden props which held the sides from slipping were beginning to rot; the hole must have been dug since the rains. It didn't seem enough, that hole, to have brought out Mr Lever with his plans and estimates for a new crusher. He was used to big industrial concerns, the sight of pitheads, the smoke of chimneys, the dingy rows of cottages back to back, the leather armchair in the office, the good cigar, the masonic hand-grips, and again it seemed to him, as it had seemed in Mr Lucas's office, that he had fallen very low. It was as if he was expected to do business beside a hole a child had dug in an overgrown and abandoned back garden; percentages wilted in the hot damp air. He shook his head; he mustn't be discouraged; this was an old hole. Davidson had probably done better since. It was only common sense to suppose that the gold rift which was mined at one end in Nigeria, at the other in Sierra Leone, would pass through the republic. Even the biggest mines had to begin with a hole in the ground. The company (he had talked to the directors in Brussels) were quite confident: all they wanted was the approval of the man on the spot that the crusher was suitable for local conditions. A signature, that was all he had to get, he told himself, staring down into the puddle of black water.

Five hours, the chief had said, but after six hours they were still walking. Mr Lever had eaten nothing; he wanted to get to Davidson first. All through the heat of the day he walked. The forest protected him from the direct sun, but it shut out the air, and the occasional clearings, shrivelled though they were in the vertical glare, seemed cooler than the shade because there was a little more air to breathe. At four o'clock the heat diminished, but he began to fear they wouldn't reach Davidson before dark. His foot pained him; he had caught a jigger the night before; it was as if someone were holding a lighted match to his toe. Then at five they came on a dead black.

Another rectangular hole in a small cleared space among the dusty greenery had caught Mr Lever's eye. He peered down and was shocked to see a face return his stare, white eyeballs like phosphorus in the black water. The black had been bent almost double to fit him in; the hole was really too small to be a grave, and he had swollen. His flesh was like a blister you could prick with a needle. Mr Lever felt sick and tired; he might have been tempted to return if he could have reached the village before dark, but now there was nothing to do but go on; the carriers luckily hadn't seen the body. He waved them forward and stumbled after them among the roots, fighting his nausea. He fanned himself with his sun helmet; his wide fat face was damp and pale. He had never seen an un-cared-for body before; his parents he had seen carefully laid out with closed eyes and washed faces; they 'fell asleep' quite in accordance with their epitaphs, but you couldn't think of sleep in connexion with the white eyeballs and the swollen face. Mr Lever would have liked very much to say a prayer, but prayers were out of place in the dead drab forest; they simply didn't 'come'.

With the dusk a little life did waken: something lived in the dry weeds and brittle trees, if only monkeys. They chattered and screamed all round you, but it was too dark to see them; you were like a blind man in the centre of a frightened crowd who wouldn't say what scared them. The carriers too were frightened. They ran under their fifty-pound loads behind the dipping light of the hurricane lamp, their huge flat carriers' feet flapping in the dust like empty gloves. Mr Lever listened nervously for mosquitoes; you would have expected them to be out by now, but he didn't hear one.

Then at the top of a rise above a small stream they came on Davidson. The ground had been cleared in a square of twelve feet and a small tent pitched; he had dug another hole; the scene came dimly into view as they climbed the path; the chop-boxes piled outside the tent, the syphon of soda water, the filter, an enamel basin. But there wasn't a light, there wasn't a sound, the flaps of the tent were not closed, and Mr Lever had to face the possibility that after all the chief might have told the truth.

Mr Lever took the lamp and stooped inside the tent. There was a body on the bed. At first Mr Lever thought Davidson was covered with blood, but then he realized it was a black vomit which stained his shirt and khaki shorts, the fair stubble on his chin. He put out a hand and touched Davidson's face, and if he hadn't felt a slight breath on his palm he would have taken him for dead; his skin was so cold. He moved the lamp closer, and now the lemon-yellow face told him all he wanted to know: he hadn't thought of that when his boy said fever. It was quite true that a man didn't die of malaria, but an odd piece of news read in New York in '98 came back to mind: there had been an outbreak of yellow jack in Rio and ninety-four per cent of the cases had been fatal. It hadn't meant anything to him then, but it did now. While he watched, Davidson was sick, quite effortlessly; he was like a tap out of which something flowed.

It seemed at first to Mr Lever to be the end of everything, of his journey, his hopes, his life with Emily. There was nothing he could do for Davidson, the man was unconscious, there were times when his pulse was so low and irregular that Mr Lever thought that he was dead until another black stream spread from his mouth; it was no use even cleaning him. Mr Lever laid his own blankets over the bed on top of Davidson's because he was so cold to the touch, but he had no idea whether he was doing the right, or even the fatally wrong, thing. The chance of survival, if there were any chance at all, depended on neither of them. Outside his carriers had built a fire and were cooking the rice they had brought with them. Mr Lever opened his folding chair and sat by the bed. He wanted to keep awake: it seemed right to keep awake. He opened his case and found his unfinished letter to Emily. He sat by Davidson's side and tried to write, but he could think of nothing but what he had already written too often: *Look after yourself. Don't forget that stout and milk.*

He fell asleep over his pad and woke at two and thought that Davidson was dead. But he was wrong again. He was very thirsty and missed his boy. Always the first thing his boy did at the end of a march was to light a fire and put on a kettle; after that, by the time his table and chair were set up, there was water ready for the filter. Mr Lever found half a cup of soda water left in Davidson's syphon; if it had been only his health at stake he would have gone down to the stream, but he had Emily to remember. There was a typewriter by the bed, and it occurred to Mr Lever that he might just as well begin to write his report of failure now; it might keep him awake; it seemed disrespectful to the dying man to sleep. He found paper under some letters which had been typed and signed but not sealed. Davidson must have been taken ill very suddenly. Mr Lever wondered whether it was he who had crammed the black into the hole; his boy perhaps, for there was no sign of a servant. He balanced the typewriter on his knee and headed the letter 'In Camp near Greh'.

It seemed to him unfair that he should have come so far, spent so much money, worn out a rather old body to meet his inevitable ruin in a dark tent beside a dying man, when he could have met it just as well at home with Emily in the plush parlour. The thought of the prayers he had uselessly uttered on his knees by the camp-bed among the jiggers, the rats and the cockroaches made him rebellious. A mosquito, the first he had heard, went humming round the tent. He slashed at it savagely; he wouldn't have recognized himself among the rotarians. He was lost and he was set free. Moralities were what enabled a man to live happily and successfully with his fellows, but Mr Lever wasn't happy and he wasn't successful, and his only fellow in the little stuffy tent wouldn't be troubled by Untruth in Advertising or by Mr Lever coveting his neighbour's oxen. You couldn't keep your ideas intact when you discovered their geographical nature. The Solemnity of Death: death wasn't solemn; it was a lemon-yellow skin and a black vomit. Honesty is the Best Policy: he saw quite suddenly how false that was. It was an anarchist who sat happily over the typewriter, an anarchist who recognized nothing but one personal relationship, his affection for Emily. Mr Lever began to type: *I have examined the plans and estimates of the new Lucas crusher* . . .

Mr Lever thought with savage happiness: I win. This letter would be the last the company would hear from Davidson. The junior partner would open it in the dapper Brussels office; he would tap his false teeth with a Waterman pen and go in to talk to M. Golz. *Taking all these factors into consideration I recommend acceptance.* . . .

They would telegraph to Lucas. As for Davidson, that trusted agent of the company would have died of yellow fever at some never accurately determined date. Another agent would come out, and the crusher . . . Mr Lever carefully copied Davidson's signature on a spare sheet of paper. He wasn't satisfied. He turned the original upside-down and copied it that way, so as not to be confused by his own idea of how a letter should be formed. That was better, but it didn't satisfy him. He searched until he found Davidson's own pen and began again to copy and copy the signature. He fell asleep copying it and woke again an hour later to find the lamp was out; it had burnt up all the oil. He sat there beside Davidson's bed till daylight; once he was bitten by a mosquito in the ankle and clapped his hand to the place too late: the brute went humming out. With the light Mr Lever saw that Davidson was dead. 'Dear, dear,' he said. 'Poor fellow.' He spat out with the words, quite delicately in a corner, the bad morning taste in his mouth. It was like a little sediment of his conventionality.

Mr Lever got two of his carriers to cram Davidson tidily into his hole. He was no longer afraid of them or of failure or of separation. He tore up his letter to Emily. It no longer represented his mood in its timidity, its secret fear, its gentle fussing phrases, *Don't forget the stout. Look after yourself.* He would be home as soon as the letter, and they were going to do things together now they'd never dreamt of doing. The money for the crusher was only the beginning. His ideas stretched farther now than Eastbourne, they stretched as far as Switzerland; he had a feeling that, if he really let himself go, they'd stretch as far as the Riviera. How happy he was on what he thought of as 'the trip home'. He was freed from what had held him back through a long pedantic career, the fear of a conscious fate that notes the dishonesty, notes the skirt in Piccadilly, notes the glass too many of Stone's special. Now he had said Boo to that goose . . .

But you who are reading this, who know so much more than Mr Lever, who can follow the mosquito's progress from the dead swollen black to Davidson's tent, to Mr Lever's ankle, you may possibly believe in God, a kindly god tender towards human frailty, ready to give Mr Lever three days of happiness, three days off the galling chain, as he carried back through the forest his amateurish forgeries and the infection of yellow fever in the blood. The story might very well have encouraged my faith in that loving omniscience if it had not been shaken by personal knowledge of the drab forest through which Mr Lever now went so merrily, where it is impossible to believe in any spiritual life, in anything outside the nature dying round you, the shrivelling of the weeds. But of course, there are two opinions about everything; it was Mr Lever's favourite expression, drinking beer in the Ruhr, Pernod in Lorraine, selling heavy machinery.

A Little Place
off the Edgware Road

CAST

CRAVEN, Tony Calvin
LANDLADY, Joyce Windsor
INSPECTOR TWEEDIE, Michael Sheard
POLICE DOCTOR, Don McKillop
NEWSBOY, Eric Holliday
CHEMIST'S ASSISTANT, David Auker
VICAR, Bill Horsley
MISS WHITING, Ann Queensberry
MAN WITH THE BEARD,
                    Roger Hammond
POLICEMEN,
        Christopher Driscoll
        Ken Kitson

Dramatised by John Mortimer
Directed by Philip Saville

A Little Place
off the Edgware Road

Craven came up past the Achilles statue in the thin summer rain. It was only just after lighting-up time, but already the cars were lined up all the way to the Marble Arch, and the sharp acquisitive faces peered out ready for a good time with anything possible which came along. Craven went bitterly by with the collar of his mackintosh tight round his throat: it was one of his bad days.

All the way up the Park he was reminded of passion, but you needed money for love. All that a poor man could get was lust. Love needed a good suit, a car, a flat somewhere, or a good hotel. It needed to be wrapped in cellophane. He was aware all the time of the stringy tie beneath the mackintosh, and the frayed sleeves: he carried his body about with him like something he hated. (There were moments of happiness in the British Museum reading-room, but the body called him back.) He bore, as his only sentiment, the memory of ugly deeds committed on park chairs. People talked as if the body died too soon – that wasn't the trouble, to Craven, at all. The body kept alive – and through the glittering tinselly rain, on his way to a rostrum, he passed a little man in a black suit carrying a banner, 'The Body shall rise again.' He remembered a dream from which three times he had woken trembling: he had been alone in the huge dark cavernous burying ground of all the world. Every grave was connected to another under the ground: the globe was honeycombed for the sake of the dead, and on each occasion of dreaming he had discovered anew the horrifying fact that the body doesn't decay. There are no worms and dissolution. Under the ground the world was littered with masses of dead flesh ready to rise again with their warts and boils and eruptions. He had lain in bed and remembered – as 'tidings of great joy' – that the body after all was corrupt.

He came up into the Edgware Road walking fast – the Guardsmen were out in couples, great languid elongated beasts – the bodies like worms in their tight trousers. He hated them, and hated his hatred because he knew what it was, envy. He was aware that every one of them had a better body than himself: indigestion creased his stomach: he felt sure that his breath was foul – but who could he ask? Sometimes he secretly touched himself here and there with scent: it was one of his ugliest secrets. Why should he be asked to believe in the resurrection of this body he wanted to forget? Sometimes he prayed at night (a hint of religious belief was lodged in his breast like a worm in a nut) that *his* body at any rate should never rise again.

He knew all the side streets round the Edgware Road only too well: when a mood was on, he simply walked until he tired, squinting at his own image in the windows of Salmon & Gluckstein and the A.B.C.s. So he noticed at once the posters outside the disused theatre in Culpar Road. They were not unusual, for sometimes Barclays Bank Dramatic Society would hire the place for an evening – or an obscure film would be trade-shown there. The theatre had been built in 1920 by an optimist who thought the cheapness of the site would more than counter-balance its disadvantage of lying a mile outside the conventional theatre zone. But no play had ever succeeded, and it was soon left to gather rat-holes and spider-webs. The covering of the seats was never renewed, and all that ever happened to the place was the temporary false life of an amateur play or a trade show.

Craven stopped and read – there were still optimists it appeared, even in 1939, for nobody but the blindest optimist could hope to make money out of the place as 'The Home of the Silent Film'. The first season of 'primitives' was announced (a high-brow phrase): there would never be a second. Well, the seats were cheap, and it was perhaps worth a shilling to him, now that he was tired, to get in somewhere out of the rain. Craven bought a ticket and went in to the darkness of the stalls.

In the dead darkness a piano tinkled something monotonous recalling Mendelssohn: he sat down in a gangway seat, and could immediately feel the emptiness all round him. No, there would never be another season. On the screen a large woman in a kind of toga wrung her hands, then wobbled with curious jerky movements towards a couch. There she sat and stared out like a sheepdog distractedly through her loose and black and stringy hair. Sometimes she seemed to dissolve altogether into dots and flashes and wiggly lines. A sub-title said, 'Pompilia betrayed by her beloved Augustus seeks an end to her troubles.'

Craven began at last to see – a dim waste of stalls. There were not twenty people in the place – a few couples whispering with their heads touching, and a number of lonely men like himself, wearing the same uniform of the cheap mackintosh. They lay about at intervals like corpses – and again Craven's obsession returned: the tooth-ache of horror. He thought miserably – I am going mad: other people don't feel like this. Even a disused theatre

148

reminded him of those interminable caverns where the bodies were waiting for resurrection.

'A slave to his passion Augustus calls for yet more wine.'

A gross middle-aged Teutonic actor lay on an elbow with his arm round a large woman in a shift. The Spring Song tinkled ineptly on, and the screen flickered like indigestion. Somebody felt his way through the darkness, scrabbling past Craven's knees – a small man: Craven experienced the unpleasant feeling of a large beard brushing his mouth. Then there was a long sigh as the newcomer found the next chair, and on the screen events had moved with such rapidity that Pompilia had already stabbed herself – or so Craven supposed – and lay still and buxom among her weeping slaves.

A low breathless voice sighed out close to Craven's ear, 'What's happened? Is she asleep?'

'No. Dead.'

'Murdered?' the voice asked with a keen interest.

'I don't think so. Stabbed herself.'

Nobody said 'Hush': nobody was enough interested to object to a voice. They drooped among the empty chairs in attitudes of weary inattention.

The film wasn't nearly over yet: there were children somehow to be considered: was it all going on to a second generation? But the small bearded man in the next seat to be interested only in Pompilia's death. The fact that he had come in at that moment apparently fascinated him. Craven heard the word 'coincidence' twice, and he went on talking to himself about it in low out-of-breath tones. 'Absurd when you come to think of it,' and then 'no blood at all'. Craven didn't listen: he sat with his hands clasped between his knees, facing the fact as he had faced it so often before, that he was in danger of going mad. He had to pull himself up, take a holiday, see a doctor (God knew what infection moved in his veins). He became aware that his bearded neighbour had addressed him directly. 'What?' he asked impatiently, 'what did you say?'

'There would be more blood than you can imagine.'

'What are you talking about?'

When the man spoke to him, he sprayed him with damp breath. There was a little bubble in his speech like an impediment. He said, 'When you murder a man . . .'

'This was a woman,' Craven said impatiently.

'That wouldn't make any difference.'

'And it's got nothing to do with murder anyway.'

'That doesn't signify.' They seemed to have got into an absurd and meaningless wrangle in the dark.

'I know, you see,' the little bearded man said in a tone of enormous conceit.

'Know what?'

'About such things,' he said with guarded ambiguity.

Craven turned and tried to see him clearly. Was he mad? Was this a warning of what he might become – babbling incomprehensibly to strangers in cinemas? He thought, By God, no, trying to see: I'll be sane yet. I *will* be sane. He could make out nothing but a small black hump of body. The man was talking to himself again. He said, 'Talk. Such talk. They'll say it was all for fifty pounds. But that's a lie. Reasons and reasons. They always take the first reason. Never look behind. Thirty years of reasons. Such simpletons,' he added again in that tone of breathless and unbounded conceit. So this was madness. So long as he could realize that, he must be sane himself – relatively speaking. Not so sane perhaps as the seekers in the park or the Guardsmen in the Edgware Road, but saner than this. It was like a message of encouragement as the piano tinkled on.

Then again the little man turned and sprayed him. 'Killed herself, you say? But who's to know that? It's not a mere question of what hand holds the knife.' He laid a hand suddenly and confidingly on Craven's: it was damp and sticky: Craven said with horror as a possible meaning came to him, 'What are you talking about?'

'I know,' the little man said. 'A man in my position gets to know almost everything.'

'What is your position?' Craven asked, feeling the sticky hand on his, trying to make up his mind whether he was being hysterical or not – after all, there were a a dozen explanations – it might be treacle.

'A pretty desperate one *you'd* say.' Sometimes the voice almost died in the throat altogether. Something incomprehensible had happened on the screen – take your eyes from these early pictures for a moment and the plot had proceeded on at such a pace.... Only the actors moved slowly and jerkily. A young woman in a nightdress seemed to be weeping in the arms of a Roman centurion: Craven hadn't seen either of them before. '*I am not afraid of death, Lucius – in your arms.*'

The little man began to titter – knowingly. He was talking to himself again. It would have been easy to ignore him altogether if it had not been for those sticky hands which he now removed: he seemed to be fumbling at the seat in front of him. His head had a habit of lolling sideways – like an idiot child's. He said distinctly and irrelevantly: 'Bayswater Tragedy.'

'What was that?' Craven said. He had seen those words on a poster before he entered the park.

'What?'

'About the tragedy.'

'To think they call Cullen Mews Bayswater.' Suddenly the little man began to cough – turning his face towards Craven and coughing right at him: it was like vindictiveness. The voice said, 'Let me see. My umbrella.' He was getting up.

'You didn't have an umbrella.'

'My umbrella,' he repeated. 'My –' and seemed to lose the word altogether. He went scrabbling out past Craven's knees.

Craven let him go, but before he had reached the billowy dusty curtains of the Exit the screen went blank and bright – the film had broken, and somebody immediately turned up one dirt-choked chandelier above the circle. It shone down just enough for Craven to see the smear on his hands. This wasn't hysteria: this was a fact. He wasn't mad: he had sat next a madman who in some mews – what was the name, Colon, Collin. . . . Craven jumped up and made his own way out: the black curtain flapped in his mouth. But he was too late: the man had gone and there were three turnings to choose from. He chose instead a telephone-box and dialled with a sense odd for him of sanity and decision 999.

It didn't take two minutes to get the right department. They were interested and very kind. Yes, there had been a murder in a mews – Cullen Mews. A man's neck had been cut from ear to ear with a bread knife – a horrid crime. He began to tell them how he had sat next the murderer in a cinema: it couldn't be anyone else: there was blood on his hands – and he remembered with repulsion as he spoke the damp beard. There must have been a terrible lot of blood. But the voice from the Yard interrupted him. 'Oh no,' it was saying, 'we have the murderer – no doubt of it at all. It's the body that's disappeared.'

Craven put down the receiver. He said to himself aloud, 'Why should this happen to *me*? Why to *me*?' He was back in the horror of his dream – the squalid darkening street outside was only one of the innumerable tunnels connecting grave to grave where the imperishable bodies lay. He said, 'It was a dream, a dream,' and leaning forward he saw in the mirror above the telephone his own face sprinkled by tiny drops of blood like dew from a scent-spray. He began to scream, 'I won't go mad. I won't go mad. I'm sane. I won't go mad.' Presently a little crowd began to collect, and soon a policeman came.

The Blue Film

CAST

BOBBIE, Betsy Blair
HARRY, Brian Cox
THE GIRL, Koo Stark
BARMAN, Al Lampert
PIANIST, Florence De Yong
and
Baron Casanov
Thick Wilson
Kate Harper
Clare Russell
Steve Emerson
Steve Kane

Dramatised by John Mortimer
Directed by Philip Saville

The Blue Film

'Other people enjoy themselves,' Mrs Carter said.

'Well,' her husband replied, 'we've seen . . .'

'The reclining Buddha, the emerald Buddha, the floating markets,' Mrs Carter said. 'We have dinner and then go home to bed.'

'Last night we went to Chez Eve. . . .'

'If you weren't with *me*,' Mrs Carter said, 'you'd find . . . you know what I mean, Spots.'

It was true, Carter thought, eyeing his wife over the coffee-cups: her slave bangles chinked in time with her coffee-spoon: she had reached an age when the satisfied woman is at her most beautiful, but the lines of discontent had formed. When he looked at her neck he was reminded of how difficult it was to unstring a turkey. Is it my fault, he wondered, or hers – or was it the fault of her birth, some glandular deficiency, some inherited characteristic? It was sad how when one was young, one so often mistook the signs of frigidity for a kind of distinction.

'You promised we'd smoke opium,' Mrs Carter said.

'Not here, darling. In Saigon. Here it's "not done" to smoke.'

'How conventional you are.'

'There'd be only the dirtiest of coolie places. You'd be conspicuous. They'd stare at you.' He played his winning card. 'There'd be cockroaches.'

'I should be taken to plenty of Spots if I wasn't with a husband.'

He tried hopefully, 'The Japanese strip-teasers . . .'

but she had heard all about them. 'Ugly women in bras,' she said. His irritation rose. He thought of the money he had spent to take his wife with him and to ease his conscience – he had been away too often without her, but there is no company more cheerless than that of a woman who is not desired. He tried to drink his coffee calmly: he wanted to bite the edge of the cup.

'You've spilt your coffee,' Mrs Carter said.

'I'm sorry.' He got up abruptly and said, 'All right. I'll fix something. Stay here.' He leant across the table. 'You'd better not be shocked,' he said. 'You've asked for it.'

'I don't think I'm usually the one who is shocked,' Mrs Carter said with a thin smile.

Carter left the hotel and walked up towards the New Road. A boy hung at his side and said, 'Young girl?'

'I've got a woman of my own,' Carter said gloomily.

'Boy?'

'No thanks.'

'French films?'

Carter paused. 'How much?'

They stood and haggled awhile at the corner of the drab street. What with the taxi, the guide, the films, it was going to cost the best part of eight pounds, but it was worth it, Carter thought, if it closed her mouth for ever from demanding 'Spots'. He went back to fetch Mrs Carter.

They drove a long way and came to a halt by a bridge over a canal, a dingy lane overcast with indeterminate smells. The guide said, 'Follow me.'

Mrs Carter put a hand on Carter's arm. 'Is it safe?' she asked.

'How would I know?' he replied, stiffening under her hand.

They walked about fifty unlighted yards and halted by a bamboo fence. The guide knocked several times. When they were admitted it was to a tiny earth-floored yard and a wooden hut. Something – presumably human – was humped in the dark under a mosquito-net. The owner showed them into a tiny stuffy room with two chairs and a portrait of the King. The screen was about the size of a folio volume.

The first film was peculiarly unattractive and showed the rejuvenation of an elderly man at the hands of two blonde masseuses. From the style of the women's hairdressing the film must have been made in the late twenties. Carter and his wife sat in mutual embarrassment as the film whirled and clicked to a stop.

'Not a very good one,' Carter said, as though he were a connoisseur.

'So that's what they call a blue film,' Mrs Carter said. 'Ugly and not exciting.'

A second film started.

There was very little story in this. A young man – one couldn't see his face because of the period soft hat – picked up a girl in the street (her cloche hat extinguished her like a meat-cover) and accompanied her to her room. The actors were young: there was some charm and excitement in the picture. Carter thought, when the girl took off her hat, I know that face, and a memory which had been buried for more than a quarter of a century moved. A doll over a telephone, a pin-up girl of the period over the double bed. The girl undressed, folding her clothes very neatly: she leant over to adjust the bed, exposing herself to the camera's eye and to the young

158

man: he kept his head turned from the camera. Afterwards, she helped him in turn to take off his clothes. It was only then he remembered – that particular playfulness confirmed by the birthmark on the man's shoulder.

Mrs Carter shifted on her chair. 'I wonder how they find the actors,' she said hoarsely.

'A prostitute,' he said. 'It's a bit raw, isn't it? Wouldn't you like to leave?' he urged her, waiting for the man to turn his head. The girl knelt on the bed and held the youth around the waist – she couldn't have been more than twenty. No, he made a calculation, twenty-one.

'We'll stay,' Mrs Carter said, 'we've paid.' She laid a dry hot hand on his knee.

'I'm sure we could find a better place than this.'

'No.'

The young man lay on his back and the girl for a moment left him. Briefly, as though by accident, he looked at the camera. Mrs Carter's hand shook on his knee. 'Good God,' she said, 'it's you.'

'It *was* me,' Carter said, 'thirty years ago.' The girl was climbing back on to the bed.

'It's revolting,' Mrs Carter said.

'I don't remember it as revolting,' Carter replied.

'I suppose you went and gloated, both of you.'

'No, I never saw it.'

'Why did you do it? I can't look at you. It's shameful.'

'I asked you to come away.'

'Did they pay you?'

'They paid her. Fifty pounds. She needed the money badly.'

'And you had your fun for nothing?'

'Yes.'

'I'd never have married you if I'd known. Never.'

'That was a long time afterwards.'

'You still haven't said why. Haven't you any excuse?' She stopped. He knew she was watching, leaning forward, caught up herself in the heat of that climax more than a quarter of a century old.

Carter said, 'It was the only way I could help her. She'd never acted in one before. She wanted a friend.'

'A friend,' Mrs Carter said.

'I loved her.'

'You couldn't love a tart.'

'Oh yes, you can. Make no mistake about that.'

'You queued for her, I suppose.'

'You put it too crudely,' Carter said.

'What happened to her?'

'She disappeared. They always disappear.'

The girl leant over the young man's body and put out the light. It was the end of the film. 'I have new ones coming next week,' the Siamese said, bowing deeply. They followed their guide back down the dark lane to the taxi.

In the taxi Mrs Carter said, 'What was her name?'

'I don't remember.' A lie was easiest.

As they turned into the New Road she broke her bitter silence again. 'How could you have brought yourself . . . ? It's so degrading. Suppose someone you knew – in business – recognized you.'

'People don't talk about seeing things like that. Anyway, I wasn't in business in those days.'

'Did it never worry you?'

'I don't believe I have thought of it once in thirty years.'

'How long did you know her?'

'Twelve months perhaps.'

'She must look pretty awful by now if she's alive. After all she was common even then.'

'I thought she looked lovely,' Carter said.

They went upstairs in silence. He went straight to the bathroom and locked the door. The mosquitoes gathered around the lamp and the great jar of water. As he undressed he caught glimpses of himself in the small mirror: thirty years had not been kind: he felt his thickness and his middle age. He thought: I hope to God she's dead. Please, God, he said, let her be dead. When I go back in there, the insults will start again.

But when he returned Mrs Carter was standing by the mirror. She had partly undressed. Her thin bare legs reminded him of a heron waiting for fish. She came and put her arms round him: a slave bangle joggled against his shoulder. She said, 'I'd forgotten how nice you looked.'

'I'm sorry. One changes.'

'I didn't mean that. I like you as you are.'

She was dry and hot and implacable in her desire. 'Go on,' she said, 'go on,' and then she screamed like an angry and hurt bird. Afterwards she said, 'It's years since that happened,' and continued to talk for what seemed a long half hour excitedly at his side. Carter lay in the dark silent, with a feeling of loneliness and guilt. It seemed to him that he had betrayed that night the only woman he loved.

The Root of All Evil

CAST

PUCKLER, Donald Pleasence
SCHMIDT, John Le Mesurier
CONSTABLE HESSE, Bill Fraser
THE SUPERINTENDENT, Peter Jones
BRAUN, Ray Mort
WEISS, Gordon Rollings
MULLER, Michael Logan
FRAU MULLER, Molly Weir
FRAU SCHMIDT, Dorothea Phillips
FRAU BRAUN, Pamela Cundell
FRAU WEISS, Barbara Hicks
FRAU PUCKLER, Jane Wenham
THE MADAM, Katherine Kath
HARLOTS,
      Edina Ronay
      Lynda Westover
WOMAN IN STREET, Joan Young
FATHER, James Berwick
SON, Ashley Knight

Dramatised by Clive Exton
Directed by Alastair Reid

The Root of All Evil

This story was told me by my father who heard it directly from his father, the brother of one of the participants; otherwise I doubt whether I would have credited it. But my father was a man of absolute rectitude, and I have no reason to believe that this virtue did not then run in the family.

The events happened in 189–, as they say in old Russian novels, in the small market town of B—. My father was German, and when he settled in England he was the first of the family to go further than a few kilometres from the home commune, province, canton or whatever it was called in those parts. He was a Protestant who believed in his faith, and no one has a greater ability to believe, without doubt or scruple, than a Protestant of that type. He would not even allow my mother to read us fairy-stories, and he walked three miles to church rather than go to one with pews. 'We've nothing to hide,' he said. 'If I sleep I sleep, and let the world know the weakness of my flesh. Why,' he added, and the thought touched my imagination strongly and perhaps had some influence on my future, 'they could play cards in those pews and no one the wiser.'

That phrase is linked in my mind with the fashion in which he would begin this story. 'Original sin gave man a tilt towards secrecy,' he would say. 'An open sin is only half a sin, and a secret innocence is only half innocent. When you have secrets, there, sooner or later, you'll have sin. I wouldn't let a Freemason cross my threshold. Where

I come from secret societies were illegal, and the government had reason. Innocent though they might be at the start, like that club of Schmidt's.'

It appears that among the old people of the town where my father lived were a couple whom I shall continue to call Schmidt, being a little uncertain of the nature of the laws of libel and how limitations and the like affect the dead. Herr Schmidt was a big man and a heavy drinker, but most of his drinking he preferred to do at his own board to the discomfort of his wife, who never touched a drop of alcohol herself. Not that she wished to interfere with her husband's potations; she had a proper idea of a wife's duty, but she had reached an age (she was over sixty and he well past seventy) when she had a great yearning to sit quietly with another woman knitting something or other for her grandchildren and talking about their latest maladies. You can't do that at ease with a man continually on the go to the cellar for another litre. There is a man's atmosphere and a woman's atmosphere, and they don't mix except in the proper place, under the sheets. Many a time Frau Schmidt in her gentle way had tried to persuade him to go out of an evening to the inn. 'What and pay more for every glass?' he would say. Then she tried to persuade him that he had need of men's company and men's conversation. 'Not when I'm tasting a good wine,' he said.

So last of all she took her trouble to Frau Muller who suffered in just the same manner as herself. Frau Muller was a stronger type of woman and she set out to build an organization. She found four other women starved of female company and female interests, and they arranged to forgather once a week with their sewing and take their evening coffee together. Between them they could summon up more than two dozen grandchildren, so you can imagine they were never short of subjects to talk about. When one child had finished with the chicken-pox, at least two would have started the measles. There were all the varying treatments to compare, and there was one school of thought which took the motto 'starve a cold' to mean 'if you starve a cold you will feed a fever' and another school which took the more traditional view. But their debates were never heated like those they had with their husbands, and they took it in turn to act hostess and make the cakes.

But what was happening all this time to the husbands? You might think they would be content to go on drinking alone, but not a bit of it. Drinking's like reading a 'romance' (my father used the term with contempt, he had never turned the pages of a novel in his life); you don't need talk, but you need company, otherwise it begins to feel like work. Frau Muller had thought of that and she suggested to her husband – very gently, so that he hardly noticed – that, when the women were meeting elsewhere, he should ask the other husbands in with their own drinks (no need to spend extra money at the bar) and they could sit as silent as they wished with their glasses till bedtime. Not, of course, that they would be silent all the time. Now and then no doubt one of them would remark on the wet or the fine day, and another would mention the prospects for the harvest, and a third would say that they'd never had so warm a summer as the summer of 188–. Men's talk, which, in the absence of women, would never become heated.

But there was one snag in this arrangement and it was the one which caused the disaster. Frau Muller roped in a seventh woman, who had been widowed by something other than drink, by her husband's curiosity. Frau Puckler had a husband whom none of them could abide, and, before they could settle down to their friendly evenings, they had to decide what to do about him. He was a little vinegary man with a squint and a completely bald head who would empty any bar when he came into it. His eyes, coming together like that, had the effect of a gimlet, and he would stay in conversation with one man for ten minutes on end with his eyes fixed on the other's forehead until you expected sawdust to come out. Unfortunately Frau Puckler was highly respected. It was essential to keep from her any idea that her husband was unwelcome, so for some weeks they had to reject Frau Muller's proposal. They were quite happy, they said, sitting alone at home with a glass when what they really meant was that even loneliness was preferable to the company of Herr Puckler. But they got so miserable all this time that often, when their wives returned home, they would find their husbands tucked up in bed and asleep.

It was then Herr Schmidt broke his customary silence. He called round at Herr Muller's door, one evening when the wives were away, with a four-litre jug of wine, and he hadn't got through more than two litres when he broke silence. This lonely drinking, he said, must come to an end – he had had more sleep the last few weeks than he had had in six months and it was sapping his strength. 'The grave yawns for us,' he said, yawning himself from habit.

'But Puckler?' Herr Muller objected. 'He's worse than the grave.'

'We shall have to meet in secret,' Herr Schmidt said. 'Braun has a fine big cellar,' and that was how the secret began; and from secrecy, my father would moralize, you can grow every sin in the calendar. I pictured secrecy like the dark mould in the cellar where we cultivated our mushrooms, but the mushrooms were good to eat, so that their secret growth . . . I always found an ambivalence in my father's moral teaching.

It appears that for a time all went well. The men were happy drinking together – in the absence, of course, of Herr Puckler, and so were the women, even Frau Puckler, for she always found her husband in bed at night ready for domesticities. He was far too proud to tell her of his ramblings in search of company between the strokes of the town-clock. Every night he would try a different house and every night he found only the closed door and the darkened window. Once in Herr Braun's cellar the husbands heard the knocker hammering overhead. At the Gasthof too he would look regularly in – and sometimes irregularly, as though he hoped that he might catch them off their guard. The street-lamp shone on his bald head, and often some late drinker going home would be confronted by those gimlet-eyes which believed nothing you said. 'Have you seen Herr Muller tonight?' or 'Herr Schmidt, is he at home?' he would demand of another reveller. He sought them here, he sought them there – he had been content enough aforetime drinking in his own home and sending his wife down to the cellar for a refill, but he knew only too well, now he was alone, that there was no pleasure possible for a solitary drinker. If Herr Schmidt and Herr Muller were not at home, where were they? And the other four with whom he had never been well acquainted, where were they? Frau Puckler was the very reverse of her husband, she had no curiosity, and Frau Muller and Frau Schmidt had mouths which clicked shut like the clasp of a well-made handbag.

Inevitably after a certain time Herr Puckler went to the police. He refused to speak to anyone lower than the Superintendent. His gimlet-eyes bored like a migraine into the Superintendent's forehead. While the eyes rested on the one spot, his words wandered ambiguously. There had been an anarchist outrage at Schloss – I can't remember the name; there were rumours of an attempt on a Grand Duke. The Superintendent shifted a little this way and a little that way on his seat, for these were big affairs which did not concern him, while the squinting eyes bored continuously at the sensitive spot above his nose where his migraine always began. Then the Superintendent blew loudly and said, 'The times are evil,' a phrase which he had remembered from the service on Sunday.

'You know the law about secret societies,' Herr Puckler said.

'Naturally.'

'And yet here, under the nose of the police,' and the squint-eyes bored deeper, 'there exists just such a society.'

'If you would be a little more explicit . . .'

So Herr Puckler gave him the whole row of names, beginning with Herr Schmidt. 'They meet in secret,' he said. 'None of them stays at home.'

'They are not the kind of men I would suspect of plotting.'

'All the more dangerous for that.'

'Perhaps they are just friends.'

'Then why don't they meet in public?'

'I'll put a policeman on the case,' the Superintendent said half-heartedly, so now at night there were two men looking around to find where the six had their meeting-place. The policeman was a simple man who began by asking direct questions, but he had been seen several times in the company of Puckler, so the six assumed quickly enough that he was trying to track them down on Puckler's behalf and they became more careful than ever to avoid discovery. They stocked up Herr Braun's cellar with wine, and they took elaborate precautions not to be seen entering – each one sacrificed a night's drinking in order to lead Herr Puckler and the policeman astray. Nor could they confide in their wives for fear that it might come to the ears of Frau Puckler, so they pretended the scheme had not worked and it was every man for himself again now in drinking. That meant they had to tell a lot of lies if they failed to be the first home – and so, my father said, sin began to enter in.

One night too, Herr Schmidt, who happened to be the decoy, led Herr Puckler a long walk into the suburbs, and then seeing an open door and a light burning in the window with a comforting red glow and being by that time very dry in the mouth, he mistook the house in his distress for a quiet inn and walked inside. He was warmly welcomed by a stout lady and shown into a parlour, where he expected to be served with wine. Three young ladies sat on a sofa in various stages of undress and greeted Herr Schmidt with giggles and warm words. Herr Schmidt was afraid to leave the house at once, in case Puckler was lurking outside, and while he hesitated the stout lady entered with a bottle of champagne on ice and a number of glasses. So for the sake of the drink (though champagne was not his preference – he would have liked the local wine) he stayed, and thus out of secrecy, my father said, came the second sin. But it didn't end there with lies and fornication.

When the time came to go, if he were not to overstay

his welcome, Herr Schmidt took a look out of the window, and there, in place of Puckler, was the policeman walking up and down the pavement. He must have followed Puckler at a distance, and then taken on his watch while Puckler went rabbiting after the others. What to do? It was growing late; soon the wives would be drinking their last cup and closing the file on the last grandchild. Herr Schmidt appealed to the kind stout lady; he asked her whether she hadn't a back-door so that he might avoid the man he knew in the street outside. She had no back-door, but she was a woman of great resource, and in no time she had decked Herr Schmidt out in a great cartwheel of a skirt, like peasant-women in those days wore at market, a pair of white stockings, a blouse ample enough and a floppy hat. The girls hadn't enjoyed themselves so much for a long time, and they amused themselves decking his face with rouge, eye-shadow and lipstick. When he came out of the door, the policeman was so astonished by the sight that he stood rooted to the spot long enough for Herr Schmidt to billow round the corner, take to his heels down a side-street and arrive safely home in time to scour his face before his wife came in.

If it had stopped there all might have been well, but the policeman had not been deceived, and now he reported to the Superintendent that members of the secret society dressed themselves as women and in that guise frequented the gay houses of the town. 'But why dress as women to do that?' the Superintendent asked, and Puckler hinted at orgies which went beyond the natural order of things. 'Anarchy,' he said, 'is out to upset everything, even the proper relationship of man and woman.'

'Can't you be more explicit?' the Superintendent

asked him for the second time; it was a phrase of which he was pathetically fond, but Puckler left the details shrouded in mystery.

It was then that Puckler's fanaticism took a morbid turn; he suspected every large woman he saw in the street at night of being a man in disguise. Once he actually pulled the wig off a certain Frau Hackenfurth (no one till that day, not even her husband, knew that she wore a wig), and presently he sallied out into the streets himself dressed as a woman with the belief that one transvestite would recognize another and that sooner or later he would find himself enlisted in the secret orgies. He was a small man and he played the part better than Herr Schmidt had done – only his gimlet-eyes would have betrayed him to an acquaintance in daylight.

The men had been meeting happily enough now for two weeks in Herr Braun's cellar, the policeman had tired of his search, the Superintendent was in hopes that all had blown over, when a disastrous decision was taken. Frau Schmidt and Frau Muller in the old days had the habit of cooking pasties for their husbands to go with the wine, and the two men began to miss this treat which they described to their fellow drinkers, their mouths wet with the relish of the memory. Herr Braun suggested that they should bring in a woman to cook for them – it would mean only a small contribution from each, for no one would charge very much for a few hours' work at the end of the evening. Her duty would be to bring in fresh warm pasties every half an hour or so as long as their wine-session lasted. He advertised the position openly enough in the local paper, and Puckler, taking a long chance – the advertisement had referred to a men's club – applied, dressed up in his wife's best Sunday blacks. He was accepted by Herr Braun, who was the only one who did not know Herr Puckler except by repute, and so Puckler found himself installed at the very heart of the mystery, with a grand opportunity to hear all their talk. The only trouble was that he had little skill at cooking and often with his ears to the cellar-door he allowed the pasties to burn. On the second evening Herr Braun told him that, unless the pasties improved, he would find another woman.

However Puckler was not worried by that because he had all the information he required for the Superintendent, and it was a real pleasure to make his report in the presence of the policeman, who contributed nothing at all to the inquiry.

Puckler had written down the dialogue as he had heard it, leaving out only the long pauses, the gurgle of the wine-jugs, and the occasional rude tribute that wind makes to the virtue of young wine. His report read as follows:

Inquiry into the Secret Meetings held in the Cellar of Herr Braun's House at 27 —strasse. The following dialogue was overheard by the investigator.

Muller: If the rain keeps off another month, the wine harvest will be better than last year.

Unidentified voice: Ugh.

Schmidt: They say the postman nearly broke his ankle last week. Slipped on a step.

Braun: I remember sixty-one vintages.

Dobel: Time for a pasty.

Unidentified voice: Ugh.

Muller: Call in that cow.

The investigator was summoned and left a tray of pasties.

Braun: Careful. They are hot.

Schmidt: This one's burnt to a cinder.

Dobel: Uneatable.

Kastner: Better sack her before worse happens.

Braun: She's paid till the end of the week. We'll give her till then.

Muller: It was fourteen degrees midday.

Dobel: The town-hall clock's fast.

Schmidt: Do you remember that dog the mayor had with black spots?

Unidentified voice: Ugh.

Kastner: No, why?

Schmidt: I can't remember.

Muller: When I was a boy we had plum-duff they never make now.

Dobel: It was the summer of '87.

Unidentified voice: What was?

Muller: The year Mayor Kalnitz died.

Schmidt: '88.

Muller: There was a hard frost.

Dobel: Not as hard as '86.

Braun: That was a shocking year for wine.

So it went on for twelve pages. 'What's it all about?' the Superintendent asked.

'If we knew that, we'd know all.'

'It sounds harmless.'

'Then why do they meet in secret?'

The policeman said 'Ugh' like the unidentified voice.

'My feeling is,' Puckler said, 'a pattern will emerge. Look at all those dates. They need to be checked.'

'There was a bomb thrown in '86,' the Superintendent said doubtfully. 'It killed the Grand Duke's best grey.'

'A shocking year for wine,' Puckler said. 'They missed. No wine. No royal blood.'

'The attempt was mistimed,' the Superintendent remembered.

'The town-hall clock's fast,' Puckler quoted.

'I can't believe it all the same.'

'A code. To break a code we have need of more material.'

The Superintendent agreed with some reluctance that the report should continue, but then there was the difficulty of the pasties. 'We need a good assistant-cook for the pasties,' Puckler said, 'and then I can listen without interruption. They won't object if I tell them that it will cost no more.'

The Superintendent said to the policeman, 'Those were good pasties I had in your house.'

'I cooked them myself,' the policeman said gloomily.

'Then that's no help.'

'Why no help?' Puckler demanded. 'If I can dress up as a woman, so can he.'

'His moustache?'

'A good blade and a good lather will see to that.'

'It's an unusual thing to demand of a man.'

'In the service of the law.'

So it was decided, though the policeman was not at all happy about the affair. Puckler, being a small man, was able to dress in his wife's clothes, but the policeman had no wife. In the end Puckler was forced to agree to buy the clothes himself; he did it late in the evening, when the assistants were in a hurry to leave and were unlikely to recognize his gimlet-eyes, as they judged the size of the skirt, blouse, knickers. There had been lies, fornication: I don't know in what further category my father placed the strange shopping expedition, which didn't, as it happened, go entirely unnoticed. Scandal – perhaps that was the third offence which secrecy produced, for a late customer coming into the shop did in fact recognize Puckler, just as he was holding up the bloomers to see if the seat seemed large enough. You can imagine how quickly that story got around, to every woman except Frau Puckler, and she felt at the next sewing-party an odd – well, it might have been deference or it might have been compassion. Everyone stopped to listen when she spoke; no one contradicted or argued with her, and she was not allowed to carry a tray or pour a cup. She began to feel so like an invalid that she developed a headache and decided to go home early. She could see them all nodding at each other as though they knew what was the matter better than she did, and Frau Muller volunteered to see her home.

Of course she hurried straight back to tell them about it. 'When we arrived,' she said, 'Herr Puckler was not at home. Of course the poor woman pretended not to know where he could be. She got in quite a state about it. She said he was always there to welcome her when she came in. She had half a mind to go round to the police-station and report him missing, but I dissuaded her. I almost began to believe that she didn't know what he was up to. She muttered about the strange goings-on in town, anarchists and the like, and would you believe it, she said that Herr Puckler told her a policeman had seen Herr Schmidt dressed up in women's clothes.'

'The little swine,' Frau Schmidt said, naturally referring to Puckler, for Herr Schmidt had the figure of one of his own wine-barrels. 'Can you imagine such a thing?'

'Distracting attention,' Frau Muller said, 'from his own

vices. For look what happened next. We come to the bedroom, and Frau Puckler finds her wardrobe door wide
open, and she looks inside, and what does she find – her
black Sunday dress missing. "There's truth in the story
after all," she said, "and I'm going to look for Herr
Schmidt," but I pointed out to her that it would have to
be a very small man indeed to wear her dress.'

'Did she blush?'

'I really believe she knows nothing about it.'

'Poor, poor woman,' Frau Dobel said. 'And what do
you think he does when he's all dressed up?' and they
began to speculate. So thus it was, my father would say,
that foul talk was added to the other sins of lies, fornication, scandal. Yet there still remained the most serious
sin of all.

That night Puckler and the policeman turned up at
Herr Braun's door, but little did they know that the story
of Puckler had already reached the ears of the drinkers,
for Frau Muller had reported the strange events to Herr
Muller, and at once he remembered the gimlet-eyes of
the cook Anna peering at him out of the shadows. When
the men met, Herr Braun reported that the cook was to
bring an assistant to help her with the pasties and as she
had asked for no extra money he had consented. You can
imagine the babble of voices that broke out from these
silent men when Herr Muller told his story. What was
Puckler's motive? It was a bad one or it would not have
been Puckler. One theory was that he was planning with
the help of an assistant to poison them with the pasties in
revenge for being excluded. 'It's not beyond Puckler,'
Herr Dobel said. They had good reason to be suspicious,
so my father, who was a just man, did not include un-
worthy suspicion among the sins of which the secret

society was the cause. They began to prepare a reception for Puckler.

Puckler knocked on the door and the policeman stood just behind him, enormous in his great black skirt with his white stockings crinkling over his boots because Puckler had forgotten to buy him suspenders. After the second knock the bombardment began from the upper windows. Puckler and the policeman were drenched with unmentionable liquids, they were struck with logs of wood. Their eyes were endangered from falling forks. The policeman was the first to take to his heels, and it was a strange sight to see so huge a woman go beating down the street. The blouse had come out of the waist-band and flapped like a sail as its owner tacked to avoid the flying objects – which now included a toilet-roll, a broken teapot and a portrait of the Grand Duke.

Puckler, who had been hit on the shoulder with a rolling-pin, did not at first run away. He had his moment of courage or bewilderment. But when the frying-pan he had used for pasties struck him, he turned too late to follow the policeman. It was then that he was struck on the head with a chamber-pot and lay in the street with the pot fitting over his head like a vizor. They had to break it with a hammer to get it off, and by that time he was dead, whether from the blow on the head or the fall or from fear or from being stifled by the chamber-pot nobody knew, though suffocation was the general opinion. Of course there was an inquiry which went on for many months into the existence of an anarchist plot, and before the end of it the Superintendent had become secretly affianced to Frau Puckler, for which nobody blamed her, for she was a popular woman – except my father who resented the secrecy of it all. (He suspected that the

Superintendent's love for Frau Puckler had extended the inquiry, since he pretended to believe her husband's accusations.)

Technically, of course, it was murder – death arising from an illegal assault – but the courts after about six months absolved the six men. 'But there's a greater court,' my father would always end his story, 'and in that court the sin of murder never goes unrequited. You begin with a secret,' and he would look at me as though he knew my pockets were stuffed with them, as indeed they were, including the note I intended to pass the next day at school to the yellow-haired girl in the second row, 'and you end with every sin in the calendar.' He began to recount them over again for my benefit. 'Lies, drunkenness, fornication, scandal-bearing, murder, the subornation of authority.'

'Subornation of authority?'

'Yes,' he said and fixed me with his glittering eye. I think he had Frau Puckler and the Superintendent in mind. He rose towards his climax. 'Men in women's clothes – the terrible sin of Sodom.'

'And what's that?' I asked with excited expectation.

'At your age,' my father said, 'some things must remain secret.'

A Drive in the Country

CAST

FATHER, Arthur White
MOTHER, Amanda Walker
DAUGHTER, Lesley Dunlop
SISTER, Susan Skipper
FRED, John Hurt
MIKE, Ronald Lacey
GIRL, Nicolette McKenzie

Dramatised by Philip Mackie
Directed by Alan Cooke

A Drive in the Country

As every other night she listened to her father going round the house, locking the doors and windows. He was head clerk at Bergson's Export Agency, and lying in bed she would think with dislike that his home was like his office, run on the same lines, its safety preserved with the same meticulous care, so that he could present a faithful steward's account to the managing-director. Regularly every Sunday he presented the account, accompanied by his wife and two daughters, in the little neo-Gothic church in Park Road. They always had the same pew, they were always five minutes early, and her father sang loudly with no sense of tune, holding an out-size prayer book on the level of his eyes. 'Singing songs of exultation' – he was presenting the week's account (one household duly safeguarded) – 'marching to the Promised Land.' When they came out of church, she looked carefully away from the corner by the 'Bricklayers' Arms' where Fred always stood, a little lit because the Arms had been open for half an hour, with his air of unbalanced exultation.

She listened: the back door closed, she could hear the catch of the kitchen window click, and the restless pad of his feet going back to try the front door. It wasn't only the outside doors he locked: he locked the empty rooms, the bathroom, the lavatory. He was locking something out, but obviously it was something capable of penetrating his first defences. He raised his second line all the way up to bed.

She laid her ear against the thin wall of the jerry-built

villa and could hear the faint voices from the neighbouring room; as she listened they came clearer as though she were turning the knob of a wireless set. Her mother said . . . 'margarine in the cooking . . .' and her father said '. . . much easier in fifteen years'. Then the bed creaked and there were dim sounds of tenderness and comfort between the two middle-aged strangers in the next room. In fifteen years, she thought unhappily, the house will be his; he had paid twenty-five pounds down and the rest he was paying month by month as rent. 'Of course,' he was in the habit of saying after a good meal, 'I've improved the property,' and he expected at least one of them to follow him into his study. 'I've wired this room for power,' he padded back past the little downstairs lavatory, 'this radiator,' the final stroke of satisfaction, 'the garden,' and if it was a fine evening he would fling the french window of the dining-room open on the little carpet of grass as carefully kept as a college lawn. 'A pile of bricks,' he'd say, 'that's all it was.' Five years of Saturday afternoons and fine Sundays had gone into the patch of turf, the surrounding flower-bed, the one apple-tree which regularly produced one crimson tasteless apple more each year.

'Yes,' he said, 'I've improved the property,' looking round for a nail to drive in, a weed to be uprooted. 'If we had to sell now, we should get back more than I've paid from the society.' It was more than a sense of property, it was a sense of honesty. Some people who bought their houses through the society let them go to rack and ruin and then cleared out.

She stood with her ear against the wall, a small, furious, immature figure. There was no more to be heard from the other room, but in her inner ear she still heard the chorus of a property owner, the tap-tap of a hammer, the scrape of a spade, the whistle of radiator steam, a key turning, a bolt pushed home, the little trivial sounds of men building barricades. She stood planning her treachery.

It was a quarter-past ten; she had an hour in which to leave the house, but it did not take so long. There was really nothing to fear. They had played their usual rubber of three-handed bridge while her sister altered a dress for the local 'hop' next night; after the rubber she had boiled a kettle and brought in a pot of tea; then she had filled the hot-water bottles and put them in the beds while her father locked up. He had no idea whatever that she was an enemy.

She put on a scarf and a heavy coat because it was still cold at night; the spring was late that year, as her father commented, watching for the buds on the apple-tree. She didn't pack a suitcase; that would have reminded her too much of week-ends at the sea, a family expedition to Ostend from all of which one returned; she wanted to match the odd reckless quality of Fred's mind. This time she wasn't going to return. She went softly downstairs into the little crowded hall, unlocked the door. All was quiet upstairs, and she closed the door behind her.

She was touched by a faint feeling of guilt because she couldn't lock it from the outside. But her guilt vanished by the time she reached the end of the crazy paved path and turned to the left down the road which after five years was still half made, past the gaps between the villas where the wounded fields remained grimly alive in the form of thin grass and heaps of clay and dandelions.

She walked fast, passing a long line of little garages like the graves in a Latin cemetery where the coffin lies below the fading photograph of its occupant. The cold night air touched her with exhilaration. She was ready for anything, as she turned by the Belisha beacon into the shuttered shopping street; she was like a recruit in the first months of a war. The choice made she could surrender her will to the strange, the exhilarating, the gigantic event.

Fred, as he had promised, was at the corner where the road turned down towards the church; she could taste the spirit on his lips as they kissed, and she was satisfied that no one else could have so adequately matched the occasion; his face was bright and reckless in the lamp-light, he was as exciting and strange to her as the adventure. He took her arm and ran her into a blind un-lighted alley, then left her for a moment until two head-lamps beamed softly at her out of the cavern. She cried with astonishment, 'You've got a car?' and felt the jerk of his nervous hand urging her towards it. 'Yes,' he said, 'do you like it?' grinding into second gear, changing clumsily into top as they came out between the shuttered windows.

She said, 'It's lovely. Let's drive a long way.'

'We will,' he said, watching the speedometer needle go quivering to fifty-five.

'Does it mean you've got a job?'

'There are no jobs,' he said, 'they don't exist any more than the Dodo. Did you see that bird?' he asked sharply, turning his headlights full on as they passed the turning to the housing estate and quite suddenly came out into the country between a café ('Draw in here'), a boot-shop ('Buy the shoes worn by your favourite film star'), and an undertaker's with a large white angel lit by a Neon light.

'I didn't see any bird.'

'Not flying at the windscreen?'

'No.'

'I nearly hit it,' he said. 'It would have made a mess. Bad as those fellows who run someone down and don't stop. Should *we* stop?' he asked, turning out his switchboard light so that they couldn't see the needle vibrate to sixty.

'Whatever you say,' she said, sitting deep in a reckless dream.

'You going to love me tonight?'

'Of course I am.'

'Never going back there?'

'No,' she said, abjuring the tap of hammer, the click of latch, the pad of slippered feet making the rounds.

'Want to know where we are going?'

'No.' A little flat cardboard copse ran forward into the green light and darkly by. A rabbit turned its scut and vanished into a hedge. He said, 'Have you any money?'

'Half a crown.'

'Do you love me?' For a long time she expended on his lips all she had patiently had to keep in reserve, looking the other way on Sunday mornings, saying nothing when his name came up at meals with disapproval. She expended herself against dry unresponsive lips as the car leapt ahead and his foot trod down on the accelerator. He said, 'It's the hell of a life.'

She echoed him, 'The hell of a life.'

He said, 'There's a bottle in my pocket. Have a drink.'

'I don't want one.'

'Give me one then. It has a screw top,' and with one hand on her and one on the wheel he tipped his head, so that she could pour a little whisky into his mouth out of the quarter bottle. 'Do you mind?' he said.

'Of course I don't mind.'

'You can't save,' he said, 'on ten shillings a week pocket-money. I lay it out the best I can. It needs a hell of a lot of thought. To give variety. Half a crown on Weights. Three and six on whisky. A shilling on the pictures. That leaves three shillings for beer. I take my fun once a week and get it over.'

The whisky had dribbled on to his tie and the smell filled the small coupé. It pleased her. It was *his* smell. He said, 'They grudge it me. They think I ought to get a job. When you're that age you don't realize there aren't any jobs for some of us – any more for ever.'

'I know,' she said. 'They are old.'

'How's your sister?' he asked abruptly; the bright glare swept the road ahead of them clean of small scurrying birds and animals.

'She's going to the hop tomorrow. I wonder where we shall be.'

He wouldn't be drawn; he had his own idea and kept it to himself.

'I'm loving this.'

He said, 'There's a club out this way. At a road-house. Mick made me a member. Do you know Mick?'

'No.'

'Mick's all right. If they know you, they'll serve you drinks till midnight. We'll look in there. Say hullo to Mick. And then in the morning – we'll decide that later when we've had a few drinks.'

'Have you the money?' A small village, a village fast asleep already behind closed doors and windows, sailed down the hill towards them as if it was being carried

187

smoothly by a landslide into the scarred plain from which they'd come. A low grey Norman church, an inn without a sign, a clock striking eleven. He said, 'Look in the back. There's a suitcase there.'

'It's locked.'

'I forgot the key,' he said.

'What's in it?'

'A few things,' he said vaguely. 'We could pop them for drinks.'

'What about a bed?'

'There's the car. You are not scared, are you?'

'No,' she said. 'I'm not scared. This is –' but she hadn't words for the damp cold wind, the darkness, the strangeness, the smell of whisky and the rushing car. 'It moves,' she said. 'We must have gone a long way already. This is real country,' seeing an owl sweep low on furry wings over a ploughed field.

'You've got to go farther than this for real country,' he said. 'You won't find it yet on *this* road. We'll be at the road-house soon.'

She discovered in herself a nostalgia for their dark windy solitary progress. She said, 'Need we go to the club? Can't we go farther into the country?'

He looked sideways at her; he had always been open to *any* suggestion: like some meteorological instrument, he was made for the winds to blow through. 'Of course,' he said, 'anything you like.' He didn't give the club a second thought; they swept past it a moment later, a long lit Tudor bungalow, a crash of voices, a bathing-pool filled for some reason with hay. It was immediately behind them, a patch of light whipping round a corner out of sight.

He said, 'I suppose this is country now. They none of

them get farther than the club. We're quite alone now. We could lie in these fields till doomsday as far as *they* are concerned, though I suppose a ploughman . . . if they do plough here.' He raised his foot from the accelerator and let the car's speed gradually diminish. Somebody had left a wooden gate open into a field and he turned the car in; they jolted a long way down the field beside the hedge and came to a standstill. He turned out the headlamps and they sat in the tiny glow of the switchboard light. 'Peaceful,' he said uneasily; and they heard a screech owl hunting overhead and a small rustle in the hedge where something went into hiding. They belonged to the city; they hadn't a name for anything round them; the tiny buds breaking in the bushes were nameless. He nodded at a group of dark trees at the hedge end. 'Oaks?'

'Elms?' she asked, and their mouths went together in a mutual ignorance. The touch excited her; she was ready for the most reckless act; but from his mouth, the dry spiritous lips, she gained a sense that he was less excited than he had hoped to be.

She said, to reassure herself, 'It's good to be here – miles away from anyone we know.'

'I dare say Mick's there. Down the road.'

'Does he know?'

'Nobody knows.'

She said, 'That's how I wanted it. How did you get this car?'

He grinned at her with unbalanced amusement. 'I saved from the ten shillings.'

'No but how? Did someone lend it you?'

'Yes,' he said. He suddenly pushed the door open and said, 'Let's take a walk.'

'We've never walked in the country before.' She took his arm, and she could feel the tense nerves responding to her touch. It was what she liked; she couldn't tell what he would do next. She said, 'My father calls you crazy. I like you crazy. What's all this stuff?' kicking at the ground.

'Clover,' he said, 'isn't it? I don't know.' It was like being in a foreign city where you can't understand the names on shops, the traffic signs: nothing to catch hold of, to hold you down to this and that, adrift together in a dark vacuum. 'Shouldn't you turn on the headlamps?' she said. 'It won't be so easy finding our way back. There's not much moon.' Already they seemed to have gone a long way from the car; she couldn't see it clearly any longer.

'We'll find our way,' he said. 'Somehow. Don't worry.' At the hedge end they came to the trees. He pulled a twig down and felt the sticky buds. 'What is it? Beech?'

'I don't know.'

He said, 'If it had been warmer, we could have slept out here. You'd think we might have had that much luck, tonight of all nights. But it's cold and it's going to rain.'

'Let's come in the summer,' but he didn't answer. Some other wind had blown, she could tell it, and already he had lost interest in her. There was something hard in his pocket; it hurt her side; she put her hand in. The metal chamber had absorbed all the cold there had been in the windy ride. She whispered fearfully, 'Why are you carrying that?' She had always before drawn a line round his recklessness. When her father had said he was crazy she had secretly and possessively smiled because she thought she knew the extent of his craziness. Now, while she waited for him to answer her, she could feel his craziness go on and on, out of her reach, out of her sight; she couldn't see where it ended; it had no end, she couldn't possess it any more than she could possess a darkness or a desert.

'Don't be scared,' he said. 'I didn't mean you to find that tonight.' He suddenly became more tender than he had ever been; he put his hand on her breast; it came from his fingers, a great soft meaningless flood of tenderness. He said, 'Don't you see? Life's hell. There's nothing we can do.' He spoke very gently, but she had never been more aware of his recklessness: he was open to every wind, but the wind now seemed to have set from the east: it blew like sleet through his words. 'I haven't a penny,' he said. 'We can't live on nothing. It's no good hoping that I'll get a job.' He repeated, 'There aren't any more jobs any more. And every year, you know, there's less chance, because there are more people younger than I am.'

'But why,' she said, 'have we come –?'

He became softly and tenderly lucid. 'We do love each other, don't we? We can't live without each other. It's no good hanging around, is it, waiting for our luck to change. We don't even get a fine night,' he said, feeling for rain with his hand. 'We can have a good time tonight – in the car – and then in the morning –'

'No, no,' she said. She tried to get away from him. 'I couldn't. It's horrible. I never said –'

'You wouldn't know anything,' he said gently and inexorably. Her words, she could realize now, had never made any real impression; he was swayed by them but no more than he was swayed by anything: now that the wind had set, it was like throwing scraps of paper towards the sky to speak at all, or to argue. He said, 'Of course we neither of us believe in God, but there may be

a chance, and it's company, going together like that.'
He added with pleasure, 'It's a gamble,' and she remembered more occasions than she could count when their last coppers had gone ringing down in fruit machines.

He pulled her closer and said with complete assurance, 'We love each other. It's the only way, you know. You can trust me.' He was like a skilled logician; he knew all the stages of the argument. She despaired of catching him out on any point but the premise: we love each other. *That* she doubted for the first time, faced by the mercilessness of his egotism. He repeated, 'It will be company.'

She said, 'There must be some way . . .'

'Why *must*?'

'Otherwise people would be doing it all the time – everywhere!'

'They are,' he said triumphantly, as if it were more important for him to find his argument flawless than to find – well, a way, a way to go on living. 'You've only got to read the papers,' he said. He whispered gently, endearingly, as if he thought the very sound of the words tender enough to dispel all fear. 'They call it a suicide pact. It's happening all the time.'

'I couldn't. I haven't the nerve.'

'You needn't do anything,' he said. 'I'll do it all.'

His calmness horrified her. 'You mean – you'd kill me?'

He said, 'I love you enough for that, I promise it won't hurt you.' He might have been persuading her to play some trivial and uncongenial game. 'We shall be together always.' He added rationally, 'Of course, if there *is* an always,' and suddenly she saw his love as a mere flicker of gas flame playing on the marshy depth of his irresponsibility, but now she realized that it was without any limit at all; it closed over the head. She pleaded, 'There are things we can sell. That suitcase.'

She knew that he was watching her with amusement, that he had rehearsed all her arguments and had an answer; he was only pretending to take her seriously. 'We might get fifteen shillings,' he said. 'We could live a day on that – but we shouldn't have much fun.'

'The things inside it?'

'Ah, that's another gamble. They might be worth thirty shillings. Three days, that would give us – with economy.'

'We might get a job.'

'I've been trying for a good many years now.'

'Isn't there the dole?'

'I'm not an insured worker. I'm one of the ruling class.'

'Your people, they'd give us something.'

'But we've got our pride, haven't we?' he said with remorseless conceit.

'The man who lent you the car?'

He said, 'You remember Cortez, the fellow who burnt his boats? I've burned mine. I've *got* to kill myself. You see, I stole that car. We'd be stopped in the next town. It's too late even to go back.' He laughed; he had reached the climax of his argument and there was nothing more to dispute about. She could tell that he was perfectly satisfied and perfectly happy. It infuriated her. '*You've* got to, maybe. But I haven't. Why should I kill myself? What right have you – ?' She dragged herself away from him and felt against her back the rough massive trunk of the living tree.

'Oh,' he said in an irritated tone, 'of course if you like

to go on without me.' She had admired his conceit; he had always carried his unemployment with a manner. Now you could no longer call it conceit: it was a complete lack of any values. 'You can go home,' he said, 'though I don't quite know how – I can't drive you back because I'm staying here. You'll be able to go to the hop tomorrow night. And there's a whist-drive, isn't there, in the church hall? My dear, I wish you joy of home.'

There was a savagery in his manner. He took security, peace, order in his teeth and worried them so that she couldn't help feeling a little pity for what they had joined in despising: a hammer tapped at her heart, driving in a nail here and a nail there. She tried to think of a bitter retort, for after all there was something to be said for the negative virtues of doing no injury, of simply going on, as her father was going on for another fifteen years. But the next moment she felt no anger. They had trapped each other. He had always wanted this: the dark field, the weapon in his pocket, the escape and the gamble; but she less honestly had wanted a little of both worlds: irresponsibility and a safe love, danger and a secure heart.

He said, 'I'm going now. Are you coming?'

'No,' she said. He hesitated; the recklessness for a moment wavered; a sense of something lost and bewildered came to her through the dark. She wanted to say: Don't be a fool. Leave the car where it is. Walk back with me, and we'll get a lift home, but she knew any thought of hers had occurred to him and been answered already: ten shillings a week, no job, getting older. Endurance was a virtue of one's fathers.

He suddenly began to walk fast down the hedge; he couldn't see where he was going; he stumbled on a root

and she heard him swear. 'Damnation' – the little commonplace sound in the darkness overwhelmed her with
pain and horror. She cried out, 'Fred. Fred. Don't do it,'
and began to run in the opposite direction. She couldn't
stop him and she wanted to be out of hearing. A twig
broke under her foot like a shot, and the owl screamed
across the ploughed field beyond the hedge. It was like a
rehearsal with sound effects. But when the real shot came,
it was quite different: a thud like a gloved hand striking
a door and no cry at all. She didn't notice it at first and
afterwards she thought that she had never been conscious
of the exact moment when her lover ceased to exist.

She bruised herself against the car, running blindly; a
blue-spotted Woolworth handkerchief lay on the seat in
the light of the switchboard bulb. She nearly took it, but
no, she thought, no one must know that I have been here.
She turned out the light and picked her way as quietly
as she could across the clover. She could begin to be sorry
when she was safe. She wanted to close a door behind her,
thrust a bolt down, hear the catch grip.

It wasn't ten minutes walk down the deserted lane to
the road-house. Tipsy voices spoke a foreign language,
though it was the language Fred had spoken. She could
hear the clink of coins in fruit machines, the hiss of soda;
she listened to these sounds like an enemy, planning her
escape. They frightened her like something mindless:
there was no appeal one could make to that egotism. It
was simply a Want to be satisfied; it gaped at her like a
mouth. A man was trying to wind up his car; the self-
starter wouldn't work. He said, 'I'm a Bolshie. Of course
I'm a Bolshie. I believe –'

A thin girl with red hair sat on the step and watched
him. 'You're all wrong,' she said.

'I'm a Liberal Conservative.'

'You *can't* be a liberal Conservative.'

'Do you love me?'

'I love Joe.'

'You *can't* love Joe.'

'Let's go home, Mike.'

The man tried to wind up the car again, and she came up to them as if she'd come out of the club and said, 'Give me a lift?'

'Course. Delighted. Get in.'

'Won't the car go?'

'No.'

'Have you flooded –?'

'That's an idea.' He lifted the bonnet and she pressed the self-starter. It began to rain slowly and heavily and drenchingly, the kind of rain you always expect to fall on graves, and her thoughts went down the lane towards the field, the hedge, the trees – oak, beech, elm? She imagined the rain on his face, the pool collecting in each eye-socket and streaming down on either side the nose. But she could feel nothing but gladness because she had escaped from him.

'Where are you going?' she said.

'Devizes.'

'I thought you might be going to London.'

'Where do *you* want to go to?'

'Golding's Park.'

'Let's go to Golding's Park.'

The red-haired girl said, 'I'm going in, Mike. It's raining.'

'Aren't you coming?'

'I'm going to find Joe.'

'All right.' He smashed his way out of the little car-park, bending his mudguard on a wooden post, scraping the paint of another car.

'That's the wrong way,' she said.

'We'll turn.' He backed the car into a ditch and out again. 'Was a good party,' he said. The rain came down harder; it blinded the windscreen and the electric wiper wouldn't work, but her companion didn't care. He drove straight on at forty miles an hour; it was an old car, it wouldn't do any more; the rain leaked through the hood. He said, 'Twis' that knob. Have a tune,' and when she turned it and the dance music came through, he said, 'That's Harry Roy. Know him anywhere,' driving into the thick wet night carrying the hot music with them. Presently he said, 'A friend of mine, one of the best, you'd know him, Peter Weatherall. You know him.'

'No.'

'You must know Peter. Haven't seen him about lately. Goes off on the drink for weeks. They sent out an SOS for Peter once in the middle of the dance music. "Missing from Home." We were in the car. We had a laugh about that.'

She said, 'Is that what people do – when people are missing?'

'Know this tune,' he said. 'This isn't Harry Roy. This is Alf Cohen.'

She said suddenly, 'You're Mike, aren't you? Wouldn't *you* lend –'

He sobered up. 'Stony broke,' he said. 'Comrades in misfortune. Try Peter. Why do you want to go to Golding's Park?'

'My home.'

'You mean you live there?'

'Yes.' She said, 'Be careful. There's a speed limit here.'

He was perfectly obedient. He raised his foot and let the car crawl at fifteen miles an hour. The lamp standards marched unsteadily to meet them and lit his face: he was quite old, forty if a day, ten years older than Fred. He wore a striped tie and she could see his sleeve was frayed. He had more than ten shillings a week, but perhaps not so very much more. His hair was going thin.

'You can drop me here,' she said. He stopped the car and she got out and the rain went on. He followed her on to the road. 'Let me come in?' he asked. She shook her head; the rain wetted them through; behind her was the pillar-box, the Belisha beacon, the road through the housing estate. 'Hell of a life,' he said politely, holding her hand, while the rain drummed on the hood of the cheap car and ran down his face, across his collar and the school tie. But she felt no pity, no attraction, only a faint horror and repulsion. A kind of dim recklessness gleamed in his wet eye, as the hot music of Alf Cohen's band streamed from the car, a faded irresponsibility. 'Le's go back,' he said, 'le's go somewhere. Le's go for a ride in the country. Le's go to Maidenhead,' holding her hand limply.

She pulled it away, he didn't resist, and walked down the half-made road to No. 64. The crazy paving in the front garden seemed to hold her feet firmly up. She opened the door and heard through the dark and the rain a car grind into second gear and drone away – certainly not towards Maidenhead or Devizes or the country. Another wind must have blown.

Her father called down from the first landing: 'Who's there?'

'It's me,' she said. She explained, 'I had a feeling you'd left the door unbolted.'

'And had I?'

'No,' she said gently, 'it's bolted all right,' driving the bolt softly and firmly home. She waited till his door closed. She touched the radiator to warm her fingers – he had put it in himself, he had improved the property; in fifteen years, she thought, it will be ours. She was quite free from pain, listening to the rain on the roof; he had been over the whole roof that winter inch by inch; there was nowhere for the rain to enter. It was kept outside, drumming on the shabby hood, pitting the clover field. She stood by the door, feeling only the faint repulsion she always had for things weak and crippled, thinking, 'It isn't tragic at all,' and looking down with an emotion like tenderness at the flimsy bolt from a sixpenny store any man could have broken, but which a Man had put in, the head clerk of Bergson's.

The Case for the Defence

CAST

ADAMS/ADAMS'S TWIN, Brian Glover
MRS SALMON, Kathleen Harrison
RANSOM, Michael Gough
SIR HENRY CLINTON, Ronald Radd
MR JUSTICE CAGE, Roland Culver
MISS GARFITT, Liz Gebhardt
MR MONTAGUE TEWSON,
Roger Brierley
HENRY MACDOUGALL, Hilary Wontner
COLIN WHEELER, Colin Higgins
CAROL, Seretta Wilson
INSPECTOR, Terence Sewards
DOORMAN, Joseph Grieg

Dramatised by John Mortimer
Directed by Peter Hammond

The Case for the Defence

It was the strangest murder trial I ever attended. They named it the Peckham murder in the headlines, though Northwood Street, where the old woman was found battered to death, was not strictly speaking in Peckham. This was not one of those cases of circumstantial evidence in which you feel the jurymen's anxiety – because mistakes *have* been made – like domes of silence muting the court. No, this murderer was all but found with the body; no one present when the Crown counsel outlined his case believed that the man in the dock stood any chance at all.

He was a heavy stout man with bulging bloodshot eyes. All his muscles seemed to be in his thighs. Yes, an ugly customer, one you wouldn't forget in a hurry – and that was an important point because the Crown proposed to call four witnesses who hadn't forgotten him, who had seen him hurrying away from the little red villa in Northwood Street. The clock had just struck two in the morning.

Mrs Salmon in 15 Northwood Street had been unable to sleep; she heard a door click shut and thought it was her own gate. So she went to the window and saw Adams (that was his name) on the steps of Mrs Parker's house. He had just come out and he was wearing gloves. He had a hammer in his hand and she saw him drop it into the laurel bushes by the front gate. But before he moved away, he had looked up – at her window. The fatal instinct that tells a man when he is watched exposed him in the light of a street-lamp to her gaze – his eyes suffused with horrifying and brutal fear, like an animal's when you raise a whip. I talked afterwards to Mrs Salmon, who naturally after the astonishing verdict went in fear herself. As I imagine did all the witnesses – Henry MacDougall, who had been driving home from Benfleet late and nearly ran Adams down at the corner of North-wood Street. Adams was walking in the middle of the road looking dazed. And old Mr Wheeler, who lived next door to Mrs Parker, at No. 12, and was wakened by a noise – like a chair falling – through the thin-as-paper villa wall, and got up and looked out of the window, just as Mrs Salmon had done, saw Adams's back and, as he turned, those bulging eyes. In Laurel Avenue he had been seen by yet another witness – his luck was badly out; he might as well have committed the crime in broad daylight.

'I understand,' counsel said, 'that the defence pro-poses to plead mistaken identity. Adams's wife will tell you that he was with her at two in the morning on February 14, but after you have heard the witnesses for the Crown and examined carefully the features of the prisoner, I do not think you will be prepared to admit the possibility of a mistake.'

It was all over, you would have said, but the hang-ing.

After the formal evidence had been given by the police-man who had found the body and the surgeon who examined it, Mrs Salmon was called. She was the ideal witness, with her slight Scotch accent and her expression of honesty, care and kindness.

The counsel for the Crown brought the story gently out. She spoke very firmly. There was no malice in her, and no sense of importance at standing there in the

Central Criminal Court with a judge in scarlet hanging on her words and the reporters writing them down. Yes, she said, and then she had gone downstairs and rung up the police station.

'And do you see the man here in court?'

She looked straight at the big man in the dock, who stared hard at her with his pekingese eyes without emotion.

'Yes,' she said, 'there he is.'

'You are quite certain?'

She said simply, 'I couldn't be mistaken, sir.'

It was all as easy as that.

'Thank you, Mrs Salmon.'

Counsel for the defence rose to cross-examine. If you had reported as many murder trials as I have, you would have known beforehand what line he would take. And I was right, up to a point.

'Now, Mrs Salmon, you must remember that a man's life may depend on your evidence.'

'I do remember it, sir.'

'Is your eyesight good?'

'I have never had to wear spectacles, sir.'

'You are a woman of fifty-five?'

'Fifty-six, sir.'

'And the man you saw was on the other side of the road?'

'Yes, sir.'

'And it was two o'clock in the morning. You must have remarkable eyes, Mrs Salmon?'

'No, sir. There was moonlight, and when the man looked up, he had the lamplight on his face.'

'And you have no doubt whatever that the man you saw is the prisoner?'

I couldn't make out what he was at. He couldn't have expected any other answer than the one he got.

'None whatever, sir. It isn't a face one forgets.'

Counsel took a look round the court for a moment. Then he said, 'Do you mind, Mrs Salmon, examining again the people in court? No, not the prisoner. Stand up, please, Mr Adams,' and there at the back of the court with thick stout body and muscular legs and a pair of bulging eyes, was the exact image of the man in the dock. He was even dressed the same – tight blue suit and striped tie.

'Now think very carefully, Mrs Salmon. Can you still swear that the man you saw drop the hammer in Mrs Parker's garden was the prisoner – and not this man, who is his twin brother?'

Of course she couldn't. She looked from one to the other and didn't say a word.

There the big brute sat in the dock with his legs crossed, and there he stood too at the back of the court and they both stared at Mrs Salmon. She shook her head.

What we saw then was the end of the case. There wasn't a witness prepared to swear that it was the prisoner he'd seen. And the brother? He had his alibi, too; he was with his wife.

And so the man was acquitted for lack of evidence. But whether – if he did the murder and not his brother – he was punished or not, I don't know. That extraordinary day had an extraordinary end. I followed Mrs Salmon out of court and we got wedged in the crowd who were waiting, of course, for the twins. The police tried to drive the crowd away, but all they could do was keep the road-way clear for traffic. I learned later that they tried to get the twins to leave by a back way, but they wouldn't.

One of them – no one knew which – said, 'I've been acquitted, haven't I?' and they walked bang out of the front entrance. Then it happened. I don't know how, though I was only six feet away. The crowd moved and somehow one of the twins got pushed on to the road right in front of a bus.

He gave a squeal like a rabbit and that was all; he was dead, his skull smashed just as Mrs Parker's had been. Divine vengeance? I wish I knew. There was the other Adams getting on his feet from beside the body and looking straight over at Mrs Salmon. He was crying, but whether he was the murderer or the innocent man nobody will ever be able to tell. But if you were Mrs Salmon, could you sleep at night?

Chagrin in Three Parts

CAST

MADAME DEJOIE, Geneviéve Page
MADAME VOLET, Zouzou
AUTHOR, Anthony Bate
GASTON, Guy Deghy
MADAME GASTON, Nancy Nevinson
WAITER, Gilles Dattas

Dramatised by John Mortimer
Directed by Peter Hammond

Chagrin in Three Parts

[1]

It was February in Antibes. Gusts of rain blew along the ramparts, and the emaciated statues on the terrace of the Château Grimaldi dripped with wet, and there was a sound absent during the flat blue days of summer, the continual rustle below the ramparts of the small surf. All along the Côte the summer restaurants were closed, but lights shone in Félix au Port and one Peugeot of the latest model stood in the parking-rank. The bare masts of the abandoned yachts stuck up like tooth-picks and the last plane in the winter-service dropped, in a flicker of green, red and yellow lights, like Christmas-tree baubles, towards the airport of Nice. This was the Antibes I always enjoyed; and I was disappointed to find I was not alone in the restaurant as I was most nights of the week.

Crossing the road I saw a very powerful lady dressed in black who stared out at me from one of the window-tables, as though she were willing me not to enter, and when I came in and took my place before the other window, she regarded me with too evident distaste. My raincoat was shabby and my shoes were muddy and in any case I was a man. Momentarily, while she took me in, from balding top to shabby toe, she interrupted her conversation with the *patronne* who addressed her as Madame Dejoie.

Madame Dejoie continued her monologue in a tone of firm disapproval: it was unusual for Madame Volet to be late, but she hoped nothing had happened to her on the

208

ramparts. In winter there were always Algerians about, she added with mysterious apprehension, as though she were talking of wolves, but nonetheless Madame Volet had refused Madame Dejoie's offer to be fetched from her home. 'I did not press her under the circumstances. Poor Madame Volet.' Her hand clutched a huge pepper-mill like a bludgeon and I pictured Madame Volet as a weak timid old lady, dressed too in black, afraid even of protection by so formidable a friend.

How wrong I was. Madame Volet blew suddenly in with a gust of rain through the side door beside my table, and she was young and extravagantly pretty, in her tight black pants, and with a long neck emerging from a wine-red polo-necked sweater. I was glad when she sat down side by side with Madame Dejoie, so that I need not lose the sight of her while I ate.

'I am late,' she said, 'I know that I am late. So many little things have to be done when you are alone, and I am not yet accustomed to being alone,' she added with a pretty little sob which reminded me of a cut-glass Victorian tear-bottle. She took off thick winter gloves with a wringing gesture which made me think of handker-chiefs wet with grief, and her hands looked suddenly small and useless and vulnerable.

'*Pauvre cocotte*,' said Madame Dejoie, 'be quiet here with me and forget awhile. I have ordered a *bouillabaisse* with *langouste*.'

'But I have no appetite, Emmy.'

'It will come back. You'll see. Now here is your *porto* and I have ordered a bottle of *blanc de blancs*.'

'You will make me *tout à fait saoule*.'

'We are going to eat and drink and for a little while we are both going to forget everything. I know exactly how you are feeling, for I too lost a beloved husband.'

'By death,' little Madame Volet said. 'That makes a great difference. Death is quite bearable.'

'It is more irrevocable.'

'Nothing can be more irrevocable than my situation. Emmy, he loves the little bitch.'

'All I know of her is that she has deplorable taste – or a deplorable hairdresser.'

'But that was exactly what I told him.'

'You were wrong. I should have told him, not you, for he might have believed me and in any case my criticism would not have hurt his pride.'

'I love him,' Madame Volet said, 'I cannot be prudent,' and then suddenly became aware of my presence. She whispered something to her companion, and I heard the reassurance, '*Un anglais.*' I watched her as covertly as I could – like most of my fellow writers I have the spirit of a *voyeur* – and I wondered how stupid married men could be. I was temporarily free, and I very much wanted to console her, but I didn't exist in her eyes, now she knew that I was English, nor in the eyes of Madame Dejoie. I was less than human – I was only a reject from the Common Market.

I ordered a small *rouget* and a half bottle of Pouilly and tried to be interested in the Trollope I had brought with me. But my attention strayed.

'I adored my husband,' Madame Dejoie was saying, and her hand again grasped the pepper-mill, but this time it looked less like a bludgeon.

'I still do, Emmy. That is the worst of it. I know that if he came back . . .'

'Mine can never come back,' Madame Dejoie retorted, touching the corner of one eye with her handkerchief and then examining the smear of black left behind.

In a gloomy silence they both drained their *portos*. Then Madame Dejoie said with determination, 'There is no turning back. You should accept that as I do. There remains for us only the problem of adaptation.'

'After such a betrayal I could never look at another man,' Madame Volet replied. At that moment she looked right through me. I felt invisible. I put my hand between the light and the wall to prove that I had a shadow, and the shadow looked like a beast with horns.

'I would never suggest another man,' Madame Dejoie said. 'Never.'

'What then?'

'When my poor husband died from an infection of the bowels I thought myself quite inconsolable, but I said to myself, Courage, courage. You must learn to laugh again.'

'To laugh,' Madame Volet exclaimed. 'To laugh at what?' But before Madame Dejoie could reply, Monsieur Félix had arrived to perform his neat surgical operation upon the fish for the *bouillabaisse*. Madame Dejoie watched with real interest; Madame Volet, I thought, watched for politeness' sake while she finished a glass of *blanc de blancs*.

When the operation was over Madame Dejoie filled the glasses and said, 'I was lucky enough to have *une amie* who taught me not to mourn for the past.' She raised her glass and cocking a finger as I had seen men do, she added, '*Pas de mollesse.*'

'*Pas de mollesse,*' Madame Volet repeated with a wan enchanting smile.

I felt decidedly ashamed of myself – a cold literary observer of human anguish. I was afraid of catching poor

Madame Volet's eyes (what kind of a man was capable of betraying her for a woman who took the wrong sort of rinse?) and I tried to occupy myself with sad Mr Crawley's courtship as he stumped up the muddy lane in his big clergyman's boots. In any case the two of them had dropped their voices; a gentle smell of garlic came to me from the *bouillabaisse*, the bottle of *blanc de blancs* was nearly finished, and, in spite of Madame Volet's protestation, Madame Dejoie had called for another. 'There are no half bottles,' she said. 'We can always leave something for the gods.' Again their voices sank to an intimate murmur as Mr Crawley's suit was accepted (though how he was to support an inevitably large family would not appear until the succeeding volume). I was startled out of my forced concentration by a laugh: a musical laugh: it was Madame Volet's.

'*Cochon*,' she exclaimed. Madame Dejoie regarded her over her glass (the new bottle had already been broached) under beetling brows. 'I am telling you the truth,' she said. 'He would crow like a cock.'

'But what a joke to play!'

'It began as a joke, but he was really proud of himself. *Après seulement deux coups* . . .'

'*Jamais trois?*' Madame Volet asked and she giggled and splashed a little of her wine down her polo-necked collar.

'*Jamais.*'

'*Je suis saoule.*'

'*Moi aussi, cocotte.*'

Madame Volet said, 'To crow like a cock – at least it was a *fantaisie*. My husband has no *fantaisies*. He is strictly classical.'

'*Pas de vices?*'

'*Hélas, pas de vices.*'

'And yet you miss him?'

'He worked hard,' Madame Volet said and giggled. 'To think that at the end he must have been working hard for both of us.'

'You found it a little boring?'

'It was a habit – how one misses a habit. I wake now at five in the morning.'

'At five?'

'It was the hour of his greatest activity.'

'My husband was a very small man,' Madame Dejoie said. 'Not in height of course. He was two metres high.'

'Oh, Paul is big enough – but always the same.'

'Why do you continue to love that man?' Madame Dejoie sighed and put her large hand on Madame Volet's knee. She wore a signet-ring which perhaps had belonged to her late husband. Madame Volet sighed too and I thought melancholy was returning to the table, but then she hiccuped and both of them laughed.

'*Tu es vraiment saoule, cocotte.*'

'Do I truly miss Paul, or is it only that I miss his habits?' She suddenly met my eye and blushed right down into the wine-coloured wine-stained polo-necked collar.

Madame Dejoie repeated reassuringly, '*Un anglais – ou un américain.*' She hardly bothered to lower her voice at all. 'Do you know how limited my experience was when my husband died? I loved him when he crowed like a cock. I was glad he was so pleased. I only wanted him to be pleased. I adored him, and yet in those days – *j'ai peut-être joui trois fois par semaine.* I did not expect more. It seemed to me a natural limit.'

'In my case it was three times a day,' Madame Volet

said and giggled again. '*Mais toujours d'une façon classique.*' She put her hands over her face and gave a little sob. Madame Dejoie put an arm round her shoulders. There was a long silence while the remains of the *bouillabaisse* were cleared away.

[2]

'Men are curious animals,' Madame Dejoie said at last. The coffee had come and they divided one *marc* between them, in turn dipping lumps of sugar which they inserted into one another's mouths. 'Animals too lack imagination. A dog has no *fantaisie.*'

'How bored I have been sometimes,' Madame Volet said. 'He would talk politics continually and turn on the news at eight in the morning. At eight! What do I care for politics? But if I asked his advice about anything important he showed no interest at all. With you I can talk about anything, about the whole world.'

'I adored my husband,' Madame Dejoie said, 'yet it was only after his death I discovered my capacity for love. With Pauline. You never knew Pauline. She died five years ago. I loved her more than I ever loved Jacques, and yet I felt no despair when she died. I knew that it was not the end, for I knew by then my capacity.'

'I have never loved a woman,' Madame Volet said.

'*Chérie*, then you do not know what love can mean. With a woman you do not have to be content with *une façon classique* three times a day.'

'I love Paul, but he is so different from me in every way . . .'

'Unlike Pauline, he is a man.'

214

'Oh Emmy, you describe him so perfectly. How well you understand. A man!'

'When you really think of it, how comic that little object is. Hardly enough to crow about, one would think.'

Madame Volet giggled and said, '*Cochon.*'

'Perhaps smoked like an eel one might enjoy it.'

'Stop it. Stop it.' They rocked up and down with little gusts of laughter. They were drunk, of course, but in the most charming way.

[3]

How distant now seemed Trollope's muddy lane, the heavy boots of Mr Crawley, his proud shy courtship. In time we travel a space as vast as any astronaut's. When I looked up Madame Volet's head rested on Madame Dejoie's shoulder. 'I feel so sleepy,' she said.

'Tonight you shall sleep, *chérie.*'

'I am so little good to you. I know nothing.'

'In love one learns quickly.'

'But am I in love?' Madame Volet asked, sitting up very straight and staring into Madame Dejoie's sombre eyes.

'If the answer were no, you wouldn't ask the question.'

'But I thought I could never love again.'

'Not another man,' Madame Dejoie said. '*Chérie*, you are almost asleep. Come.'

'The bill?' Madame Volet asked as though perhaps she were trying to delay the moment of decision.

'I will pay tomorrow. What a pretty coat this is – but not warm enough, *chérie*, in February. You need to be cared for.'

'You have given me back my courage,' Madame Volet said. 'When I came in here I was *si démoralisée* . . .'

'Soon – I promise – you will be able to laugh at the past . . .'

'I have already laughed,' Madame Volet said. 'Did he really crow like a cock?'

'Yes.'

'I shall never be able to forget what you said about smoked eel. Never. If I saw one now. . . .' She began to giggle again and Madame Dejoie steadied her a little on the way to the door.

I watched them cross the road to the car-park. Suddenly Madame Volet gave a little hop and skip and flung her arms around Madame Dejoie's neck, and the wind, blowing through the archway of the port, carried the faint sound of her laughter to me where I sat alone *chez* Félix. I was glad she was happy again. I was glad that she was in the kind reliable hands of Madame Dejoie. What a fool Paul had been, I reflected, feeling chagrin myself now for so many wasted opportunities.

Two Gentle People

Two Gentle People

They sat on a bench in the Parc Monceau for a long time without speaking to one another. It was a hopeful day of early summer with a spray of white clouds lapping across the sky in front of a small breeze: at any moment the wind might drop and the sky become empty and entirely blue, but it was too late now – the sun would have set first.

In younger people it might have been a day for a chance encounter – secret behind the long barrier of perambulators with only babies and nurses in sight. But they were both of them middle-aged, and neither was inclined to cherish an illusion of possessing a lost youth, though he was better looking than he believed, with his silky old-world moustache like a badge of good behaviour, and she was prettier than the looking-glass ever told her. Modesty and disillusion gave them something in common; though they were separated by five feet of green metal they could have been a married couple who had grown to resemble each other. Pigeons like old grey tennis balls rolled unnoticed around their feet. They each occasionally looked at a watch, though never at one another. For both of them this period of solitude and peace was limited.

The man was tall and thin. He had what are called sensitive features, and the cliché fitted him; his face was comfortably, though handsomely, banal – there would be no ugly surprises when he spoke, for a man may be sensitive without imagination. He had carried with him an umbrella which suggested caution. In her case one noticed first the long and lovely legs as unsensual as those in a society portrait. From her expression she found the summer day sad, yet she was reluctant to obey the command of her watch and go – somewhere – inside.

They would never have spoken to each other if two teen-aged louts had not passed by, one with a blaring radio slung over his shoulder, the other kicking out at the preoccupied pigeons. One of his kicks found a random mark, and on they went in a din of pop, leaving the pigeon lurching on the path.

The man rose, grasping his umbrella like a riding-whip. 'Infernal young scoundrels,' he exclaimed, and the phrase sounded more Edwardian because of the faint American intonation – Henry James might surely have employed it.

'The poor bird,' the woman said. The bird struggled upon the gravel, scattering little stones. One wing hung slack and a leg must have been broken too, for the pigeon swivelled round in circles unable to rise. The other pigeons moved away, with disinterest, searching the gravel for crumbs.

'If you would look away for just a minute,' the man said. He laid his umbrella down again and walked rapidly to the bird where it thrashed around; then he picked it up, and quickly and expertly he wrung its neck – it was a kind of skill anyone of breeding ought to possess. He looked round for a refuse bin in which he tidily deposited the body.

'There was nothing else to do,' he remarked apologetically when he returned.

'I could not myself have done it,' the woman said, carefully grammatical in a foreign tongue.

'Taking life is *our* privilege,' he replied with irony rather than pride.

When he sat down the distance between them had narrowed; they were able to speak freely about the weather and the first real day of summer. The last week had been unseasonably cold, and even today. . . . He admired the way in which she spoke English and apologized for his own lack of French, but she reassured him: it was no ingrained talent. She had been 'finished' at an English school at Margate.

'That's a seaside resort, isn't it?'

'The sea always seemed very grey,' she told him, and for a while they lapsed into separate silences. Then perhaps thinking of the dead pigeon she asked him if he had been in the army. 'No, I was over forty when the war came,' he said. 'I served on a government mission, in India. I became very fond of India.' He began to describe to her Agra, Lucknow, the old city of Delhi, his eyes alight with memories. The new Delhi he did not like, built by a Britisher – Lut-Lut-Lut? No matter. It reminded him of Washington.

'Then you do not like Washington?'

'To tell you the truth,' he said, 'I am not very happy in my own country. You see, I like old things. I found myself more at home – can you believe it? – in India, even with the British. And now in France I find it's the same. My grandfather was British Consul in Nice.'

'The Promenade des Anglais was very new then,' she said.

'Yes, but it aged. What we Americans build never ages beautifully. The Chrysler Building, Hilton hotels . . .'

'Are you married?' she asked. He hesitated a moment before replying, 'Yes,' as though he wished to be quite, quite accurate. He put out his hand and felt for his umbrella – it gave him confidence in this surprising situation of talking so openly to a stranger.

'I ought not to have asked you,' she said, still careful with her grammar.

'Why not?' He excused her awkwardly.

'I was interested in what you said.' She gave him a little smile. 'The question came. It was *imprévu*.'

'Are *you* married?' he asked, but only to put her at her ease, for he could see her ring.

'Yes.'

By this time they seemed to know a great deal about each other, and he felt it was churlish not to surrender his identity. He said, 'My name is Greaves. Henry C. Greaves.'

'Mine is Marie-Claire. Marie-Claire Duval.'

'What a lovely afternoon it has been,' the man called Greaves said.

'But it gets a little cold when the sun sinks.' They escaped from each other again with regret.

'A beautiful umbrella you have,' she said, and it was quite true – the gold band was distinguished, and even from a few feet away one could see there was a monogram engraved there – an H certainly, entwined perhaps with a C or a G.

'A present,' he said without pleasure.

'I admired so much the way you acted with the pigeon. As for me I am *lâche*.'

'That I am quite sure is not true,' he said kindly.

'Oh, it is. It is.'

'Only in the sense that we are all cowards about something.'

'You are not,' she said, remembering the pigeon with gratitude.

'Oh yes, I am,' he replied, 'in one whole area of life.' He seemed on the brink of a personal revelation, and she clung to his coat-tail to pull him back; she literally clung to it, for lifting the edge of his jacket she exclaimed, 'You have been touching some wet paint.' The ruse succeeded; he became solicitous about her dress, but examining the bench they both agreed the source was not there. 'They have been painting on my staircase,' he said.

'You have a house here?'

'No, an apartment on the fourth floor.'

'With an *ascenseur*?'

'Unfortunately not,' he said sadly. 'It's a very old house in the *dix-septième*.'

The door of his unknown life had opened a crack, and she wanted to give something of her own life in return, but not too much. A 'brink' would give her vertigo. She said, 'My apartment is only too depressingly new. In the *huitième*. The door opens electrically without being touched. Like in an airport.'

A strong current of revelation carried them along. He learned how she always bought her cheeses in the Place de la Madeleine – it was quite an expedition from her side of the *huitième*, near the Avenue George V, and once she had been rewarded by finding Tante Yvonne, the General's wife, at her elbow choosing a Brie. He on the other hand bought his cheeses in the Rue de Tocqueville, only round the corner from his apartment.

'You yourself?'

'Yes, I do the marketing,' he said in a voice suddenly abrupt.

She said, 'It is a little cold now. I think we should go.'

'Do you come to the Parc often?'

'It is the first time.'

'What a strange coincidence,' he said. 'It's the first time for me too. Even though I live close by.'

'And I live quite far away.'

They looked at one another with a certain awe, aware of the mysteries of providence. He said, 'I don't suppose you would be free to have a little dinner with me.'

Excitement made her lapse into French. '*Je suis libre, mais vous . . . votre femme . . . ?*'

'She is dining elsewhere,' he said. 'And your husband?'

'He will not be back before eleven.'

He suggested the Brasserie Lorraine, which was only a few minutes' walk away, and she was glad that he had not chosen something more chic or more flamboyant. The heavy bourgeois atmosphere of the *brasserie* gave her confidence, and, though she had small appetite herself, she was glad to watch the comfortable military progress down the ranks of the sauerkraut trolley. The menu too was long enough to give them time to readjust to the startling intimacy of dining together. When the order had been given, they both began to speak at once. 'I never expected . . .'

'It's funny the way things happen,' he added, laying unintentionally a heavy inscribed monument over that conversation.

'Tell me about your grandfather, the consul.'

'I never knew him,' he said. It was much more difficult to talk on a restaurant sofa than on a park bench.

'Why did your father go to America?'

'The spirit of adventure perhaps,' he said. 'And I suppose it was the spirit of adventure which brought me back to live in Europe. America didn't mean Coca-Cola and *Time-Life* when my father was young.'

'And have you found adventure? How stupid of me to ask. Of course you married here?'

'I brought my wife with me,' he said. 'Poor Patience.'

'Poor?'

'She is fond of Coca-Cola.'

'You can get it here,' she said, this time with intentional stupidity.

'Yes.'

The wine-waiter came and he ordered a Sancerre. 'If that will suit you?'

'I know so little about wine,' she said.

'I thought all French people . . .'

'We leave it to our husbands,' she said, and in his turn he felt an obscure hurt. The sofa was shared by a husband now as well as a wife, and for a while the *sole meunière* gave them an excuse not to talk. And yet silence was not a genuine escape. In the silence the two ghosts would have become more firmly planted, if the woman had not found the courage to speak.

'Have you any children?' she asked.

'No. Have you?'

'No.'

'Are you sorry?'

She said, 'I suppose one is always sorry to have missed something.'

'I'm glad at least I did not miss the Parc Monceau today.'

'Yes, I am glad too.'

The silence after that was a comfortable silence: the two ghosts went away and left them alone. Once their fingers touched over the sugar-castor (they had chosen strawberries). Neither of them had any desire for further questions; they seemed to know each other more completely than they knew anyone else. It was like a happy marriage; the stage of discovery was over – they had passed the test of jealousy, and now they were tranquil in their middle age. Time and death remained the only enemies, and coffee was like the warning of old age. After that it was necessary to hold sadness at bay with a brandy, though not successfully. It was as though they had experienced a lifetime, which was measured as with butterflies in hours.

He remarked of the passing head waiter, 'He looks like an undertaker.'

'Yes,' she said. So he paid the bill and they went outside. It was a death-agony they were too gentle to resist for long. He asked, 'Can I see you home?'

'I would rather not. Really not. You live so close.'

'We could have another drink on the *terrasse*?' he suggested with half a sad heart.

'It would do nothing more for us,' she said. 'The evening was perfect. *Tu es vraiment gentil*.' She noticed too late that she had used '*tu*' and she hoped his French was bad enough for him not to have noticed. They did not exchange addresses or telephone numbers, for neither of them dared to suggest it: the hour had come too late in both their lives. He found her a taxi and she drove away towards the great illuminated Arc, and he walked home by the Rue Jouffroy, slowly. What is cowardice in the young is wisdom in the old, but all the same one can be ashamed of wisdom.

Marie-Claire walked through the self-opening doors and thought, as she always did, of airports and escapes. On the sixth floor she let herself into the flat. An abstract painting in cruel tones of scarlet and yellow faced the door and treated her like a stranger.

225

She went straight to her room, as softly as possible, locked the door and sat down on her single bed. Through the wall she could hear her husband's voice and laugh. She wondered who was with him tonight – Toni or François. François had painted the abstract picture, and Toni, who danced in ballet, always claimed, especially before strangers, to have modelled for the little stone phallus with painted eyes that had a place of honour in the living-room. She began to undress. While the voice next door spun its web, images of the bench in the Parc Monceau returned and of the sauerkraut trolley in the Brasserie Lorraine. If he had heard her come in, her husband would soon proceed to action: it excited him to know that she was a witness. The voice said, 'Pierre, Pierre,' reproachfully. Pierre was a new name to her. She spread her fingers on the dressing-table to take off her rings and she thought of the sugar-castor for the strawberries, but at the sound of the little yelps and giggles from next door the sugar-castor turned into the phallus with painted eyes. She lay down and screwed beads of wax into her ears, and she shut her eyes and thought how different things might have been if fifteen years ago she had sat on a bench in the Parc Monceau, watching a man with pity killing a pigeon.

'I can smell a woman on you,' Patience Greaves said with pleasure, sitting up against two pillows. The top pillow was punctured with brown cigarette burns.

'Oh no, you can't. It's your imagination, dear.'

'You said you would be home by ten.'

'It's only twenty past now.'

'You've been up in the Rue de Douai, haven't you, in one of those bars, looking for a *fille*.'

226

'I sat in the Parc Monceau and then I had dinner at the Brasserie Lorraine. Can I give you your drops?'

'You want me to sleep so that I won't expect anything. That's it, isn't it, you're too old now to do it twice.'

He mixed the drops from the carafe of water on the table between the twin beds. Anything he might say would be wrong when Patience was in a mood like this. Poor Patience, he thought, holding out the drops towards the face crowned with red curls, how she misses America – she will never believe that the Coca-Cola tastes the same here. Luckily this would not be one of their worst nights, for she drank from the glass without further argument, while he sat beside her and remembered the street outside the *brasserie* and how—by accident he was sure—he had been called '*tu*'.

'What are you thinking?' Patience asked. 'Are you still in the Rue de Douai?'

'I was only thinking that things might have been different,' he said.

It was the biggest protest he had ever allowed himself to make against the condition of life.

The Over-night Bag

CAST

HENRY, Tim Brooke-Taylor
1ST AIRPORT GIRL, Diana Berriman
2ND AIRPORT GIRL, Daphne Lawson
WOMAN ON PLANE,
Eleanor Summerfield
CUSTOMS OFFICER, Neville Phillips
HIRE-CAR DRIVER, Dudley Sutton
MOTHER, Joyce Carey

Dramatised by Clive Exton
Directed by Peter Hammond

The Over-night Bag

The little man who came to the information desk in Nice airport when they demanded 'Henry Cooper, passenger on BEA flight 105 for London' looked like a shadow cast by the brilliant glitter of the sun. He wore a grey town-suit and black shoes; he had a grey skin which carefully matched his suit, and since it was impossible for him to change his skin, it was possible that he had no other suit.

'Are you Mr Cooper?'

'Yes.' He carried a BOAC over-night bag and he laid it tenderly on the ledge of the information desk as though it contained something precious and fragile like an electric razor.

'There is a telegram for you.'

He opened it and read the message twice over. '*Bon voyage*. Much missed. You will be welcome home, dear boy. Mother.' He tore the telegram once across and left it on the desk, from which the girl in the blue uniform, after a discreet interval, picked the pieces and with natural curiosity joined them together. Then she looked for the little grey man among the passengers who were now lining up at the tourist gate to join the Trident. He was among the last, carrying his blue BOAC bag.

Near the front of the plane Henry Cooper found a window-seat and placed the bag on the central seat beside him. A large woman in pale blue trousers too tight for the size of her buttocks took the third seat. She squeezed a very large handbag in beside the other on the central seat, and she laid a large fur coat on top of both. Henry Cooper said, 'May I put it on the rack, please?'

She looked at him with contempt. 'Put what?'

'Your coat.'

'If you want to. Why?'

'It's a very heavy coat. It's squashing my over-night bag.'

He was so small he could stand nearly upright under the rack. When he sat down he fastened the seat-belt over the two bags before he fastened his own. The woman watched him with suspicion. 'I've never seen anyone do that before,' she said.

'I don't want it shaken about,' he said. 'There are storms over London.'

'You haven't got an animal in there, have you?'

'Not exactly.'

'It's cruel to carry an animal shut up like that,' she said, as though she disbelieved him.

As the Trident began its run he laid his hand on the bag as if he were reassuring something within. The woman watched the bag narrowly. If she saw the least movement of life she had made up her mind to call the stewardess. Even if it were only a tortoise. . . . A tortoise needed air, or so she supposed, in spite of hibernation. When they were safely airborne he relaxed and began to read a *Nice-Matin* – he spent a good deal of time on each story as though his French were not very good. The woman struggled angrily to get her big cavernous bag from under the seat-belt. She muttered 'Ridiculous' twice for his benefit. Then she made up, put on thick horn-rimmed glasses and began to re-read a letter which began 'My darling Tiny' and ended 'Your own cuddly Bertha'. After a while she grew tired of the weight on her knees and dropped it on to the BOAC over-night bag.

The little man leapt in distress. 'Please,' he said, 'please.' He lifted her bag and pushed it quite rudely into a corner of the seat. 'I don't want it squashed,' he said. 'It's a matter of respect.'

'What have you got in your precious bag?' she asked him angrily.

'A dead baby,' he said. 'I thought I had told you.'

'On the left of the aircraft,' the pilot announced through the loud-speaker, 'you will see Montélimar. We shall be passing Paris in –'

'You are not serious,' she said.

'It's just one of those things,' he replied in a tone that carried conviction.

'But you can't take dead babies – like that – in a bag – in the economy class.'

'In the case of a baby it is so much cheaper than freight. Only a week old. It weighs so little.'

'But it should be in a coffin, not an over-night bag.'

'My wife didn't trust a foreign coffin. She said the materials they use are not durable. She's rather a conventional woman.'

'Then it's *your* baby?' Under the circumstances she seemed almost prepared to sympathize.

'My wife's baby,' he corrected her.

'What's the difference?'

He said sadly, 'There could well be a difference,' and turned the page of *Nice-Matin*.

'Are you suggesting . . . ?' But he was deep in a column dealing with a Lions Club meeting in Antibes and the rather revolutionary suggestion made there by a member from Grasse. She read over again her letter from 'cuddly Bertha', but it failed to hold her attention. She kept on stealing glances at the over-night bag.

'You don't anticipate trouble with the customs?' she asked him after a while.

'Of course I shall have to declare it,' he said. 'It was acquired abroad.'

When they landed, exactly on time, he said to her with old-fashioned politeness, 'I have enjoyed our flight.' She looked for him with a certain morbid curiosity in the customs – Channel 10 – but then she saw him in Channel 12, for passengers carrying hand-baggage only. He was speaking, earnestly, to the officer who was poised, chalk in hand, over the over-night bag. Then she lost sight of him as her own inspector insisted on examining the contents of her cavernous bag, which yielded up a number of undeclared presents for Bertha.

Henry Cooper was the first out of the arrivals door and he took a hired car. The charge for taxis rose every year when he went abroad and it was his one extravagance not to wait for the airport-bus. The sky was overcast and the temperature only a little above freezing, but the driver was in a mood of euphoria. He had a dashing comradely air – he told Henry Cooper that he had won fifty pounds on the pools. The heater was on full blast, and Henry Cooper opened the window, but an icy current of air from Scandinavia flowed round his shoulders. He closed the window again and said, 'Would you mind turning off the heater?' It was as hot in the car as in a New York hotel during a blizzard.

'It's cold outside,' the driver said.

'You see,' Henry Cooper said, 'I have a dead baby in my bag.'

'Dead baby?'

'Yes.'

'Ah well,' the driver said, 'he won't feel the heat, will he? It's a he?'

'Yes. A he. I'm anxious he shouldn't – deteriorate.'

'They keep a long time,' the driver said. 'You'd be surprised. Longer than old people. What did you have for lunch?'

Henry Cooper was a little surprised. He had to cast his mind back. He said, '*Carré d'agneau à la provençale.*'

'Curry?'

'No, not curry, lamb chops with garlic and herbs. And then an apple-tart.'

'And you drank something I wouldn't be surprised?'

'A half bottle of *rosé*. And a brandy.'

'There you are, you see.'

'I don't understand.'

'With all that inside you, *you* wouldn't keep so well.'

Gillette Razors were half hidden in icy mist. The driver had forgotten or had refused to turn down the heat, but he remained silent for quite a while, perhaps brooding on the subject of life and death.

'How did the little perisher die?' he asked at last.

'They die so easily,' Henry Cooper answered.

'Many a true word's spoken in jest,' the driver said, a little absent-mindedly because he had swerved to avoid a car which braked too suddenly, and Henry Cooper instinctively put his hand on the over-night bag to steady it.

'Sorry,' the driver said. 'Not my fault. Amateur drivers! Anyway, you don't need to worry – they can't bruise after death, or can they? I read something about it once in *The Cases of Sir Bernard Spilsbury*, but I don't remember now exactly what. That's always the trouble about reading.'

'I'd be much happier,' Henry Cooper said, 'if you would turn off the heat.'

'There's no point in your catching a chill, is there? Or

234

me either. It won't help *him* where he's gone – if any-where at all. The next thing you know you'll be in the same position yourself. Not in an over-night bag, of course. That goes without saying.'

The Knightsbridge tunnel as usual was closed because of flooding. They turned north through the park. The trees dripped on empty benches. The pigeons blew out their grey feathers the colour of soiled city snow.

'Is he yours?' the driver asked. 'If you don't mind my inquiring.'

'Not exactly.' Henry Cooper added briskly and brightly, 'My wife's, as it happens.'

'It's never the same if it's not your own,' the driver said thoughtfully. 'I had a nephew who died. He had a split palate – that wasn't the reason, of course, but it made it easier to bear for the parents. Are you going to an undertaker's now?'

'I thought I would take it home for the night and see about the arrangements tomorrow.'

'A little perisher like that would fit easily into the frig. No bigger than a chicken. As a precaution only.'

They entered the large whitewashed Bayswater square. The houses resembled the above-ground tombs you find in continental cemeteries, except that, unlike the tombs, they were divided into flatlets and there were rows and rows of bell-pushes to wake the inmates. The driver watched Henry Cooper get out with the over-night bag at a portico entitled Stare House. 'Bloody orful aircraft company,' he said mechanically when he saw the letters BOAC – without ill-will, it was only a Pavlov response.

Henry Cooper went up to the top floor and let himself in. His mother was already in the hall to greet him. 'I saw your car draw up, dear.' He put the over-night bag on a chair so as to embrace her better.

'You've come quickly. You got my telegram at Nice?'

'Yes, Mother. With only an over-night bag I walked straight through the customs.'

'So clever of you to travel light.'

'It's the drip-dry shirt that does it,' Henry Cooper said. He followed his mother into their sitting-room. He noticed she had changed the position of his favourite picture – a reproduction from *Life* magazine of a painting by Hieronymus Bosch. 'Just so that I don't see it from *my* chair, dear,' his mother explained, interpreting his glance. His slippers were laid out by his armchair and he sat down with an air of satisfaction at being home again.

'And now, dear,' his mother said, 'tell me how it was. Tell me everything. Did you make some new friends?'

'Oh yes, Mother, wherever I went I made friends.' Winter had fallen early on the House of Stare. The over-night bag disappeared in the darkness of the hall like a blue fish into blue water.

'And adventures? What adventures?'

Once, while he talked, his mother got up and tiptoed to draw the curtains and to turn on a reading lamp, and once she gave a little gasp of horror. 'A little toe? In the marmalade?'

'Yes, Mother.'

'It wasn't English marmalade?'

'No, Mother, foreign.'

'I could have understood a finger – an accident slicing the orange – but a toe!'

'As I understood it,' Henry Cooper said, 'in those parts they use a kind of guillotine worked by the bare foot of a peasant.'

'You complained, of course?'

'Not in words, but I put the toe very conspicuously at the edge of the plate.'

After one more story it was time for his mother to go and put the shepherd's pie into the oven and Henry Cooper went into the hall to fetch the over-night bag. 'Time to unpack,' he thought. He had a tidy mind.

Dream of a Strange Land

CAST

THE MAN, Ian Hendry
THE PROFESSOR, Niall MacGinnis
THE COLONEL, Graham Crowden
THE GENERAL, Esmond Knight
1ST SUBALTERN, Richard Heffer
2ND SUBALTERN, Michael Petrovitch
GIRL, Normaline

Dramatised by Robin Chapman
Directed by Peter Hammond

Dream of a Strange Land

[1]

The house of the Herr Professor was screened on every side by the plantation of fir-trees which grew among great grey rocks. Although it was only twenty minutes' ride from the capital and then a few minutes from the main road to the north, a visitor had the impression that he was in deep country; he felt himself to be hundreds of miles away from the cafés, the kiosks, the opera-houses and the theatres.

The Herr Professor had virtually retired two years ago when he reached the age of sixty-five. His appointment at the hospital had been filled, he had closed his consulting-room in the capital, and if he continued to work it was only for a few favoured patients who were compelled to drive out to see him, or if they were poor (for he had not clung to a few rich patients only) to take a bus which landed them about ten minutes' walk away at the edge of the trees and the rocks.

It was one of these poorer patients who stood now in the doctor's study listening to his doom. The study had folding pitchpine doors leading to the living-room, which the patient had never seen. A heavy dark bookcase stood against the wall full of heavy dark books, all obviously medical in character (no one had ever seen the Herr Professor with any lighter literature, nor heard him give an opinion of even the most respected classic. Once questioned on Madame Bovary's poisoning, he had professed complete ignorance of the book, and another time he had shown himself to be equally ignorant of Ibsen's treatment of syphilis in *Ghosts*). The desk was as heavy and dark as the bookcase; it was only a desk as heavy which could have borne without cracking the massive bronze paperweight more than a foot high that represented Prometheus chained to his rock with a hovering eagle thrusting its beak into his liver. (Sometimes, when breaking the news to a patient with cirrhosis, the Professor had referred to his paperweight with dry humour.)

The patient wore a shabby-genteel suit of dark cloth; the cuffs had frayed and been repaired. He wore stout boots which had seen just as long a service, and through the open door in the hall behind him hung an overcoat and an umbrella, while a pair of goloshes stood in the steel trough under the umbrella, the snow not yet melted from their uppers. He was a man past fifty who had spent all his adult years behind the counter of a bank and by patient labour and courtesy he had risen to the position of second cashier. He would never be first cashier, for the first cashier was at least five years younger.

The Herr Professor had a short grey beard and he wore old-fashioned glasses, steel-rimmed, for his short sight. His rather hairy hands were scattered with grave-marks. As he seldom smiled one had very little opportunity to see his strong and perfect teeth. He said firmly, caressing Prometheus as he spoke, 'I warned you when you first came that my treatment might have started too late – to arrest the disease. Now the smear-test shows . . .'

'But, Herr Professor, you have been treating me all these months. No one knows about it. I can go on working at the bank. Can't you continue to treat me a little longer?'

241

'I would be breaking the law,' the Herr Professor explained, making a motion as though his thumb and forefinger clutched a chalk. 'Contagious cases must always go to the hospital.'

'But you yourself, Herr Professor, have said that it is one of the most difficult of all diseases to catch.'

'And yet you caught it.'

'How? How?' the patient asked himself with the weariness of a man who has confronted the same question time without mind.

'Perhaps it was when you were working on the coast. There are many contacts in a port.'

'Contacts?'

'I assume you are a man like other men.'

'But that was seven years ago.'

'One has known the disease to take ten years to develop.'

'It will be the end of my work, Herr Professor. The bank will never take me back. My pension will be very small.'

'You take an exaggerated view. After a certain period . . . Hansen's disease is eventually curable.'

'Why don't you call it by its proper name?'

'The International Congress decided five years ago to change the name.'

'The world hasn't changed the name, Herr Professor. If you send me to that hospital, everyone will know that I am a leper.'

'I have no choice. But I assure you you will find it very comfortable. There is television, I believe, in every room, and a golf-course.'

The Herr Professor showed no impatience at all, unless the fact that he did not ask the patient to sit and stood himself, stiff and straight-backed behind Prometheus and the eagle, was a sign of it.

'Herr Professor, I implore you. I will not breathe a word to a soul. You can treat me just as well as the hospital can. You've said yourself that the risk of contagion is very small, Herr Professor. I have my savings – they are not very great, but I will give them all . . .'

'My dear sir, you must not try to bribe me. It is not only insulting, it is a gross error of taste. I am sorry. I must ask you to go now. My time is very much occupied.'

'Herr Professor, you have no idea what it means to me. I lead a very simple life, but if a man is alone in the world he grows to love his habits. I go to a café by the lake every day at seven o'clock and stay there till eight. They all know me in the café. Sometimes I play a game of checkers. On Sunday I take the lake steamer to –'

'Your habits will have to be interrupted for a year or two,' the Herr Professor said sharply.

'Interrupted? You say interrupted? But I can never go back. Never. Leprosy is a word – it isn't a disease. They'll never believe leprosy can be cured. You can't cure a word.'

'You will be getting a certificate signed by the hospital authorities,' the Herr Professor said.

'A certificate! I might just as well carry a bell.'

He moved to the door, the hall, his umbrella and the goloshes; the Herr Professor, with a sigh of relief which was almost inaudible beyond the room, seated himself at his desk. But again the patient had turned back. 'Is it that you don't trust me to keep quiet, Herr Professor?'

'I have every belief, I can assure you, that you would keep quiet. For your own sake. But you cannot expect a doctor of my standing to break the law. A sensible and

243

necessary law. If it had not been infringed somewhere by someone you would not be standing here today. Good-bye, Herr –', but the patient had already closed the outer door and had begun to walk back amongst the rocks and firs towards the road, the bus-stop and the capital. The Herr Professor went to the window to make sure that he was truly gone and saw him among the snow-flakes which drifted lightly between the trees; he paused once and gesticulated with his hands as though a new argument had occurred to him which he was practising on a rock. Then he padded on and disappeared from sight.

The Herr Professor opened the sliding doors of the dining-room and made his accurate way to the sideboard, which was heavy like his desk. Instead of the Prometheus there stood on it a large silver flagon inscribed with the Herr Professor's name and a date more than forty years past – an award for fencing – and beside it lay a large silver epergne, also inscribed, a present from the staff of the hospital on his retirement. The Herr Professor took a hard green apple and walked back to his study. He sat down at his desk again and his teeth went crunch, crunch, crunch.

[2]

Later that morning the Herr Professor received another caller, but this one arrived before the house in a Mercedes-Benz car and the Herr Professor went himself to the door to show him in.

'Herr Colonel,' he said as he pulled forward the only chair of any comfort to be found in his study, 'this I hope is only a friendly call and not a professional one.'

'I am never ill,' the Colonel said with a look of irritated amusement at the very idea. 'My blood-pressure is normal, my weight is what it should be, and my heart's sound. I function like a machine. Indeed I find it difficult to believe that this machine need ever wear out. I have no worries, my nervous system is perfectly adjusted . . .'

'Then I'm relieved to know, Herr Colonel, that this is a social call.'

'The army,' the Colonel went on, crossing his long slim legs encased in English tweed, 'is the most healthy profession possible – naturally I mean in a neutral country like ours. The annual manoeuvres do one a world of good, brace the system, clean the blood . . .'

'I wish I could recommend them to my patients.'

'Oh, we can't have sick men in the army.' The Colonel added with a dry laugh, 'We leave that to the warring nations. They can never have our efficiency.'

The Herr Professor offered the Colonel a cigar. The Colonel took a cutter from a little leather case and prepared the cigar. 'You have met the Herr General?' he asked.

'On one or two occasions.'

'He is celebrating his seventieth birthday tonight.'

'Really? A very well preserved man.'

'Naturally. Now his friends – of whom I count myself the chief – have been arranging a very special occasion for him. You know, of course, his favourite hobby?'

'I can't say . . .'

'The tables. For the last fifty years he has spent most of his leaves at Monte Carlo.'

'He too must have a good nervous system.'

'Of course. Now it occurred to his friends, since he cannot spend his birthday at Monte Carlo for reasons of a quite temporary indisposition, to bring, as it were, the tables to him.'

'How can that be possible?'

'Everything was satisfactorily arranged. A croupier from Cannes and two assistants. All the necessary equipment. One of my friends was to have lent us his house in the country. You understand that everything has to be very discreet because of our absurd laws. You would think the police on such an occasion would turn a blind eye, but among the higher officials there is a great jealousy of the army. I once heard the Commissioner remark – at a party to which I was surprised to see that he had been invited – that the only wars in which our country had ever been engaged were fought by *his* men.'

'I don't follow.'

'Oh, he was referring to crime. An absurd comparison. What has crime to do with war?'

The Herr Professor said, 'You were telling me that everything had been satisfactorily arranged . . . ?'

'With the Herr General Director of the National Bank. But suddenly today he telephoned to say that a child – a girl as one might expect – had developed scarlatina. The household therefore is in quarantine.'

'The Herr General will be disappointed.'

'The Herr General knows nothing of all this. He understands that a party is being given in his honour in the country – that is all.'

'And you come to me,' the Herr Professor said, trying to hide mystification which he regarded as a professional weakness, 'in case I can suggest . . . ?'

'I come to you, Herr Professor, quite simply to borrow your house for this evening. The problem can be reduced to very simple terms. The house has to be in the country – I have explained to you why. It must have a *salon* of a certain size – to receive the tables; we can hardly have less than three, since the guests will number about a hundred. And the owner of the house must naturally be acceptable to the Herr General. There are houses a great deal larger than yours that the General could not be expected to enter as a guest. We can hardly, in this case, requisition.'

'I am honoured, of course, Herr Colonel, but . . .'

'These doors slide back, I suppose, and can form a room sufficiently large . . . ?'

'Yes, but . . .'

'Pardon me. You were saying?'

'I had the impression that the party was for tonight?'

'Yes.'

'I don't see how there could be time . . .'

'A matter of logistics, Herr Professor. Leave logistics to the army.' He took a notebook from his pocket and wrote down 'lights'. He explained to the Herr Professor, 'We shall have to hang chandeliers. A casino is unthinkable without chandeliers. May I see the other room, please?'

He paced it with his long tweed-clad legs. 'It will make a fine *salle privée* with the doors folded back and the chandeliers substituted for these – forgive me for saying so – rather commonplace centre lights. Your furniture we can store upstairs? Of course we will bring our own chairs. This sideboard, however, can serve as a bar. I see you were a fencer in your time, Herr Professor?'

'Yes.'

'The Herr General used to be very keen on fencing.

247

Now tell me, where do you think we could put the orchestra?'

'Orchestra?'

'My regiment will supply the musicians. If the worst came to the worst I suppose they could play on the stairs.' He stood at the window of the *salon*, looking out at the wintry garden bounded by the dark wood of fir-trees. 'Is that a summerhouse?'

'Yes.'

'The oriental touch is very suitable. If they played there, and if we left a window a little open, the music will surely carry faintly . . .'

'The cold . . .'

'You have a fine stove and the curtains are heavy.'

'The summerhouse is altogether unheated.'

'The men can wear their military overcoats. And then for a fiddler, you know, the exercise . . .'

'And all this for tonight?'

'For tonight.'

The Herr Professor said, 'I have never before violated the law,' and then smiled a quick false smile to cover his failure of nerve.

'You could hardly do so in a better cause,' the Herr Colonel replied.

[3]

Long before dark the furniture-vans began to arrive. The chandeliers came first, with the wine-glasses, and remained crated in the hall until the electricians drove up, and then the waiters arrived simultaneously with the van that contained seventy-four small gilt chairs. The mover's men had beer in the kitchen with the Herr Professor's housekeeper, waiting for a lorry to turn up with the three roulette-tables. The roulette-wheels, the cloths and the boxes of plastic tokens, of varying colours and shapes according to value, were brought later in a smart private car with the three croupiers, serious men in black suits. The Herr Professor had never seen so many cars parked before his house. He felt a stranger, a guest, and lingered at his bedroom-window, afraid to go out on the stairs and meet the workmen. The long passage outside his room became littered with the furniture from below.

As the red winter sun sank in early afternoon below the black firs the cars began to multiply upon the drive. First a fleet of taxis arrived one behind the other, all bright yellow in colour like an amber chain, and out of these scrambled many burly men in military overcoats carrying musical instruments, which too often stuck in the doors and had to be extricated with care and difficulty: it was hard indeed to understand how the 'cello had ever fitted in – the neck came out first like a dressmaker's dummy and then the shoulders proved too wide. The men in overcoats stood around holding violin-bows like rifles at the ready, and a small man with a triangle shouted advice. Presently they had all disappeared from the front of the house and discordant sounds of tuning came across the snow from the summerhouse built in oriental taste. Something broke in the passage outside, and the Herr Professor, looking out, saw that it was one of the central lamps criticized by the Herr Colonel, which had fallen off the occasional table on which it had been propped. The passage was nearly blocked by the heavy desk from the study, the glass-fronted bookcase and his three filing cabinets. The Herr Professor salvaged Prometheus and carried the bronze into his bedroom for safety, though it was the least fragile thing in all the house. There was a sound of hammers below and the Herr Colonel's voice could be heard giving orders. The Herr Professor went back into his bedroom. He sat on the bed and read a little Schopenhauer to soothe himself.

It was some three-quarters of an hour later that the Herr Colonel found him there. He came briskly in, wearing regimental evening-dress, which made his legs thinner and longer than ever. 'Zero hour approaches,' he said, 'and we are all but ready. You would not recognize your house, Herr Professor. It is quite transformed. The Herr General will feel himself in a sunnier and more liberal clime. The musicians will play a pot-pourri of Strauss and Offenbach with a little of Lehar, which the Herr General finds more easy to recognize. I've seen to it that suitable paintings hang on the walls. You will realize when you come down and see the *salle privée* that this has been no ordinary military exercise. A care for detail marks a good soldier. Tonight, Herr Professor, your house has become a casino, by the Mediterranean. I had thought of masking the trees in some way, but there was no way of getting rid of the snow which continues to fall.'

'Astonishing,' the Herr Professor said. 'Quite astonishing.' From the distant summerhouse he could hear a melody from *La Belle Hélène*, and on the drive outside cars continually braked. He felt far from home as though he were living in a strange country.

'If you will excuse me,' he said, 'I will leave everything tonight in your hands. I hardly know the Herr General. I will have a sandwich quietly in my room.'

'Quite impossible,' the Herr Colonel said. 'You are the host. By this time the Herr General knows your name, although of course he hardly expects the sight which will greet . . . Ah, the guests are now beginning to arrive. I asked them to come early so that by the time the Herr General puts in his appearance everything will be in full swing, the wheels turning, the stakes laid, the croupiers calling . . . the field of battle stretched before him, *rouge et noir*. Come, Herr Professor, a little flutter at the tables – it is time for the two of us to open the ball.'

[4]

The road was treacherous under the thin and new-fallen snow; the bus from the capital proceeded at a pace no smarter than a practice-runner who is unwilling to strain a muscle before the great race. The patient's feet felt chilled even through his goloshes, or perhaps it was the cold of his errand, a fool's errand. There was a lot of traffic on the road that night: yellow taxis frequently passed the bus, and small sports-cars full of young men in uniform or evening-dress, laughing or singing, and once at a particularly imperious siren – which might have been that of a police-car or an ambulance – the bus slithered awkwardly to a stop beside the blue heaps of snow on the margin, and a large Mercedes went by; in it the patient saw an old man sitting stiffly upright with a long grey moustache which might have dated from the neutrality of 1914, wearing an old-fashioned uniform with a fur hat on his head, pulled down over his ears.

The patient alighted at a halt beside the road; the moon was nearly full, but he still required the pocket-torch which he carried with him to show the way through the woods: no headlights of cars helped him now on the private drive to the Herr Professor's house. As he walked through the loose snow at the edge of the road he tried to practise his final appeal. If that failed there was nothing for him but the hospital, unless he could summon enough courage to enter the icy water of the lake and never to return. He felt very little hope, and, for some reason that he could not understand, when he tried to visualize the Herr Professor at his desk – angry and impatient at this so late and unforeseen a visit – he could see only the half-spread wings of the bronze eagle and the jutting beak fastened in the intestines of the prisoner.

He pleaded in an undertone beneath the trees, 'There would be no danger to anyone at all, Herr Professor. I have always been a lonely man. I have no parents. My only sister died last year. I see no one, speak to no one except the clients in the bank. An occasional game of checkers in the café perhaps – that is all. I would cut myself off even further, Herr Professor, if you thought it wiser. As for the bank, I have always been in the habit of wearing gloves when I handle the notes – so many are filthy. I will take any precaution you suggest if you will go on treating me in private, Herr Professor. I am a law-abiding man, but surely the spirit is more important than the letter. I will abide by the spirit.'

The eagle gripped Prometheus with its unrelenting beak, and the patient said sadly as though to prevent the repetition of a phrase he could not bear to hear again, 'I don't like television, Herr Professor – it makes my eyes water, and I have never played golf.'

He halted under the trees, and a lump of snow from a burdened branch fell with a plomp upon his umbrella. It seemed very unlikely, but he thought that he heard strains of distant music borne on a gust of wind and borne away again. He even thought he recognized the melody, something from *La Vie Parisienne*, a waltz sounding for a moment from where the darkness and the snow lay all around. He had seen this place before only in daylight; the snow touched his face, and the stars crackled overhead between the firs; he felt as though he must have missed his path and entered a strange estate where perhaps a dance was in progress . . .

But when he reached the circular drive before the house he recognized the portico, the shape of the windows, the steep slope of the roof from which at intervals the snow slid with a crunch like the sound of a man eating apples. It was all that he could recognize, for he had never seen the house like this, ablaze with light and noisy with voices. Perhaps two neighbouring estates had been built by the same architect, and somehow in the wood he had taken the wrong turning. To make sure, he approached the windows, the hard snow breaking like biscuits under his goloshes.

Two young officers, who were obviously the worse for drink, staggered out from the open doorway. 'I have been betrayed by nineteen,' one of them said, 'that confounded nineteen.'

'And I by zero. I have been faithful to zero for an hour but not once . . .'

The first young man took a revolver from the holster at his side and waved it in the moonlight. 'All that is required now,' he said, 'is a suicide. The atmosphere is imperfect without one.'

'Be careful. It might be loaded.'

'It *is* loaded. Who is that man?'

'I don't know. The gardener probably. Don't fool about with that thing.'

'More bubbly is required,' the first man said. He tried

to put his revolver back into the holster, but it slid down into the snow and he carefully secured the empty holster. 'More bubbly,' he repeated, 'before the dream fades.' They moved erratically back into the house. The dark object made a pocket in the snow.

The patient went up to the window, which should, if he had taken the right path, have been the window of the Herr Professor's study, but now he realized for certain that in the darkness he had come to the wrong house. Instead of a small square room with heavy desk and heavy bookcase and steel filing-cabinets was a long room brilliantly lit with cut-glass chandeliers, the walls hung with pictures of dubious taste – young women in diaphanous nightgowns leaning over waterfalls or paddling among water-lilies in a stooping position. A crowd of men wearing uniform and evening-dress swarmed around three roulette tables, and the croupiers' cries came thinly out into the night, '*Faites vos jeux, messieurs, faites vos jeux,*' while somewhere in the black garden an orchestra was playing 'The Blue Danube'. The patient stood motionless in the snow, with his face pressed to the glass, and he thought, The wrong house ? But this is not the wrong house; it is the wrong country. He felt that he could never find his way home from here – it was too far away.

At one of the tables, on the right of the croupier, sat the old man whom he had seen pass in the Mercedes. One hand was playing with his moustache, the other with a pile of tokens before him, counting and rearranging them while the ball span and jumped and span, and one foot beat in time to the tune from *The Merry Widow*. A champagne cork from the bar shot diagonally up and struck the chandelier while the croupiers cried again,

'*Faites vos jeux, messieurs,*' and the stem of a glass went crack in somebody's fingers.

Then the patient saw the Herr Professor standing with his back to the window at the other end of the great room, beyond the second chandelier, and they regarded each other, with the laughter and cries and glitter of light between them.

The Herr Professor could not properly see the patient – only the outline of a face pressed to the exterior of the pane, but the patient could see the Herr Professor very clearly between the tables, in the light of the chandelier. He could even see his expression, the lost look on his face like that of someone who has come to the wrong party. The patient raised his hand, as though to indicate to the other that he was lost too, but of course the Herr Professor could not see the gesture in the dark. The patient realized quite clearly that, though they had once been well known to each other, it was quite impossible for them to meet, in this house to which they had both strayed by some strange accident. There was no consulting-room here, no file on his case, no desk, no Prometheus, no doctor even to whom he could appeal. '*Faites vos jeux, messieurs,*' the croupiers cried, '*faites vos jeux.*'

[5]

The Herr Colonel said, 'My dear Herr Professor, after all, you are the host. You should at least lay one stake upon the table.' He took the Herr Professor by his sleeve and led him to the board where the Herr General sat, beating tip, tap, tip to the music of Lehar.

'The Herr Professor wishes to follow your fortune, Herr General.'

'I have little luck tonight, but let him . . .' and the General's fingers wove a design over the cloth. 'At the same time guard yourself with the zero.'

The ball span and jumped and span and came to rest. 'Zero,' the croupier announced and began to rake the other stakes in.

'At least you have not lost, Herr Professor,' the Herr General said. Somewhere far away behind the voices there was a faint explosion.

'The corks are popping,' the Herr Colonel said. 'Another glass of champagne, Herr General?'

'I had hoped it was a shot,' the Herr General said with a rather freezing smile. 'Ah, the old days . . . I remember once in Monte Carlo . . .'

The Herr Professor looked at the window, where he had thought a moment ago that someone looked in as lost as himself, but no one was there.

Under the Garden

Under the Garden

PART ONE

[1]

It was only when the doctor said to him, 'Of course the fact that you don't smoke is in your favour,' Wilditch realized what it was he had been trying to convey with such tact. Dr Cave had lined up along one wall a series of X-ray photographs, the whorls of which reminded the patient of those pictures of the earth's surface taken from a great height that he had pored over at one period during the war, trying to detect the tiny grey seed of a launching ramp.

Dr Cave had explained, 'I want you clearly to understand my problem.' It was very similar to an intelligence briefing of such 'top secret' importance that only one officer could be entrusted with the information. Wilditch felt gratified that the choice had fallen on him, and he tried to express his interest and enthusiasm, leaning forward and examining more closely than ever the photographs of his own interior.

'Beginning at this end,' Dr Cave said, 'let me see, April, May, June, three months ago, the scar left by pneumonia is quite obvious. You can see it here.'

'Yes, sir,' Wilditch said absent-mindedly. Dr Cave gave him a puzzled look.

'Now if we leave out the intervening photographs for the moment and come straight to yesterday's, you will

258

observe that this latest one is almost entirely clear, you can only just detect . . .'

'Good,' Wilditch said. The doctor's finger moved over what might have been tumuli or traces of prehistoric agriculture.

'But not entirely, I'm afraid. If you look now along the whole series you will notice how very slow the progress has been. Really by this stage the photographs should have shown no trace.'

'I'm sorry,' Wilditch said. A sense of guilt had taken the place of gratification.

'If we had looked at the last plate in isolation I would have said there was no cause for alarm.' The doctor tolled the last three words like a bell. Wilditch thought, is he suggesting tuberculosis?

'It's only in relation to the others, the slowness . . . it suggests the possibility of an obstruction.'

'Obstruction?'

'The chances are that it's nothing, nothing at all. Only I wouldn't be *quite* happy if I let you go without a deep examination. Not *quite* happy.' Dr Cave left the photographs and sat down behind his desk. The long pause seemed to Wilditch like an appeal to his friendship.

'Of course,' he said, 'if it would make you happy . . .'

It was then the doctor used those revealing words, 'Of course the fact that you don't smoke is in your favour.'

'Oh.'

'I think we'll ask Sir Nigel Sampson to make the examination. In case there is something there, we couldn't have a better surgeon . . . for the operation.'

Wilditch came down from Wimpole Street into Cavendish Square looking for a taxi. It was one of those summer days which he never remembered in childhood: grey and dripping. Taxis drew up outside the tall liver-coloured buildings partitioned by dentists and were immediately caught by the commissionaires for the victims released. Gusts of wind barely warmed by July drove the rain aslant across the blank eastern gaze of Epstein's virgin and dripped down the body of her fabulous son. 'But it hurt,' the child's voice said behind him. 'You make a fuss about nothing,' a mother – or a governess – replied.

[2]

This could not have been said of the examination Wilditch endured a week later, but he made no fuss at all, which perhaps aggravated his case in the eyes of the doctors who took his calm for lack of vitality. For the unprofessional to enter a hospital or to enter the services has very much the same effect; there is a sense of relief and indifference; one is placed quite helplessly on a conveyor-belt with no responsibility any more for anything. Wilditch felt himself protected by an organization, while the English summer dripped outside on the coupés of the parked cars. He had not felt such freedom since the war ended.

The examination was over – a bronchoscopy; and there remained a nightmare memory, which survived through the cloud of anaesthetic, of a great truncheon forced down his throat into the chest and then slowly withdrawn; he woke next morning bruised and raw so that even the act of excretion was a pain. But that, the nurse told him, would pass in one day or two; now he could dress and go home. He was disappointed at the abruptness with which they were thrusting him off the belt into the world of choice again.

'Was everything satisfactory?' he asked, and saw from the nurse's expression that he had shown indecent curiosity.

'I couldn't say, I'm sure,' the nurse said. 'Sir Nigel will look in, in his own good time.'

Wilditch was sitting on the end of the bed tying his tie when Sir Nigel Sampson entered. It was the first time Wilditch had been conscious of seeing him: before he had been a voice addressing him politely out of sight as the anaesthetic took over. It was the beginning of the week-end and Sir Nigel was dressed for the country in an old tweed jacket. He had tousled white hair and he looked at Wilditch with a far-away attention as though he were a float bobbing in mid-stream.

'Ah, feeling better,' Sir Nigel said incontrovertibly.

'Perhaps.'

'Not very agreeable,' Sir Nigel said, 'but you know we couldn't let you go, could we, without taking a look?'

'Did you see anything?'

Sir Nigel gave the impression of abruptly moving down-stream to a quieter reach and casting his line again.

'Don't let me stop you dressing, my dear fellow.' He looked vaguely around the room before choosing a strictly upright chair, then lowered himself on to it as though it were a tuffet which might 'give'. He began feeling in one of his large pockets – for a sandwich?

'Any news for me?'

'I expect Dr Cave will be along in a few minutes. He was caught by a rather garrulous patient.' He drew a large silver watch out of his pocket – for some reason it was tangled up in a piece of string. 'Have to meet my wife at Liverpool Street. Are *you* married?'

'No.'

'Oh well, one care the less. Children can be a great responsibility.'

'I have a child – but she lives a long way off.'

'A long way off? I see.'

'We haven't seen much of each other.'

'Doesn't care for England?'

'The colour-bar makes it difficult for her.' He realized how childish he sounded directly he had spoken, as though he had been trying to draw attention to himself by a bizarre confession, without even the satisfaction of success.

'Ah yes,' Sir Nigel said. 'Any brothers or sisters? You, I mean.'

'An elder brother. Why?'

'Oh well, I suppose it's all on the record,' Sir Nigel said, rolling in his line. He got up and made for the door. Wilditch sat on the bed with the tie over his knee. The door opened and Sir Nigel said, 'Ah, here's Dr Cave. Must run along now. I was just telling Mr Wilditch that I'll be seeing him again. You'll fix it, won't you?' and he was gone.

'Why should I see him again?' Wilditch asked and then, from Dr Cave's embarrassment, he saw the stupidity of the question. 'Oh yes, of course, you did find something?'

'It's really very lucky. If caught in time . . .'

'There's sometimes hope?'

'Oh, there's always hope.'

So, after all, Wilditch thought, I am – if I so choose – on the conveyor-belt again.

Dr Cave took an engagement-book out of his pocket and said briskly, 'Sir Nigel has given me a few dates. The tenth is difficult for the clinic, but the fifteenth – Sir

Nigel doesn't think we should delay longer than the fifteenth.'

'Is he a great fisherman?'

'Fisherman? Sir Nigel? I have no idea.' Dr Cave looked aggrieved, as though he were being shown an incorrect chart. 'Shall we say the fifteenth?'

'Perhaps I could tell you after the week-end. You see, I have not made up my mind to stay as long as that in England.'

'I'm afraid I haven't properly conveyed to you that this is serious, really serious. Your only chance – I repeat your only chance,' he spoke like an official cable, 'is to have the obstruction removed in time.'

'And then, I suppose, life can go on for a few more years.'

'It's impossible to guarantee . . . but there have been complete cures.'

'I don't want to appear dialectical,' Wilditch said, 'but I do have to decide, don't I, whether I want my particular kind of life prolonged.'

'It's the only one we have,' Dr Cave said.

'I see you are not a religious man – oh, please don't misunderstand me, nor am I. I have no curiosity at all about the future.'

[3]

The past was another matter. Wilditch remembered a leader in the Civil War who rode from an undecided battle mortally wounded. He revisited the house where he was born, the house in which he was married, greeted a few retainers who did not recognize his condition, seeing him only as a tired man upon a horse, and finally –

but Wilditch could not recollect how the biography had ended: he saw only a figure of exhaustion slumped over the saddle, as he also took, like Sir Nigel Sampson, a train from Liverpool Street. At Colchester he changed onto the branch line to Winton, and suddenly summer began, the kind of summer he always remembered as one of the conditions of life at Winton. Days had become so much shorter since then. They no longer began at six in the morning before the world was awake.

Winton Hall had belonged, when Wilditch was a child, to his uncle, who had never married, and every summer he lent the house to Wilditch's mother. Winton Hall had been virtually Wilditch's, until school cut the period short, from late June to early September. In memory his mother and brother were shadowy background figures. They were less established even than the machine upon the platform of 'the halt' from which he bought Fry's chocolates for a penny a bar: than the oak tree spreading over the green in front of the red-brick wall – under its shade as a child he had distributed apples to soldiers halted there in the hot August of 1914: the group of silver birches on the Winton lawn and the broken fountain, green with slime. In his memory he did not share the house with others: he owned it.

Nevertheless the house had been left to his brother not to him; he was far away when his uncle died and he had never returned since. His brother married, had children (for them the fountain had been mended), the paddock behind the vegetable garden and the orchard, where he used to ride the donkey, had been sold (so his brother had written to him) for building council-houses, but the hall and the garden which he had so scrupulously remembered nothing could change.

Why then go back now and see it in other hands? Was it that at the approach of death one must get rid of everything? If he had accumulated money he would now have been in the mood to distribute it. Perhaps the man who had ridden the horse around the countryside had not been saying goodbye, as his biographer imagined, to what he valued most: he had been ridding himself of illusions by seeing them again with clear and moribund eyes, so that he might be quite bankrupt when death came. He had the will to possess at that absolute moment nothing but his wound.

His brother, Wilditch knew, would be faintly surprised by this visit. He had become accustomed to the fact that Wilditch never came to Winton; they would meet at long intervals at his brother's club in London, for George was a widower by this time, living alone. He always talked to others of Wilditch as a man unhappy in the country, who needed a longer range and stranger people. It was lucky, he would indicate, that the house had been left to him, for Wilditch would probably have sold it in order to travel further. A restless man, never long in one place, no wife, no children, unless the rumours were true that in Africa . . . or it might have been in the East . . . Wilditch was well aware of how his brother spoke of him. His brother was the proud owner of the lawn, the goldfish-pond, the mended fountain, the laurel-path which they had known when they were children as the Dark Walk, the lake, the island . . . Wilditch looked out at the flat hard East Anglian countryside, the meagre hedges and the stubbly grass, which had always seemed to him barren from the salt of Danish blood. All these years his brother had been in occupation, and yet he had no idea of what might lie underneath the garden.

[4]

The chocolate-machine had gone from Winton Halt, and the halt had been promoted – during the years of nationalization – to a station; the chimneys of a cement-factory smoked along the horizon and council-houses now stood three deep along the line.

Wilditch's brother waited in a Humber at the exit. Some familiar smell of coal-dust and varnish had gone from the waiting-room and it was a mere boy who took his ticket instead of a stooped and greying porter. In childhood nearly all the world is older than oneself.

'Hullo, George,' he said in remote greeting to the stranger at the wheel.

'How are things, William?' George asked as they ground on their way – it was part of his character as a countryman that he had never learnt how to drive a car well.

The long chalky slope of a small hill – the highest point before the Ural mountains he had once been told – led down to the village between the bristly hedges. On the left was an abandoned chalk-pit – it had been just as abandoned forty years ago, when he had climbed all over it looking for treasure, in the form of brown nuggets of iron pyrites which when broken showed an interior of starred silver.

'Do you remember hunting for treasure?'

'Treasure?' George said. 'Oh, you mean that iron stuff.'

Was it the long summer afternoons in the chalk-pit

266

which had made him dream – or so vividly imagine – the discovery of a real treasure ? If it was a dream it was the only dream he remembered from those years, or, if it was a story which he had elaborated at night in bed, it must have been the final effort of a poetic imagination that afterwards had been rigidly controlled. In the various services which had over the years taken him from one part of the world to another, imagination was usually a quality to be suppressed. One's job was to provide facts, to a company (import and export), a newspaper, a government department. Speculation was discouraged. Now the dreaming child was dying of the same disease as the man. He was so different from the child that it was odd to think the child would not outlive him and go on to quite a different destiny.

George said, 'You'll notice some changes, William. When I had the bathroom added, I found I had to disconnect the pipes from the fountain. Something to do with pressure. After all there are no children now to enjoy it.'

'It never played in my time either.'

'I had the tennis-lawn dug up during the war, and it hardly seemed worth while to put it back.'

'I'd forgotten that there *was* a tennis-lawn.'

'Don't you remember it, between the pond and the goldfish-tank ?'

'The pond ? Oh, you mean the lake and the island.'

'Not much of a lake. You could jump on to the island with a short run.'

'I had thought of it as much bigger.'

But all measurements had changed. Only for a dwarf does the world remain the same size. Even the red-brick wall which separated the garden from the village was lower than he remembered – a mere five feet, but in order to look over it in those days he had always to scramble to the top of some old stumps covered deep with ivy and dusty spiders' webs. There was no sign of these when they drove in: everything was very tidy everywhere, and a handsome piece of ironmongery had taken the place of the swing-gate which they had ruined as children.

'You keep the place up very well,' he said.

'I couldn't manage it without the market-garden. That enables me to put the gardener's wages down as a professional expense. I have a very good accountant.'

He was put into his mother's room with a view of the lawn and the silver birches; George slept in what had been his uncle's. The little bedroom next door which had once been his was now converted into a tiled bathroom – only the prospect was unchanged. He could see the laurel bushes where the Dark Walk began, but they were smaller too. Had the dying horseman found as many changes?

Sitting that night over coffee and brandy, during the long family pauses, Wilditch wondered whether as a child he could possibly have been so secretive as never to have spoken of his dream, his game, whatever it was. In his memory the adventure had lasted for several days. At the end of it he had found his way home in the early morning when everyone was asleep: there had been a dog called Joe who bounded towards him and sent him sprawling in the heavy dew of the lawn. Surely there must have been some basis of fact on which the legend had been built. Perhaps he had run away, perhaps he had been out all night – on the island in the lake or hidden in the Dark Walk – and during those hours he had invented the whole story.

Wilditch took a second glass of brandy and asked tentatively, 'Do you remember much of those summers when we were children here?' He was aware of something unconvincing in the question: the apparently harmless opening gambit of a wartime interrogation.

'I never cared for the place much in those days,' George said surprisingly. 'You were a secretive little bastard.'

'Secretive?'

'And uncooperative. I had a great sense of duty towards you, but you never realized that. In a year or two you were going to follow me to school. I tried to teach you the rudiments of cricket. You weren't interested. God knows what you were interested in.'

'Exploring?' Wilditch suggested, he thought with cunning.

'There wasn't much to explore in fourteen acres. You know, I had such plans for this place when it became mine. A swimming-pool where the tennis-lawn was – it's mainly potatoes now. I meant to drain the pond too – it breeds mosquitoes. Well, I've added two bathrooms and modernized the kitchen, and even that has cost me four acres of pasture. At the back of the house now you can hear the children caterwauling from the council-houses. It's all been a bit of a disappointment.'

'At least I'm glad you haven't drained the lake.'

'My dear chap, why go on calling it a lake? Have a look at it in the morning and you'll see the absurdity. The water's nowhere more than two feet deep.' He added, 'Oh well, the place won't outlive me. My children aren't interested, and the factories are beginning to come out this way. They'll get a reasonably good price for the land – I haven't much else to leave them.' He put some more sugar in his coffee. 'Unless of course, you'd like to take it on when I am gone?'

'I haven't the money and anyway there's no cause to believe that I won't be dead first.'

'Mother was against my accepting the inheritance,' George said. 'She never liked the place.'

'I thought she loved her summers here.' The great gap between their memories astonished him. They seemed to be talking about different places and different people.

'It was terribly inconvenient, and she was always in trouble with the gardener. You remember Ernest? She said she had to wring every vegetable out of him. (By the way he's still alive, though retired of course – you ought to look him up in the morning. It would please him. He still feels he owns the place.) And then, you know, she always thought it would have been better for us if we could have gone to the seaside. She had an idea that she was robbing us of a heritage – buckets and spades and seawater-bathing. Poor mother, she couldn't afford to turn down Uncle Henry's hospitality. I think in her heart she blamed father for dying when he did without providing for holidays at the sea.'

'Did you talk it over with her in those days?'

'Oh no, not then. Naturally she had to keep a front before the children. But when I inherited the place – you were in Africa – she warned Mary and me about the difficulties. She had very decided views, you know, about any mysteries, and that turned her against the garden. Too much shrubbery, she said. She wanted everything to be very clear. Early Fabian training, I daresay.'

'It's odd. I don't seem to have known her very well.'

'You had a passion for hide-and-seek. She never liked that. Mystery again. She thought it a bit morbid. There

270

was a time when we couldn't find you. You were away for hours.'

'Are you sure it was hours? Not a whole night?'

'I don't remember it at all myself. Mother told me.' They drank their brandy for a while in silence. Then George said, 'She asked Uncle Henry to have the Dark Walk cleared away. She thought it was unhealthy with all the spiders' webs, but he never did anything about it.'

'I'm surprised *you* didn't.'

'Oh, it was on my list, but other things had priority, and now it doesn't seem worth while to make more changes.' He yawned and stretched. 'I'm used to early bed. I hope you don't mind. Breakfast at 8.30?'

'Don't make any changes for me.'

'There's just one thing I forgot to show you. The flush is tricky in your bathroom.'

George led the way upstairs. He said, 'The local plumber didn't do a very good job. Now, when you've pulled this knob, you'll find the flush never quite finishes. You have to do it a second time – sharply like this.'

Wilditch stood at the window looking out. Beyond the Dark Walk and the space where the lake must be, he could see the splinters of light given off by the council-houses; through one gap in the laurels there was even a street-light visible, and he could hear the faint sound of television-sets joining together different programmes like the discordant murmur of a mob.

He said, 'That view would have pleased mother. A lot of the mystery gone.'

'I rather like it this way myself,' George said, 'on a winter's evening. It's a kind of companionship. As one gets older one doesn't want to feel quite alone on a sinking ship. Not being a churchgoer myself . . .' he added, leaving the sentence lying like a torso on its side.

'At least we haven't shocked mother in that way, either of us.'

'Sometimes I wish I'd pleased her, though, about the Dark Walk. And the pond – how she hated that pond too.'

'Why?'

'Perhaps because you liked to hide on the island. Secrecy and mystery again. Wasn't there something you wrote about it once? A story?'

'Me? A story? Surely not.'

'I don't remember the circumstances. I thought – in a school magazine? Yes, I'm sure of it now. She was very angry indeed and she wrote rude remarks in the margin with a blue pencil. I saw them somewhere once. Poor mother.'

George led the way into the bedroom. He said, 'I'm sorry there's no bedside light. It was smashed last week, and I haven't been into town since.'

'It's all right. I don't read in bed.'

'I've got some good detective-stories downstairs if you wanted one.'

'Mysteries?'

'Oh, mother never minded those. They came under the heading of puzzles. Because there was always an answer.'

Beside the bed was a small bookcase. He said, 'I brought some of mother's books here when she died and put them in her room. Just the ones that she had liked and no bookseller would take.' Wilditch made out a title, *My Apprenticeship* by Beatrice Webb. 'Sentimental, I suppose, but I didn't want actually to *throw away* her favourite books. Good night.' He repeated, 'I'm sorry about the light.'

'It really doesn't matter.'

George lingered at the door. He said, 'I'm glad to see you here, William. There were times when I thought you were avoiding the place.'

'Why should I?'

'Well, you know how it is. I never go to Harrods now because I was there with Mary a few days before she died.'

'Nobody has died here. Except Uncle Henry, I suppose.'

'No, of course not. But why did you, suddenly, decide to come?'

'A whim,' Wilditch said.

'I suppose you'll be going abroad again soon?'

'I suppose so.'

'Well, good night.' He closed the door.

Wilditch undressed, and then, because he felt sleep too far away, he sat down on the bed under the poor centre-light and looked along the rows of shabby books. He opened Mrs Beatrice Webb at some account of a trade union congress and put it back. (The foundations of the future Welfare State were being truly and uninterestingly laid.) There were a number of Fabian pamphlets heavily scored with the blue pencil which George had remembered. In one place Mrs Wilditch had detected an error of one decimal point in some statistics dealing with agricultural imports. What passionate concentration must have gone to that discovery. Perhaps because his own life was coming to an end, he thought how little of this, in the almost impossible event of a future, she would have carried with her. A fairy-story in such an event would be a more valuable asset than a Fabian graph, but his mother had not approved of fairy-stories. The only children's book on these shelves was a history of England. Against an enthusiastic account of the battle of Agincourt she had pencilled furiously,

> And what good came of it at last?
> Said little Peterkin.

The fact that his mother had quoted a poem was in itself remarkable.

The storm which he had left behind in London had travelled east in his wake and now overtook him in short gusts of wind and wet that slapped at the pane. He thought, for no reason, It will be a rough night on the island. He had been disappointed to discover from George that the origin of the dream which had travelled with him round the world was probably no more than a story invented for a school-magazine and forgotten again, and just as that thought occurred to him, he saw a bound volume called *The Warburian* on the shelf.

He took it out, wondering why his mother had preserved it, and found a page turned down. It was the account of a cricket-match against Lancing and Mrs Wilditch had scored the margin: 'Wilditch One did good work in deep field.' Another turned-down leaf produced a passage under the heading Debating Society: 'Wilditch One spoke succinctly to the motion.' The motion was 'That this House has no belief in the social policies of His Majesty's Government'. So George in those days had been a Fabian too.

He opened the book at random this time and a letter fell out. It had a printed heading, Dean's House, Warbury, and it read, 'Dear Mrs Wilditch, I was sorry to receive your letter of the 3rd and to learn that you were displeased with the little fantasy published by your younger son in *The Warburian*. I think you take a rather extreme view of the tale which strikes me as quite a good imaginative exercise for a boy of thirteen. Obviously he has been influenced by the term's reading of *The Golden Age* – which after all, fanciful though it may be, was written by a governor of the Bank of England.' (Mrs Wilditch had made several blue exclamation marks in the margin – perhaps representing her view of the Bank.) 'Last term's *Treasure Island* too may have contributed. It is always our intention at Warbury to foster the imagination – which I think you rather harshly denigrate when you write of "silly fancies". We have scrupulously kept our side of the bargain, knowing how strongly you feel, and the boy is not "subjected", as you put it, to any religious instruction at all. Quite frankly, Mrs Wilditch, I cannot see any trace of religious feeling in this little fancy – I have read it through a second time before writing to you – indeed the treasure, I'm afraid, is only too material, and quite at the mercy of those "who break in and steal".'

Wilditch tried to find the place from which the letter had fallen, working back from the date of the letter. Eventually he found it: 'The Treasure on the Island' by W.W.

Wilditch began to read.

[5]

'*In the middle of the garden there was a great lake and in the middle of the lake an island with a wood. Not everybody knew about the lake, for to reach it you had to find your way down a long dark walk, and not many people's nerves were strong enough to reach the end. Tom knew that he was likely to be undisturbed in that frightening region, and so it was*

275

there that he constructed a raft out of old packing cases, and one drear wet day when he knew that everybody would be shut in the house, he dragged the raft to the lake and paddled it across to the island. As far as he knew he was the first to land there for centuries.

'It was all overgrown on the island, but from a map he had found in an ancient sea-chest in the attic he made his measurements, three paces north from the tall umbrella pine in the middle and then two paces to the right. There seemed to be nothing but scrub, but he had brought with him a pick and a spade and with the dint of almost superhuman exertions he uncovered an iron ring sunk in the grass. At first he thought it would be impossible to move, but by inserting the point of the pick and levering it he raised a kind of stone lid and there below, going into the darkness, was a long narrow passage.

'Tom had more than the usual share of courage, but even he would not have ventured further if it had not been for the parlous state of the family fortunes since his father had died. His elder brother wanted to go to Oxford, but for lack of money he would probably have to sail before the mast, and the house itself, of which his mother was passionately fond, was mortgaged to the hilt to a man in the City called Sir Silas Dedham whose name did not belie his nature.'

Wilditch nearly gave up reading. He could not reconcile the childish story with the dream which he remembered. Only the 'drear wet night' seemed true as the bushes rustled and dripped and the birches swayed outside. A writer, so he had always understood, was supposed to order and enrich the experience which was the source of his story, but in that case it was plain that the young Wilditch's talents had not been for literature. He read with growing irritation, wanting to exclaim again and again to this thirteen-year-old ancestor of his, 'But why did you leave that out? Why did you alter this?'

'*The passage opened out into a great cave stacked from floor to ceiling with gold bars and chests overflowing with pieces of eight. There was a jewelled crucifix*' – Mrs Wilditch had underlined the word in blue – '*set with precious stones which had once graced the chapel of a Spanish galleon and on a marble table were goblets of precious metal.*'

But, as he remembered, it was an old kitchen-dresser, and there were no pieces of eight, no crucifix, and as for the Spanish galleon . . .

'*Tom thanked the kindly Providence which had led him first to the map in the attic*' (but there had been no map. Wilditch wanted to correct the story, page by page, much as his mother had done with her blue pencil) '*and then to this rich treasure trove*' (his mother had written in the margin, referring to the kindly Providence, 'No trace of religious feeling! !'). '*He filled his pockets with the pieces of eight and taking one bar under each arm, he made his way back along the passage. He intended to keep his discovery secret and slowly day by day to transfer the treasure to the cupboard in his room, thus surprising his mother at the end of the holidays with all this sudden wealth. He got safely home unseen by anyone and that night in bed he counted over his new riches while outside it rained and rained. Never had he heard such a storm. It was as though the wicked spirit of his old pirate ancestor raged against him*' (Mrs Wilditch had written, 'Eternal punishment I suppose!') '*and indeed the next day, when he returned to the island in the lake, whole trees had been uprooted and now lay across the entrance to the passage. Worse still there had been a landslide, and now the cavern must lie hidden forever below the waters of the lake. However,*' the young Wilditch had added briefly forty years ago, '*the treasure already recovered was sufficient to save the family home and send his brother to Oxford.*'

Wilditch undressed and got into bed, then lay on his back listening to the storm. What a trivial conventional day-dream W.W. had constructed – out of what? There had been no attic-room – probably no raft: these were preliminaries which did not matter, but why had W.W. so falsified the adventure itself? Where was the man with the beard? The old squawking woman? Of course it had all been a dream, it could have been nothing else but a dream, but a dream too was an experience, the images of a dream had their own integrity, and he felt professional anger at this false report just as his mother had felt at the mistake in the Fabian statistics.

All the same, while he lay there in his mother's bed and thought of her rigid interrogation of W.W.'s story, another theory of the falsifications came to him, perhaps a juster one. He remembered how agents parachuted into France during the bad years after 1940 had been made to memorize a cover-story which they could give, in case of torture, with enough truth in it to be checked. Perhaps forty years ago the pressure to tell had been almost as great on W.W., so that he had been forced to find relief in fantasy. Well, an agent dropped into occupied territory was always given a time-limit after capture. 'Keep the interrogators at bay with silence or lies for just so long, and then you may tell all.' The time-limit had surely been passed in his case a long time ago, his mother was beyond the possibility of hurt, and Wilditch for the first time deliberately indulged his passion to remember.

He got out of bed and, after finding some notepaper stamped, presumably for income-tax purposes, Winton

Small Holdings Limited, in the drawer of the desk, he began to write an account of what he had found – or dreamed that he found – under the garden of Winton Hall. The summer night was nosing wetly around the window just as it had done fifty years ago but, as he wrote, it began to turn grey and recede; the trees of the garden became visible, so that, when he looked up after some hours from his writing, he could see the shape of the broken fountain and what he supposed were the laurels in the Dark Walk, looking like old men humped against the weather.

PART TWO

[1]

Never mind how I came to the island in the lake, never mind whether in fact, as my brother says, it is a shallow pond with water only two feet deep (I suppose a raft can be launched on two feet of water, and certainly I must have always come to the lake by way of the Dark Walk, so that it is not at all unlikely that I built my raft there). Never mind what hour it was – I think it was evening, and I had hidden, as I remember it, in the Dark Walk because George had not got the courage to search for me there. The evening turned to rain, just as it's raining now, and George must have been summoned into the house for shelter. He would have told my mother that he couldn't find me and she must have called from the upstair windows, front and back – perhaps it was the occasion George spoke about tonight. I am not sure of these facts, they are plausible only, I can't yet *see* what I'm describing. But I know that I was not to find George and my mother again for many days . . . It cannot, whatever George says, have been less than three days and nights that I spent below the ground. Could he really have forgotten so inexplicable an experience?

And here I am already checking my story as though it were something which had really happened, for what possible relevance has George's memory to the events of a dream?

I dreamed that I crossed the lake, I dreamed . . . that is the only certain fact and I must cling to it, the fact that

I dreamed. How my poor mother would grieve if she could know that, even for a moment, I had begun to think of these events as true . . . but, of course, if it were possible for her to know what I am thinking now, there would be no limit to the area of possibility. I dreamed then that I crossed the water (either by swimming – I could already swim at seven years old – or by wading if the lake is really as small as George makes out, or by paddling a raft) and scrambled up the slope of the island. I can remember grass, scrub, brushwood, and at last a wood. I would describe it as a forest if I had not already seen, in the height of the garden-wall, how age diminishes size. I don't remember the umbrella-pine which W.W. described – I suspect he stole the sentinel-tree from *Treasure Island*, but I do know that when I got into the wood I was completely hidden from the house and the trees were close enough together to protect me from the rain. Quite soon I was lost, and yet how could I have been lost if the lake were no bigger than a pond, and the island therefore not much larger than the top of a kitchen-table?

Again I find myself checking my memories as though they were facts. A dream does not take account of size. A puddle can contain a continent, and a clump of trees stretch in sleep to the world's edge. I dreamed, I *dreamed* that I was lost and that night began to fall. I was not frightened. It was as though even at seven I was accustomed to travel. All the rough journeys of the future were already in me then, like a muscle which had only to develop. I curled up among the roots of the trees and slept. When I woke I could still hear the pit-pat of the rain in the upper branches and the steady zing of an insect near by. All these noises come as clearly back to me now as the sound of the rain on the parked cars outside the clinic in Wimpole Street, the music of yesterday.

The moon had risen and I could see more easily around me. I was determined to explore further before the morning came, for then an expedition would certainly be sent in search of me. I knew, from the many books of exploration George had read to me, of the danger to a person lost of walking in circles until eventually he dies of thirst or hunger, so I cut a cross in the bark of the tree (I had brought a knife with me that contained several blades, a small saw and an instrument for removing pebbles from horses' hooves). For the sake of future reference I named the place where I had slept Camp Hope. I had no fear of hunger, for I had apples in both pockets, and as for thirst I had only to continue in a straight line and I would come eventually to the lake again where the water was sweet, or at worst a little brackish. I go into all these details, which W.W. unaccountably omitted, to test my memory. I had forgotten until now how far or how deeply it extended. Had W.W. forgotten or was he afraid to remember?

I had gone a little more than three hundred yards – I paced the distances and marked every hundred paces or so on a tree – it was the best I could do, without proper surveying instruments, for the map I already planned to draw – when I reached a great oak of apparently enormous age with roots that coiled away above the surface of the ground. (I was reminded of those roots once in Africa where they formed a kind of shrine for a fetish – a seated human figure made out of a gourd and palm fronds and unidentifiable vegetable matter gone rotten in the rains and a great penis of bamboo. Coming on it suddenly, I was frightened, or was it the memory that it brought back which scared me?) Under one of these roots the earth had been disturbed; somebody had shaken a mound of charred tobacco from a pipe and a sequin glistened like a snail in the moist moonlight. I struck a match to examine the ground closer and saw the imprint of a foot in a patch of loose earth – it was pointing at the tree from a few inches away and it was as solitary as the print Crusoe found on the sands of another island. It was as though a one-legged man had taken a leap out of the bushes straight at the tree.

Pirate ancestor! What nonsense W.W. had written, or had he converted the memory of that stark frightening footprint into some comforting thought of the kindly scoundrel, Long John Silver, and his wooden leg?

I stood astride the imprint and stared up the tree, half expecting to see a one-legged man perched like a vulture among the branches. I listened and there was no sound except last night's rain dripping from leaf to leaf. Then – I don't know why – I went down on my knees and peered among the roots. There was no iron ring, but one of the roots formed an arch more than two feet high like the entrance to a cave. I put my head inside and lit another match – I couldn't see the back of the cave.

It's difficult to remember that I was only seven years old. To the self we remain always the same age. I was afraid at first to venture further, but so would any grown man have been, any one of the explorers I thought of as my peers. My brother had been reading aloud to me a month before from a book called *The Romance of Australian Exploration* – my own powers of reading had not advanced quite as far as that, but my memory was green and retentive and I carried in my head all kinds of new images and evocative words – aboriginal, sextant,

Murumbidgee, Stony Desert, and the points of the compass with their big capital letters E.S.E. and N.N.W. had an excitement they have never quite lost. They were like the figure on a watch which at last comes round to pointing the important hour. I was comforted by the thought that Sturt had been sometimes daunted and that Burke's bluster often hid his fear. Now, kneeling by the cave, I remembered a cavern which George Grey, another hero of mine, had entered and how suddenly he had come on the figure of a man ten feet high painted on the wall, clothed from the chin down to the ankles in a red garment. I don't know why, but I was more afraid of that painting than I was of the aborigines who killed Burke, and the fact that the feet and hands which protruded from the garment were said to be badly executed added to the terror. A foot which looked like a foot was only human, but my imagination could play endlessly with the faults of the painter – a club-foot, a claw-foot, the worm-like toes of a bird. Now I associated this strange footprint with the ill-executed painting and I hesitated a long time before I got the courage to crawl into the cave under the root. Before doing so, in reference to the footprint, I gave the spot the name of Friday's Cave.

[2]

For some yards I could not even get upon my knees, the roof grated my hair, and it was impossible for me in that position to strike another match. I could only inch along like a worm, making an ideograph in the dust. I didn't notice for a while in the darkness that I was crawling down a long slope, but I could feel on either side of me roots rubbing my shoulders like the banisters of a staircase. I was creeping through the branches of an underground tree in a mole's world. Then the impediments were passed – I was out the other side; I banged my head again on the earth-wall and found that I could rise to my knees. But I nearly toppled down again, for I had not realized how steeply the ground sloped. I was more than a man's height below ground and, when I struck a match, I could see no finish to the long gradient going down. I cannot help feeling a little proud that I continued on my way, on my knees this time, though I suppose it is arguable whether one can really show courage in a dream.

I was halted again by a turn in the path, and this time I found I could rise to my feet after I had struck another match. The track had flattened out and ran horizontally. The air was stuffy with an odd disagreeable smell like cabbage cooking, and I wanted to go back. I remembered how miners carried canaries with them in cages to test the freshness of the air, and I wished I had thought of bringing our own canary with me which had accompanied us to Winton Hall – it would have been company too in that dark tunnel with its tiny song. There was something, I remembered, called coal-damp which caused explosions, and this passage was certainly damp enough. I must be nearly under the lake by this time, and I thought to myself that, if there was an explosion, the waters of the lake would pour in and drown me.

I blew out my match at the idea, but all the same I continued on my way in the hope that I might come on an exit a little easier than the long crawl back through the roots of the trees.

Suddenly ahead of me something whistled, only it was less like a whistle than a hiss: it was like the noise a kettle makes when it is on the boil. I thought of snakes and wondered whether some giant serpent had made its nest in the tunnel. There was something fatal to man called a Black Mamba . . . I stood stock-still and held my breath, while the whistling went on and on for a long while, before it whined out into nothing. I would have given anything then to have been safe back in bed in the room next to my mother's, with the electric-light switch close to my hand and the firm bed-end at my feet. There was a strange clanking sound and a duck-like quack. I couldn't bear the darkness any more and I lit another match, reckless of coal-damp. It shone on a pile of old newspapers and nothing else – it was strange to find I had not been the first person here. I called out 'Hullo!' and my voice went on in diminishing echoes down the long passage. Nobody answered, and when I picked up one of the papers I saw it was no proof of a human presence. It was the *East Anglian Observer* for April 5th 1885 – 'with which is incorporated the *Colchester Guardian*'. It's funny how even the date remains in my mind and the Victorian Gothic type of the titling. There was a faint fishy smell about it as though – oh, eons ago – it had been wrapped around a bit of prehistoric cod. The match burnt my fingers and went out. Perhaps I was the first to come here for all those years, but suppose whoever had brought those papers were lying somewhere dead in the tunnel . . .

Then I had an idea. I made a torch of the paper in my hand, tucked the others under my arm to serve me later, and with a stronger light advanced more boldly down the passage. After all wild beasts – so George had read to me – and serpents too in all likelihood – were afraid of fire, and my fear of an explosion had been driven out by the greater terror of what I might find in the dark. But it was not a snake or a leopard or a tiger or any other cavern-haunting animal that I saw when I turned the second corner. Scrawled with the simplicity of ancient man upon the left-hand wall of the passage – done with a sharp tool like a chisel – was the outline of a gigantic fish. I held up my paper-torch higher and saw the remains of lettering either half-obliterated or in a language I didn't know.

I was trying to make sense of the symbols when a hoarse voice out of sight called, 'Maria, Maria'.

I stood very still and the newspaper burned down in my hand. 'Is that you, Maria?' the voice said. It sounded to me very angry. 'What kind of trick are you playing? What's the clock say? Surely it's time for my broth.' And then I heard again that strange quacking sound which I had heard before. There was a long whispering and after that silence.

[3]

I suppose I was relieved that there were human beings and not wild beasts down the passage, but what kind of human beings could they be except criminals hiding from justice or gypsies who are notorious for stealing children? I was afraid to think what they might do to anyone who discovered their secret. It was also possible, of course, that I had come on the home of some aboriginal tribe . . . I stood there unable to make up my mind whether to go on or to turn back. It was not a problem which my Australian peers could help me to solve, for

287

they had sometimes found the aboriginals friendly folk who gave them fish (I thought of the fish on the wall) and sometimes enemies who attacked with spears. In any case – whether these were criminals or gypsies or aboriginals – I had only a pocket-knife for my defence. I think it showed the true spirit of an explorer that in spite of my fears I thought of the map I must one day draw if I survived and so named this spot Camp Indecision.

My indecision was solved for me. An old woman appeared suddenly and noiselessly around the corner of the passage. She wore an old blue dress which came down to her ankles covered with sequins, and her hair was grey and straggly and she was going bald on top. She was every bit as surprised as I was. She stood there gaping at me and then she opened her mouth and squawked. I learned later that she had no roof to her mouth and was probably saying, 'Who are you?', but then I thought it was some foreign tongue she spoke – perhaps aboriginee – and I replied with an attempt at assurance, 'I'm English.'

The hoarse voice out of sight said, 'Bring him along here, Maria.'

The old woman took a step towards me, but I couldn't bear the thought of being touched by her hands, which were old and curved like a bird's and covered with the brown patches that Ernest, the gardener, had told me were 'grave-marks'; her nails were very long and filled with dirt. Her dress was dirty too and I thought of the sequin I'd seen outside and I imagined her scrabbling home through the roots of the tree. I backed up against the side of the passage and somehow squeezed around her. She quacked after me, but I went on. Round a second – or perhaps a third – corner I found myself in a great cave some eight feet high. On what I thought was a throne, but I later realized was an old lavatory-seat, sat a big old man with a white beard yellowing round the mouth from what I suppose now to have been nicotine. He had one good leg, but the right trouser was sewn up and looked stuffed like a bolster. I could see him quite well because an oil-lamp stood on a kitchen-table, beside a carving-knife and two cabbages, and his face came vividly back to me the other day when I was reading Darwin's description of a carrier-pigeon: 'Greatly elongated eyelids, very large external orifices to the nostrils, and a wide gape of mouth.'

He said, 'And who would you be and what are you doing here and why are you burning my newspaper?'

The old woman came squawking around the corner and then stood still behind me, barring my retreat.

I said, 'My name's William Wilditch, and I come from Winton Hall.'

'And where's Winton Hall?' he asked, never stirring from his lavatory-seat.

'Up there,' I said and pointed at the roof of the cave.

'That means precious little,' he said. 'Why, everything is up there, China and all America too and the Sandwich Islands.'

'I suppose so,' I said. There was a kind of reason in most of what he said, as I came to realize later.

'But down here there's only us. We are exclusive,' he said, 'Maria and me.'

I was less frightened of him now. He spoke English. He was a fellow-countryman. I said, 'If you'll tell me the way out I'll be going on my way.'

'What's that you've got under your arm?' he asked me sharply. 'More newspapers?'

'I found them in the passage . . .'

'Finding's not keeping here,' he said, 'whatever it may be up there in China. You'll soon discover that. Why, that's the last lot of papers Maria brought in. What would we have for reading if we let you go and pinch them?'

'I didn't mean . . .'

'Can you read?' he asked, not listening to my excuses.

'If the words aren't too long.'

'Maria can read, but she can't see very well any more than I can, and she can't articulate much.'

Maria went kwahk, kwahk behind me, like a bull-frog it seems to me now, and I jumped. If that was how she read I wondered how he could understand a single word.

He said, 'Try a piece.'

'What do you mean?'

'Can't you understand plain English? You'll have to work for your supper down here.'

'But it's not supper-time. It's still early in the morning,' I said.

'What o'clock is it, Maria?'

'Kwahk,' she said.

'Six. That's supper-time.'

'But it's six in the morning, not the evening.'

'How do you know? Where's the light? There aren't such things as mornings and evenings here.'

'Then how do you ever wake up?' I asked. His beard shook as he laughed. 'What a shrewd little shaver he is,' he exclaimed. 'Did you hear that, Maria? "How do you ever wake up?" he said. All the same you'll find that life here isn't all beer and skittles and who's your Uncle Joe. If you are clever, you'll learn and if you are not clever . . .' He brooded morosely. 'We are deeper here than any grave was ever dug to bury secrets in. Under the earth or over the earth, it's there you'll find all that matters.' He added angrily, 'Why aren't you reading a piece as I told you to? If you are to stay with us, you've got to jump to it.'

'I don't want to stay.'

'You think you can just take a peek, is that it? and go away. You are wrong – but take all the peek you want and then get on with it.'

I didn't like the way he spoke, but all the same I did as he suggested. There was an old chocolate-stained chest of drawers, a tall kitchen-cupboard, a screen covered with scraps and transfers, and a wooden crate which perhaps served Maria for a chair, and another larger one for a table. There was a cooking-stove with a kettle pushed to one side, steaming yet. That would have caused the whistle I had heard in the passage. I could see no sign of any bed, unless a heap of potato-sacks against the wall served that purpose. There were a lot of bread-crumbs on the earth-floor and a few bones had been swept into a corner as though awaiting interment.

'And now,' he said, 'show your young paces. I've yet to see whether you are worth your keep.'

'But I don't want to be kept,' I said. 'I really don't. It's time I went home.'

'Home's where a man lies down,' he said, 'and this is where you'll lie from now on. Now take the first page that comes and read to me. I want to hear the news.'

'But the paper's nearly fifty years old,' I said. 'There's no news in it.'

'News is news however old it is.' I began to notice a way he had of talking in general statements like a lecturer or a prophet. He seemed to be less interested in conversation than in the recital of some articles of belief, odd crazy ones, perhaps, yet somehow I could never put my finger convincingly on an error. 'A cat's a cat even when it's a dead cat. We get rid of it when it's smelly, but news never smells, however long it's dead. News keeps. And it comes round again when you least expect. Like thunder.'

I opened the paper at random and read: 'Garden fête at the Grange. The fête at the Grange, Long Wilson, in aid of Distressed Gentlewomen was opened by Lady (Isobel) Montgomery.' I was a bit put out by the long words coming so quickly, but I acquitted myself with fair credit. He sat on the lavatory-seat with his head sunk a little, listening with attention. 'The Vicar presided at the White Elephant Stall.'

The old man said with satisfaction, 'They are royal beasts.'

'But these were not really elephants,' I said.

'A stall is part of a stable, isn't it? What do you want a stable for if they aren't real? Go on. Was it a good fate or an evil fate?'

'It's not that kind of fate either,' I said.

'There's no other kind,' he said. 'It's your fate to read to me. It's *her* fate to talk like a frog, and mine to listen because my eyesight's bad. This is an underground fate we suffer from here, and that was a garden fate – but it all comes to the same fate in the end.' It was useless to argue with him and I read on: 'Unfortunately the festivities were brought to an untimely close by a heavy rainstorm.'

Maria gave a kwahk that sounded like a malicious laugh, and 'You see,' the old man said, as though what I had read proved somehow he was right, 'that's fate for you.'

'The evening's events had to be transferred indoors, including the Morris Dancing and the Treasure Hunt.'

'Treasure Hunt?' the old man asked sharply.

'That's what it says here.'

'The impudence of it,' he said. 'The sheer impudence. Maria, did you hear that?'

She kwahked – this time, I thought, angrily.

'It's time for my broth,' he said with deep gloom, as though he were saying, 'It's time for my death.'

'It happened a long time ago,' I said, trying to soothe him.

'Time,' he exclaimed, 'you can — time,' using a word quite unfamiliar to me which I guessed – I don't know how – was one that I could not with safety use myself when I returned home. Maria had gone behind the screen – there must have been other cupboards there, for I heard her opening and shutting doors and clanking pots and pans.

I whispered to him quickly, 'Is she your luba?'

'Sister, wife, mother, daughter,' he said, 'what difference does it make? Take your choice. She's a woman, isn't she?' He brooded there on the lavatory-seat like a king on a throne. 'There are two sexes,' he said. 'Don't try to make more than two with definitions.' The statement sank into my mind with the same heavy mathematical certainty with which later on at school I learned the rule of Euclid about the sides of an isosceles triangle. There was a long silence.

'I think I'd better be going,' I said, shifting up and down. Maria came in. She carried a dish marked Fido filled with hot broth. Her husband, her brother, whatever he was, nursed it on his lap a long while before he drank it. He seemed to be lost in thought again, and I hesitated to disturb him. All the same, after a while, I tried again.

'They'll be expecting me at home.'

'Home?'

'Yes.'

'You couldn't have a better home than this,' he said. 'You'll see. In a bit of time – a year or two – you'll settle down well enough.'

I tried my best to be polite. 'It's very nice here, I'm sure, but . . .'

'It's no use your being restless. I didn't ask you to come, did I, but now you are here, you'll stay. Maria's a great hand with cabbage. You won't suffer any hardship.'

'But I can't stay. My mother . . .'

'Forget your mother and your father too. If you need anything from up there Maria will fetch it down for you.'

'But I can't stay here.'

'Can't's not a word that you can use to the likes of me.'

'But you haven't any right to keep me . . .'

'And what right had you to come busting in like a thief, getting Maria all disturbed when she was boiling my broth?'

'I couldn't stay here with you. It's not – sanitary.' I don't know how I managed to get that word out. 'I'd die . . .'

'There's no need to talk of dying down here. No one's ever died here, and you've no reason to believe that anyone ever will. We aren't dead, are we, and we've lived a long long time, Maria and me. You don't know how lucky you are. There's treasure here beyond all the riches of Asia. One day, if you don't go disturbing Maria, I'll show you. You know what a millionaire is?' I nodded.

'They aren't one quarter as rich as Maria and me. And they die too, and where's their treasure then? Rockefeller's gone and Fred's gone and Columbus. I sit here and just read about dying – it's an entertainment that's all. You'll find in all those papers what they call an obituary – there's one about a Lady Caroline Winterbottom that made Maria laugh and me. It's summerbottoms we have here, I said, all the year round, sitting by the stove.'

Maria kwahked in the background, and I began to cry more as a way of interrupting him than because I was really frightened.

It's extraordinary how vividly after all these years I can remember that man and the words he spoke. If they were to dig down now on the island below the roots of the tree, I would half expect to find him sitting there still on the old lavatory-seat which seemed to be detached from any pipes or drainage and serve no useful purpose, and yet, if he had really existed, he must have passed his century a long time ago. There was something of a monarch about him and something, as I said, of a prophet and something of the gardener my mother disliked and of a policeman in the next village; his expressions were often countrylike and coarse, but his ideas seemed to move on a deeper level, like roots spreading below a layer of compost. I could sit here now in this room for hours remembering the things he said – I haven't made out the sense of them all yet: they are stored in my memory like a code uncracked which waits for a clue or an inspiration.

He said to me sharply, 'We don't need salt here. There's too much as it is. You taste any bit of earth and you'll find it salt. We live in salt. We are pickled, you might say, in it. Look at Maria's hands, and you'll see the salt in the cracks.'

I stopped crying at once and looked (my attention could always be caught by bits of irrelevant information), and, true enough, there seemed to be grey-white seams running between her knuckles.

'You'll turn salty too in time,' he said encouragingly and drank his broth with a good deal of noise.

I said, 'But I really am going, Mr . . .'

'You can call me Javitt,' he said, 'but only because it's not my real name. You don't believe I'd give you that, do you? And Maria's not Maria – it's just a sound she answers to, you understand me, like Jupiter.'

'No.'

'If you had a dog called Jupiter, you wouldn't believe he was really Jupiter, would you?'

'I've got a dog called Joe.'

'The same applies,' he said and drank his soup. Sometimes I think that in no conversation since have I found the interest I discovered in those inconsequent sentences of his to which I listened during the days (I don't know how many) that I spent below the garden. Because, of course, I didn't leave that day. Javitt had his way.

He might be said to have talked me into staying, though if I had proved obstinate I have no doubt at all that Maria would have blocked my retreat, and certainly I would not have fancied struggling to escape through the musty folds of her clothes. That was the strange balance – to and fro – of those days; half the time I was frightened as though I were caged in a nightmare and half the time I only wanted to laugh freely and happily at the strangeness of his speech and the novelty of his ideas. It was as if, for those hours or days, the only important things in life were two, laughter and fear. (Perhaps the same ambivalence was there when I first began to know a woman.) There are people whose laughter has always a sense of superiority, but it was Javitt who taught me that laughter is more often a sign of equality, of pleasure and not of malice. He sat there on his lavatory-seat and he said, 'I shit dead stuff every day, do I? How wrong you are.' (I was already laughing because that was a word I knew to be obscene and I had never heard it spoken before.) 'Everything that comes out of me is alive, I tell you. It's squirming around there, germs and bacilli and the like, and it goes into the ground like a womb, and it comes out somewhere, I daresay, like my daughter did – I forgot I haven't told you about her.'

'Is she here?' I asked with a look at the curtain, wondering what monstrous woman would next emerge.

'Oh, no, she went upstairs a long time ago.'

'Perhaps I could take her a message from you,' I said cunningly.

He looked at me with contempt. 'What kind of message,' he asked, 'could the likes of you take to the likes of her?' He must have seen the motive behind my offer, for he reverted to the fact of my imprisonment. 'I'm not unreasonable,' he said, 'I'm not one to make hailstorms in harvest time, but if you went back up there you'd talk about me and Maria and the treasure we've got, and would come digging.'

'I swear I'd say nothing' (and at least I have kept that promise, whatever others I have broken, through all the years until now).

'You talk in your sleep maybe. A boy's never alone. You've got a brother, I daresay, and soon you'll be going to school and hinting of things to make you seem important. There are plenty of ways of keeping an oath and breaking it in the same moment. Do you know what I'd do then? If they came searching? I'd go further in.'

Maria kwahk-kwahked her agreement where she listened from somewhere behind the curtains.

'What do you mean?'

'Give me a hand to get off this seat,' he said. He pressed his hand down on my shoulder and it was like a mountain heaving. I looked at the lavatory-seat and I could see that it had been placed exactly to cover a hole which went down down down out of sight. 'A moit of the treasure's down there already,' he said, 'but I wouldn't let the bastards enjoy what they could find here. There's a little matter of subsidence I've got fixed up so that they'd never see the light of day again.'

'But what would you do below there for food?'

'We've got tins enough for another century or two,' he said. 'You'd be surprised at what Maria's stored away there. We don't use tins up here because there's always broth and cabbage and that's more healthy and keeps the scurvy off, but we've no more teeth to lose and our gums are fallen as it is, so if we had to fall back on tins we would. Why, there's hams and chickens and red salmons' eggs and butter and steak-and-kidney pies and caviar, venison too and marrow-bones, I'm forgetting the fish — cods' roe and sole in white wine, langouste legs, sardines, bloaters, and herrings in tomato-sauce, and all the fruits that ever grew, apples, pears, strawberries, figs, raspberries, plums and greengages and passion fruit, mangoes, grapefruit, loganberries and cherries, mulberries too and sweet things from Japan, not to speak of vegetables, Indian corn and taties, salsify and spinach and that thing they call endive, asparagus, peas and the hearts of bamboo, and I've left out our old friend the tomato.' He lowered himself heavily back on to his seat above the great hole going down.

'You must have enough for two lifetimes,' I said.

'There's means of getting more,' he added darkly, so that I pictured other channels delved through the under-soil of the garden like the section of an ant's nest, and I remembered the sequin on the island and the single footprint.

Perhaps all this talk of food had reminded Maria of her duties because she came quacking out from behind her dusty curtain, carrying two bowls of broth, one medium size for me and one almost as small as an egg-cup for herself. I tried politely to take the small one, but she snatched it away from me.

'You don't have to bother about Maria,' the old man said. 'She's been eating food for more years than you've got weeks. She knows her appetite.'

'What do you cook with?' I asked.

'Calor,' he said.

That was an odd thing about this adventure or rather this dream: fantastic though it was, it kept coming back to ordinary life with simple facts like that. The man could never, if I really thought it out, have existed all those years below the earth, and yet the cooking, as I seem to remember it, was done on a cylinder of calor-gas.

The broth was quite tasty and I drank it to the end. When I had finished I fidgeted about on the wooden box they had given me for a seat – nature was demanding something for which I was too embarrassed to ask aid.

'What's the matter with you?' Javitt asked. 'Chair not comfortable?'

'Oh, it's very comfortable,' I said.

'Perhaps you want to lie down and sleep?'

'No.'

'I'll show you something which will give you dreams,' he said. 'A picture of my daughter.'

'I want to do number one,' I blurted out.

'Oh, is that all?' Javitt said. He called to Maria, who was still clattering around behind the curtain, 'The boy wants to piss. Fetch him the golden po.' Perhaps my eyes showed interest, for he added to me diminishingly, with the wave of a hand, 'It's the least of my treasures.'

All the same it was remarkable enough in my eyes, and I can remember it still, a veritable chamber-pot of gold. Even the young dauphin of France on that long road back from Varennes with his father had only a silver cup at his service. I would have been more embarrassed, doing what I called number one in front of the old man Javitt, if I had not been so impressed by the pot. It lent the everyday affair the importance of a ceremony, almost of a sacrament. I can remember the tinkle in the pot like far-away chimes as though a gold surface resounded differently from china or base metal.

Javitt reached behind him to a shelf stacked with old papers and picked one out. He said, 'Now you look at that and tell me what you think.'

It was a kind of magazine I'd never seen before – full of pictures which are now called cheese-cake. I have no earlier memory of a woman's unclothed body, or as nearly unclothed as made no difference to me then, in the skin-tight black costume. One whole page was given up to a Miss Ramsgate, shot from all angles. She was the favourite contestant for something called Miss England and might later go on, if she were successful, to compete for the title of Miss Europe, Miss World and after that Miss

Universe. I stared at her as though I wanted to memorize her for ever. And that is exactly what I did.

'That's our daughter,' Javitt said.

'And did she become . . .'

'She was launched,' he said with pride and mystery, as though he were speaking of some moon-rocket which had at last after many disappointments risen from the pad and soared to outer space. I looked at the photograph, at the wise eyes and the inexplicable body, and I thought, with all the ignorance children have of age and generations, I never want to marry anybody but her. Maria put her hand through the curtains and quacked, and I thought, she would be my mother then, but not a hoot did I care. With that girl for my wife I could take anything, even school and growing up and life. And perhaps I could have taken them, if I had ever succeeded in finding her.

Again my thoughts were interrupted. For if I am remembering a vivid dream – and dreams do stay in all their detail far longer than we realize – how would I have known at that age about such absurdities as beauty-contests? A dream can only contain what one has experienced, or, if you have sufficient faith in Jung, what our ancestors have experienced. But calor-gas and the Ramsgate Beauty Queen? . . . They are not ancestral memories, nor the memories of a child of seven. Certainly my mother did not allow us to buy with our meagre pocket-money – sixpence a week? – such papers as that. And yet the image is there, caught once and for all, not only the expression of the eyes, but the expression of the body too, the particular tilt of the breasts, the shallow scoop of the navel like something carved in sand, the little trim buttocks – the dividing line swung between them close and regular like the single sweep of a pencil. Can a child of seven fall in love for life with a body ? And there is a further mystery which did not occur to me then: how could a couple as old as Javitt and Maria have had a daughter so young in the period when such contests were the vogue ?

'She's a beauty,' Javitt said, 'you'll never see her like where your folks live. Things grow differently underground, like a mole's coat. I ask you where there's softness softer than that?' I'm not sure whether he was referring to the skin of his daughter or the coat of a mole.

I sat on the golden po and looked at the photograph and listened to Javitt as I would have listened to my own father if I had possessed one. His sayings are fixed in my memory like the photograph. Gross some of them seem now, but they did not appear gross to me then when even the graffiti on walls were innocent. Except when he called me 'boy' or 'snapper' or something of the kind he seemed unaware of my age: it was not that he talked to me as an equal but as someone from miles away, looking down from his old lavatory-seat to my golden po, from so far away that he couldn't distinguish my age, or perhaps he was so old that anyone under a century or so seemed much alike to him. All that I write here was not said at that moment. There must have been many days or nights of conversation – you couldn't down there tell the difference – and now I dredge the sentences up, in no particular order, just as they come to mind, sitting at my mother's desk so many years later.

[4]

'You laugh at Maria and me. You think we look ugly. I tell you she could have been painted if she had chosen by

302

some of the greatest – there's one that painted women with three eyes – she'd have suited him. But she knew how to tunnel in the earth like me, when to appear and when not to appear. It's a long time now that we've been alone down here. It gets more dangerous all the time – if you can speak of time – on the upper floor. But don't think it hasn't happened before. But when I remember . . .' But what he remembered has gone from my head, except only his concluding phrase and a sense of desolation: 'Looking round at all those palaces and towers, you'd have thought they'd been made like a child's castle of the desert-sand.'

'In the beginning you had a name only the man or woman knew who pulled you out of your mother. Then there was a name for the tribe to call you by. That was of little account, but of more account all the same than the name you had with strangers; and there was a name used in the family – by your pa and ma if it's those terms you call them by nowadays. The only name without any power at all was the name you used to strangers. That's why I call myself Javitt to you, but the name the man who pulled me out knew – that was so secret I had to keep him as a friend for life, so that he wouldn't even tell me because of the responsibility it would bring – I might let it slip before a stranger. Up where you come from they've begun to forget the power of the name. I wouldn't be surprised if you only had the one name and what's the good of a name everyone knows? Do you suppose even I feel secure here with my treasure and all – because, you see, as it turned out, I got to know the first name of all. He told it me before he died, before I could stop him, with a hand over his mouth. I doubt if there's anyone in the world except me who knows his first name.

It's an awful temptation to speak it out loud – introduce it casually into the conversation like you might say by Jove, by George, for Christ's sake. Or whisper it when I think no one's attentive.'

'When I was born, time had a different pace to what it has now. Now you walk from one wall to another, and it takes you twenty steps – or twenty miles – who cares ? – between the towns. But when I was young we took a leisurely way. Don't bother me with "I must be gone now" or "I've been away so long". I can't talk to you in terms of time – your time and my time are different. Javitt isn't my usual name either even with strangers. It's one I thought up fresh for you, so that you'll have no power at all. I'll change it right away if you escape. I warn you that.'

'You get a sense of what I mean when you make love with a girl. The time isn't measured by clocks. Time is fast or slow or it stops for a while altogether. One minute is different to every other minute. When you make love it's a pulse in a man's part which measures time and when you spill yourself there's no time at all. That's how time comes and goes, not by an alarm-clock made by a man with a magnifying glass in his eye. Haven't you ever heard them say, "It's — time" up there ?' and he used again the word which I guessed was forbidden like his name, perhaps because it had power too.

'I daresay you are wondering how Maria and me could make a beautiful girl like that one. That's an illusion people have about beauty. Beauty doesn't come from beauty. All that beauty can produce is prettiness. Have you never looked around upstairs and counted the beautiful women with their pretty daughters ? Beauty diminishes all the time, it's the law of diminishing returns, and only when you get back to zero, to the real ugly base of things, there's a chance to start again free and independent. Painters who paint what they call ugly things know that. I can still see that little head with its cap of blonde hair coming out from between Maria's thighs and how she leapt out of Maria in a spasm (there wasn't any doctor down here or midwife to give her a name and rob her of power – and she's Miss Ramsgate to you and to the whole world upstairs). Ugliness and beauty; you see it in war too; when there's nothing left of a house but a couple of pillars against the sky, the beauty of it starts all over again like before the builder ruined it. Perhaps when Maria and I go up there next, there'll only be pillars left, sticking up around the flattened world like it was fucking time.' (The word had become familiar to me by this time and no longer had the power to shock.)

'Do you know, boy, that when they make those maps of the universe you are looking at the map of something that looked like that six thousand million years ago? You can't be much more out of date than that, I'll swear. Why, if they've got pictures up there of us taken yesterday, they'll see the world all covered with ice – if their photos are a bit more up to date than ours, that is. Otherwise we won't be there at all, maybe, and it might just as well be a photo of the future. To catch a star while it's alive you have to be as nippy as if you were snatching at a racehorse as it goes by.'

'You are a bit scared still of Maria and me because you've never seen anyone like us before. And you'd be scared to see our daughter too, there's no other like her in whatever country she's in now, and what good would a scared man be to her? Do you know what a rogue-plant is? And do you know that white cats with blue eyes are

305

deaf? People who keep nursery-gardens look around all the time at the seedlings and they throw away any oddities like weeds. They call them rogues. You won't find many white cats with blue eyes and that's the reason. But sometimes you find someone who wants things different, who's tired of all the plus signs and wants to find zero, and he starts breeding away with the differences. Maria and I are both rogues and we are born of generations of rogues. Do you think I lost this leg in an accident? I was born that way just like Maria with her squawk. Generations of us uglier and uglier, and suddenly out of Maria comes our daughter, who's Miss Ramsgate to you. I don't speak her name even when I'm asleep. We're unique like the Red Grouse. You ask anybody if they can tell you where the Red Grouse came from.'

'You are wondering why we are unique. It's because for generations we haven't been thrown away. Man kills or throws away what he doesn't want. Somebody once in Greece kept the wrong child and exposed the right one, and then one rogue at least was safe and it only needed another. Why, in Tierra del Fuego in starvation years they kill and eat their old women because the dogs are of more value. It's the hardest thing in the world for a rogue to survive. For hundreds of years now we've been living underground and we'll have the laugh of you yet, coming up above for keeps in a dead world. Except I'll bet you your golden po that Miss Ramsgate will be there somewhere – her beauty's rogue too. We have long lives, we – Javitts to you. We've kept our ugliness all those years and why shouldn't she keep her beauty? Like a cat does. A cat is as beautiful the last day as the first. And it keeps its spittle. Not like a dog.'

'I can see your eye light up whenever I say Miss

Ramsgate, and you still wonder how it comes Maria and I have a child like that in spite of all I'm telling you. Elephants go on breeding till they are ninety years old, don't they, and do you suppose a rogue like Javitt (which isn't my real name) can't go on longer than a beast so stupid it lets itself be harnessed and draw logs? There's another thing we have in common with elephants. No one sees us dead.'

'We know the sex-taste of female birds better than we know the sex-taste of women. Only the most beautiful in the hen's eyes survives, so when you admire a peacock you know you have the same taste as a pea-hen. But women are more mysterious than birds. You've heard of beauty and the beast, haven't you? They have rogue-tastes. Just look at me and my leg. You won't find Miss Ramsgate by going round the world preening yourself like a peacock to attract a beautiful woman – she's our daughter and she has rogue-tastes too. She isn't for some-one who wants a beautiful wife at his dinner-table to satisfy his vanity, and an understanding wife in bed who'll treat him just the same number of times as he was accus-tomed to at school – so many times a day or week. She went away, our daughter did, with a want looking for a want – and not a want you can measure in inches either or calculate in numbers by the week. They say that in the northern countries people make love for their health, so it won't be any good looking for her in the north. You might have to go as far as Africa or China. And talking of China . . .'

[5]

Sometimes I think that I learned more from Javitt – this man who never existed – than from all my schoolmasters.

He talked to me while I sat there on the po or lay upon the sacks as no one had ever done before or has ever done since. I could not have expected my mother to take time away from the Fabian pamphlets to say, 'Men are like monkeys – they don't have any season in love, and the monkeys aren't worried by this notion of dying. They tell us from pulpits we're immortal and then they try to frighten us with death. I'm more a monkey than a man. To the monkeys death's an accident. The gorillas don't bury their dead with hearses and crowns of flowers, thinking one day it's going to happen to them and they better put on a show if they want one for themselves too. If one of them dies, it's a special case, and so they can leave it in the ditch. I feel like them. But I'm not a special case yet. I keep clear of hackney-carriages and railway-trains, you won't find horses, wild dogs or machinery down here. I love life and I survive. Up there they talk about natural death, but it's natural death that's unnatural. If we lived for a thousand years – and there's no reason we shouldn't – there'd always be a smash, a bomb, tripping over your left foot – those are the natural deaths. All we need to live is a bit of effort, but nature sows booby-traps in our way.'

'Do you believe those skulls monks have in their cells are set there for contemplation? Not on your life. They don't believe in death any more than I do. The skulls are there for the same reason you'll see a queen's portrait in an embassy – they're just part of the official furniture. Do you believe an ambassador ever looks at that face on the wall with a diamond tiara and an empty smile?'

'Be disloyal. It's your duty to the human race. The human race needs to survive and it's the loyal man who dies first from anxiety or a bullet or overwork. If you have to earn a living, boy, and the price they make you pay is loyalty, be a double agent – and never let either of the two sides know your real name. The same applies to women and God. They both respect a man they don't own, and they'll go on raising the price they are willing to offer. Didn't Christ say that very thing? Was the prodigal son loyal or the lost shilling or the strayed sheep? The obedient flock didn't give the shepherd any satisfaction or the loyal son interest his father.'

'People are afraid of bringing May blossom into the house. They say it's unlucky. The real reason is it smells strong of sex and they are afraid of sex. Why aren't they afraid of fish then, you may rightly ask? Because when they smell fish they smell a holiday ahead and they feel safe from breeding for a short while.'

I remember Javitt's words far more clearly than the passage of time; certainly I must have slept at least twice on the bed of sacks, but I cannot remember Javitt sleeping until the very end – perhaps he slept like a horse or a god, upright. And the broth – that came at regular intervals, so far as I could tell, though there was no sign anywhere of a clock, and once I think they opened for me a tin of sardines from their store (it had a very Victorian label on it of two bearded sailors and a seal, but the sardines tasted good).

I think Javitt was glad to have me there. Surely he could not have been talking quite so amply over the years to Maria who could only quack in response, and several times he made me read to him from one of the newspapers. The nearest to our time I ever found was a local account of the celebrations for the relief of Mafeking. ('Riots,' Javitt said, 'purge like a dose of salts.')

Once he told me to pick up the oil-lamp and we would

go for a walk together, and I was able to see how agile he could be on his one leg. When he stood upright he looked like a rough carving from a tree-trunk where the sculptor had not bothered to separate the legs, or perhaps, as with the image on the cave, they were 'badly executed'. He put one hand on each wall and hopped gigantically in front of me, and when he paused to speak (like many old people he seemed unable to speak and move at the same time) he seemed to be propping up the whole passage with his arms as thick as pit-beams. At one point he paused to tell me that we were now directly under the lake. 'How many tons of water lie up there?' he asked me – I had never thought of water in tons before that, only in gallons, but he had the exact figure ready, I can't remember it now. Further on, where the passage sloped upwards, he paused again and said, 'Listen,' and I heard a kind of rumbling that passed overhead and after that a rattling as little cakes of mud fell around us. 'That's a motor-car,' he said, as an explorer might have said, 'That's an elephant.'

I asked him whether perhaps there was a way out near there since we were so close to the surface, and he made his answer, even to that direct question, ambiguous and general like a proverb. 'A wise man has only one door to his house,' he said.

What a boring old man he would have been to an adult mind, but a child has a hunger to learn which makes him sometimes hang on the lips of the dullest schoolmaster. I thought I was learning about the world and the universe from Javitt, and still to this day I wonder how it was that a child could have invented these details, or have they accumulated year by year, like coral, in the sea of the unconscious around the original dream?

There were times when he was in a bad humour for no apparent reason, or at any rate for no adequate reason. An example: for all his freedom of speech and range of thought, I found there were tiny rules which had to be obeyed, else the thunder of his invective broke – the way I had to arrange the spoon in the empty broth-bowl, the method of folding a newspaper after it had been read, even the arrangement of my limbs on the bed of sacks.

'I'll cut you off,' he cried once and I pictured him lopping off one of my legs to resemble him. 'I'll starve you, I'll set you alight like a candle for a warning. Haven't I given you a kingdom here of all the treasures of the earth and all the fruits of it, tin by tin, where time can't get in to destroy you and there's no day or night, and you go and defy me with a spoon laid down longways in a saucer? You come of an ungrateful generation.' His arms waved about and cast shadows like wolves on the wall behind the oil-lamp, while Maria sat squatting behind a cylinder of calor-gas in an attitude of terror.

'I haven't even seen your wonderful treasure,' I said with feeble defiance.

'Nor you won't,' he said, 'nor any lawbreaker like you. You lay last night on your back grunting like a small swine, but did I curse you as you deserved? Javitt's patient. He forgives and he forgives seventy times seven, but then you go and lay your spoon longways . . .' He gave a great sigh like a wave withdrawing. He said, 'I forgive even that. There's no fool like an old fool and you will search a long way before you find anything as old as I am – even among the tortoises, the parrots and the elephants. One day I'll show you the treasure, but not now. I'm not in the right mood now. Let time pass. Let time heal.'

I had found the way, however, on an earlier occasion to set him in a good humour and that was to talk to him about his daughter. It came quite easily to me, for I found myself to be passionately in love, as perhaps one can only be at an age when all one wants is to give and the thought of taking is very far removed. I asked him whether he was sad when she left him to go 'upstairs' as he liked to put it.

'I knew it had to come,' he said. 'It was for that she was born. One day she'll be back and the three of us will be together for keeps.'

'Perhaps I'll see her then,' I said.

'You won't live to see that day,' he said, as though it was I who was the old man, not he.

'Do you think she's married?' I asked anxiously.

'She isn't the kind to marry,' he said. 'Didn't I tell you she's a rogue like Maria and me? She has her roots down here. No one marries who has his roots down here.'

'I thought Maria and you were married,' I said anxiously.

He gave a sharp crunching laugh like a nut-cracker closing. 'There's no marrying in the ground,' he said. 'Where would you find the witnesses? Marriage is public. Maria and me, we just grew into each other, that's all, and then she sprouted.'

I sat silent for a long while, brooding on that vegetable picture. Then I said with all the firmness I could muster, 'I'm going to find her when I get out of here.'

'If you get out of here,' he said, 'you'd have to live a very long time and travel a very long way to find her.'

'I'll do just that,' I replied.

He looked at me with a trace of humour. 'You'll have to take a look at Africa,' he said, 'and Asia – and then there's America, North and South, and Australia – you might leave out the Arctic and the other Pole – she was always a warm girl.' And it occurs to me now when I think of the life I have led since, that I have been in most of those regions – except Australia where I have only twice touched down between planes.

'I will go to them all,' I said, 'and I'll find her.' It was as though the purpose of life had suddenly come to me as it must have come often enough to some future explorer when he noticed on a map for the first time an empty space in the heart of a continent.

'You'll need a lot of money,' Javitt jeered at me.

'I'll work my passage,' I said, 'before the mast.' Perhaps it was a reflection of that intention which made the young author W.W. menace his elder brother with such a fate before preserving him for Oxford of all places. The mast was to be a career sacred to me – it was not for George.

'It'll take a long time,' Javitt warned me.

'I'm young,' I said.

I don't know why it is that when I think of this conversation with Javitt the doctor's voice comes back to me saying hopelessly, 'There's always hope.' There's hope perhaps, but there isn't so much time left now as there was then to fulfil a destiny.

That night, when I lay down on the sacks, I had the impression that Javitt had begun to take a favourable view of my case. I woke once in the night and saw him sitting there on what is popularly called a throne, watching me. He closed one eye in a wink and it was like a star going out.

Next morning after my bowl of broth, he suddenly spoke up. 'Today,' he said, 'you are going to see my treasure.'

[6]

It was a day heavy with the sense of something fateful coming nearer – I call it a day but for all I could have told down there it might have been a night. And I can only compare it in my later experience with those slow hours I have sometimes experienced before I have gone to meet a woman with whom for the first time the act of love is likely to come about. The fuse has been lit, and who can tell the extent of the explosion? A few cups broken or a house in ruins?

For hours Javitt made no further reference to the subject, but after the second cup of broth (or was it perhaps, on that occasion, the tin of sardines?) Maria disappeared behind the screen and when she reappeared she wore a hat. Once, years ago perhaps, it had been a grand hat, a hat for the races, a great black straw affair; now it was full of holes like a colander decorated with one drooping scarlet flower which had been stitched and re-stitched and stitched again. I wondered when I saw her dressed like that whether we were about to go 'upstairs'. But we made no move. Instead she put a kettle upon the stove, warmed a pot and dropped in two spoonfuls of tea. Then she and Javitt sat and watched the kettle like a couple of soothsayers bent over the steaming entrails of a kid, waiting for a revelation. The kettle gave a thin preliminary whine and Javitt nodded and the tea was made. He alone took a cup, sipping it slowly, with his eyes on me, as though he were considering and perhaps revising his decision.

On the edge of his cup, I remember, was a tea-leaf. He took it on his nail and placed it on the back of my hand. I knew very well what that meant. A hard stalk of tea indicated a man upon the way and a soft leaf a woman; this was a soft leaf. I began to strike it with the palm of my other hand counting as I did so, 'One, two, three.' It lay flat, adhering to my hand. 'Four, five.' It was on my fingers now and I said triumphantly, 'In five days,' thinking of Javitt's daughter in the world above.

Javitt shook his head. 'You don't count time like that with us,' he said. 'That's five decades of years.' I accepted his correction – he must know his own country best, and it's only now that I find myself calculating, if every day down there were ten years long, what age in our reckoning could Javitt have claimed?

I have no idea what he had learned from the ceremony of the tea, but at least he seemed satisfied. He rose on his one leg, and now that he had his arms stretched out to either wall, he reminded me of a gigantic crucifix, and the crucifix moved in great hops down the way we had taken the day before. Maria gave me a little push from behind and I followed. The oil lamp in Maria's hand cast long shadows ahead of us.

First we came under the lake and I remembered the tons of water hanging over us like a frozen falls, and after that we reached the spot where we had halted before, and again a car went rumbling past on the road above. But this time we continued our shuffling march. I calculated that now we had crossed the road which led to Winton Halt; we must be somewhere under the inn called The Three Keys, which was kept by our gardener's uncle, and after that we should have arrived below the Long Mead, a field with a small minnowy stream along its northern border owned by a farmer called Howell. I had not given up all idea of escape and I noted our route carefully and the distance we had gone. I had hoped for some side-passage which might indicate another entrance to the tunnel, but there seemed to be none and I was disappointed to find that, before we travelled below the inn, we descended quite steeply, perhaps in order to avoid the cellars – indeed at one moment I heard a groaning and a turbulence as though the gardener's uncle were taking delivery of some new barrels of beer.

We must have gone nearly half a mile before the passage came to an end in a kind of egg-shaped hall. Facing us was a kitchen-dresser of unstained wood, very similar to the one in which my mother kept her stores of jam, sultanas, raisins and the like.

'Open up, Maria,' Javitt said, and Maria shuffled by me, clanking a bunch of keys and quacking with excitement, while the lamp swung to and fro like a censer.

'She's heated up,' Javitt said. 'It's many days since she saw the treasure last.' I do not know which kind of time he was referring to then, but judging from her excitement I think the days must really have represented decades – she had even forgotten which key fitted the lock and she tried them all and failed and tried again before the tumbler turned.

I was disappointed when I first saw the interior – I had expected gold bricks and a flow of Maria Theresa dollars spilling on the floor, and there were only a lot of shabby cardboard-boxes on the upper shelves and the lower shelves were empty. I think Javitt noted my disappointment and was stung by it. 'I told you,' he said, 'the moit's down below for safety.' But I wasn't to stay disappointed very long. He took down one of the biggest boxes off the top shelf and shook the contents on to the earth at my feet, as though defying me to belittle *that*.

And *that* was a sparkling mass of jewellery such as I had never seen before – I was going to say in all the colours of the rainbow, but the colours of stones have not that pale girlish simplicity. There were reds almost as deep as raw liver, stormy blues, greens like the underside of a wave, yellow sunset colours, greys like a shadow on snow, and stones without colour at all that sparkled brighter than all the rest. I say I'd seen nothing like it: it is the scepticism of middle age which leads me now to compare that treasure trove with the caskets overflowing with artificial jewellery which you sometimes see in the shop-windows of Italian touristresorts.

And there again I find myself adjusting a dream to the kind of criticism I ought to reserve for some agent's report on the import or export value of coloured glass. If this was a dream, these were real stones. Absolute reality belongs to dreams and not to life. The gold of dreams is not the diluted gold of even the best goldsmith, there are no diamonds in dreams made of paste – what seems is. 'Who seems most kingly is the king.'

I went down on my knees and bathed my hands in the treasure, and while I knelt there Javitt opened box after box and poured the contents upon the ground. There is no avarice in a child. I didn't concern myself with the value of this horde: it was simply a treasure, and a treasure is to be valued for its own sake and not for what it will buy. It was only years later, after a deal of literature and learning and knowledge at second hand, that W.W. wrote of the treasure as something with which he could save the family fortunes. I was nearer to the jackdaw in my dream, caring only for the glitter and the sparkle.

'It's nothing to what lies below out of sight,' Javitt remarked with pride.

There were necklaces and bracelets, lockets and bangles, pins and rings and pendants and buttons. There were quantities of those little gold objects which girls like to hang on their bracelets: the Vendôme column and the Eiffel Tower and a Lion of St Mark's, a champagne bottle and a tiny booklet with leaves of gold inscribed with the names of places important perhaps to a pair of lovers – Paris, Brighton, Rome, Assisi and Moreton-in-Marsh. There were gold coins too – some with the heads of Roman emperors and others of Victoria and George IV and Frederick Barbarossa. There were birds made out of precious stone with diamond-eyes, and buckles for shoes and belts, hairpins too with the rubies turned into roses, and vinaigrettes. There were toothpicks of gold, and swizzlesticks, and little spoons to dig the wax out of your ears of gold too, and cigarette-holders studded with diamonds, and small boxes of gold for pastilles and snuff, horse-shoes for the ties of hunting men, and emerald-hounds for the lapels of hunting women: fishes were there too and little carrots of ruby for luck, diamond-stars which had perhaps decorated generals or statesmen, golden key-rings with emerald-initials, and sea-shells picked out with pearls and a portrait of a dancing-girl in gold and enamel, with Haidee inscribed in what I suppose were rubies.

'Enough's enough,' Javitt said, and I had to drag myself away, as it seemed to me, from all the riches in the world, its pursuits and enjoyments. Maria would have packed everything that lay there back into the cardboard-boxes, but Javitt said with his lordliest voice, 'Let them lie,' and back we went in silence the way we had come, in the same order, our shadows going ahead. It was as if the sight of the treasure had exhausted me. I lay down on the sacks without waiting for my broth and fell asleep at once. In my dream within a dream somebody laughed and wept.

[7]

I have said that I can't remember how many days and nights I spent below the garden. The number of times I slept is really no guide, for I slept simply when I had the inclination or when Javitt commanded me to lie down, there being no light or darkness save what the oil-lamp determined, but I am almost sure it was after this sleep of exhaustion that I woke with the full intention somehow to reach home again. Up till now I had acquiesced in my captivity with little complaint; perhaps the meals of broth were palling on me, though I doubt if that was the reason, for I have fed for longer, with as little variety and less appetite, in Africa; perhaps the sight of Javitt's treasure had been a climax which robbed my story of any further interest; perhaps, and I think this is the most likely reason, I wanted to begin my search for Miss Ramsgate.

Whatever the motive, I came awake determined from my deep sleep, as suddenly as I had fallen into it. The wick was burning low in the oil-lamp and I could hardly distinguish Javitt's features and Maria was out of sight somewhere behind the curtain. To my astonishment Javitt's eyes were closed – it had never occurred to me before that there were moments when these two might sleep. Very quietly, with my eyes on Javitt, I slipped off my shoes – it was now or never. When I had got them off with less sound than a mouse makes, an idea came to me and I withdrew the laces – I can still hear the sharp ting of the metal tag ringing on the gold po beside my sacks. I thought I had been too clever by half, for Javitt stirred – but then he was still again and I slipped off my makeshift bed and crawled over to him where he sat on the lavatory-seat. I knew that, unfamiliar as I was with the tunnel, I could never outpace Javitt, but I was taken aback when I realized that it was impossible to bind together the ankles of a one-legged man.

But neither could a one-legged man travel without the help of his hands – the hands which lay now conveniently folded like a statue's on his lap. One of the things my brother had taught me was to make a slip-knot. I made one now with the laces joined and very gently, millimetre by millimetre, passed it over Javitt's hands and wrists, then pulled it tight.

I had expected him to wake with a howl of rage and even in my fear felt some of the pride Jack must have experienced at outwitting the giant. I was ready to flee at once, taking the lamp with me, but his very silence detained me. He only opened one eye, so that again I had the impression that he was winking at me. He tried to move his hands, felt the knot, and then acquiesced in their imprisonment. I expected him to call for Maria, but he did nothing of the kind, just watching me with his one open eye.

Suddenly I felt ashamed of myself. 'I'm sorry,' I said.

'Ha, ha,' he said, 'my prodigal, the strayed sheep, you're learning fast.'

'I promise not to tell a soul.'

'They wouldn't believe you if you did,' he said.

'I'll be going now,' I whispered with regret, lingering there absurdly, as though with half of myself I would have been content to stay for always.

'You better,' he said. 'Maria might have different views from me.' He tried his hands again. 'You tie a good knot.'

'I'm going to find your daughter,' I said, 'whatever you may think.'

'Good luck to you then,' Javitt said. 'You'll have to travel a long way; you'll have to forget all your schoolmasters try to teach you; you must lie like a horse-trader and not be tied up with loyalties any more than you are here, and who knows? I doubt it, but you might, you just might.'

I turned away to take the lamp, and then he spoke again. 'Take your golden po as a souvenir,' he said. 'Tell them you found it in an old cupboard. You've got to have something when you start a search to give you substance.'

'Thank you,' I said, 'I will. You've been very kind.' I began – absurdly in view of his bound wrists – to hold out my hand like a departing guest; then I stopped to pick up the po just as Maria, woken perhaps by our voices, came through the curtain. She took the situation in as quick as a breath and squawked at me – what I don't know – and made a dive with her bird-like hand.

I had the start of her down the passage and the advantage of the light, and I was a few feet ahead when I reached Camp Indecision, but at that point, what with the wind of my passage and the failing wick, the lamp went out. I dropped it on the earth and groped on in the dark. I could hear the scratch and whimper of Maria's sequin dress, and my nerves leapt when her feet set the lamp rolling on my tracks. I don't remember much after that. Soon I was crawling upwards, making better speed on my knees than she could do in her skirt, and a little later I saw a grey light where the roots of the tree parted.

When I came up into the open it was much the same early morning hour as the one when I had entered the cave. I could hear kwahk, kwahk, kwahk, come up from below the ground – I don't know if it was a curse or a menace or just a farewell, but for many nights afterwards I lay in bed afraid that the door would open and Maria would come in to fetch me, when the house was silent and asleep. Yet strangely enough I felt no fear of Javitt, then or later.

Perhaps – I can't remember – I dropped the gold po at the entrance of the tunnel as a propitiation to Maria; certainly I didn't have it with me when I rafted across the lake or when Joe, our dog, came leaping out of the house at me and sent me sprawling on my back in the dew of the lawn by the green broken fountain.

PART THREE

[1]

Wilditch stopped writing and looked up from the paper. The night had passed and with it the rain and the wet wind. Out of the window he could see thin rivers of blue sky winding between the banks of cloud, and the sun as it slanted in gleamed weakly on the cap of his pen. He read the last sentence which he had written and saw how again at the end of his account he had described his adventure as though it were one which had really happened and not something that he had dreamed during the course of a night's truancy or invented a few years later for the school magazine. Somebody, early though it was, trundled a wheelbarrow down the gravel-path beyond the fountain. The sound, like the dream, belonged to childhood.

He went downstairs and unlocked the front door. There unchanged was the broken fountain and the path which led to the Dark Walk, and he was hardly surprised when he saw Ernest, his uncle's gardener, coming towards him behind the wheelbarrow. Ernest must have been a young man in the days of the dream and he was an old man now, but to a child a man in the twenties approaches middle age and so he seemed much as Wilditch remembered him. There was something of Javitt about him, though he had a big moustache and not a beard – perhaps it was only a brooding and scrutinizing look and that air of authority and possession which had angered Mrs Wilditch when she approached him for vegetables.

323

'Why, Ernest,' Wilditch said, 'I thought you had re-tired?'

Ernest put down the handle of the wheelbarrow and regarded Wilditch with reserve. 'It's Master William, isn't it?'

'Yes. George said –'

'Master George was right in a way, but I have to lend a hand still. There's things in this garden others don't know about.' Perhaps he *had* been the model for Javitt, for there was something in his way of speech that suggested the same ambiguity.

'Such as . . . ?'

'It's not everyone can grow asparagus in chalky soil,' he said, making a general statement out of the particular in the same way Javitt had done. 'You've been away a long time, Master William.'

'I've travelled a lot.'

'We heard one time you was in Africa and another time in Chinese parts. Do you like a black skin, Master William?'

'I suppose at one time or another I've been fond of a black skin.'

'I wouldn't have thought they'd win a beauty prize,' Ernest said.

'Do you know Ramsgate, Ernest?'

'A gardener travels far enough in a day's work,' he said. The wheelbarrow was full of fallen leaves after the night's storm. 'Are the Chinese as yellow as people say?'

'No.'

There *was* a difference, Wilditch thought: Javitt never asked for information, he gave it: the weight of water, the age of the earth, the sexual habits of a monkey. 'Are there many changes in the garden,' he asked, 'since I was here?'

'You'll have heard the pasture was sold?'

'Yes. I was thinking of taking a walk before breakfast – down the Dark Walk perhaps to the lake and the island.'

'Ah.'

'Did you ever hear any story of a tunnel under the lake?'

'There's no tunnel there. For what would there be a tunnel?'

'No reason that I know. I suppose it was something I dreamed.'

'As a boy you was always fond of that island. Used to hide there from the missus.'

'Do you remember a time when I ran away?'

'You was always running away. The missus used to tell me to go and find you. I'd say to her right out, straight as I'm talking to you, I've got enough to do digging the potatoes you are always asking for. I've never known a woman get through potatoes like she did. You'd have thought she ate them. She could have been living on potatoes and not on the fat of the land.'

'Do you think I was treasure-hunting? Boys do.'

'You was hunting for something. That's what I said to the folk round here when you were away in those savage parts – not even coming back here for your uncle's funeral. "You take my word," I said to them, "he hasn't changed, he's off hunting for something, like he always did, though I doubt if he knows what he's after," I said to them. "The next we hear," I said, "he'll be standing on his head in Australia."'

Wilditch remarked with regret, 'Somehow I never looked there'; he was surprised that he had spoken aloud. 'And The Three Keys, is it still in existence?'

'Oh, it's there all right, but the brewers bought it when my uncle died and it's not a free house any more.'

'Did they alter it much?'

'You'd hardly know it was the same house with all the pipes and tubes. They put in what they call pressure, so you can't get an honest bit of beer without a bubble in it. My uncle was content to go down to the cellar for a barrel, but it's all machinery now.'

'When they made all those changes you didn't hear any talk of a tunnel under the cellar?'

'Tunnel again. What's got you thinking of tunnels? The only tunnel I know of is the railway tunnel at Bugham and that's five miles off.'

'Well, I'll be walking on, Ernest, or it will be breakfast time before I've seen the garden.'

'And I suppose now you'll be off again to foreign parts. What's it to be this time? Australia?'

'It's too late for Australia now.'

Ernest shook his brindled head at Wilditch with an air of sober disapproval. 'When I was born,' he said, 'time had a different pace to what it seems to have now,' and, lifting the handle of the wheelbarrow, he was on his way towards the new iron gate before Wilditch had time to realize he had used almost the very words of Javitt. The world was the world he knew.

[2]

The Dark Walk was small and not very dark – perhaps the laurels had thinned with the passing of time, but the cobwebs were there as in his childhood to brush his face as he went by. At the end of the walk there was the wooden gate on to the green which had always in his day been locked – he had never known why that route out of the garden was forbidden him, but he had discovered a way of opening the gate with the rim of a halfpenny. Now he could find no halfpennies in his pocket.

When he saw the lake he realized how right George had been. It was only a small pond, and a few feet from the margin there was an island the size of the room in which last night they had dined. There *were* a few bushes growing there, and even a few trees, one taller and larger than the others, but certainly it was neither the sentinel-pine of W.W.'s story nor the great oak of his memory. He took a few steps back from the margin of the pond and jumped.

He hadn't quite made the island, but the water in which he landed was only a few inches deep. Was any of the water deep enough to float a raft? He doubted it. He sloshed ashore, the water not even penetrating his shoes. So this little spot of earth had contained Camp Hope and Friday's Cave. He wished that he had the cynicism to laugh at the half-expectation which had brought him to the island.

The bushes came only to his waist and he easily pushed through them towards the largest tree. It was difficult to believe that even a small child could have been lost here. He was in the world that George saw every day, making his round of a not very remarkable garden. For perhaps a minute, as he pushed his way through the bushes, it seemed to him that his whole life had been wasted, much as a man who has been betrayed by a woman wipes out of his mind even the happy years with her. If it had not been for his dream of the tunnel and the bearded man and the hidden treasure, couldn't he have made a less restless life for himself, as George in fact had done, with marriage, children, a home? He tried to persuade himself that he was exaggerating the importance of a dream. His lot had probably been decided months before that when George was reading him *The Romance of Australian Exploration.* If a child's experience does really form his future life, surely he had been formed, not by Javitt, but by Grey and Burke. It was his pride that at least he had never taken his various professions seriously: he had been loyal to no one – not even to the girl in Africa (Javitt would have approved his disloyalty). Now he stood beside the ignoble tree that had no roots above the ground which could possibly have formed the entrance to a cave and he looked back at the house: it was so close that he could see George at the window of the bathroom lathering his face. Soon the bell would be going for breakfast and they would be sitting opposite each other exchanging the morning small talk. There was a good train back to London at 10.25. He supposed that it was the effect of his disease that he was so tired – not sleepy but achingly tired as though at the end of a long journey.

After he had pushed his way a few feet through the bushes he came on the blackened remains of an oak; it had been split by lightning probably and then sawed close to the ground for logs. It could easily have been the source of his dream. He tripped on the old roots hidden in the grass, and squatting down on the ground he laid his ear close to the earth. He had an absurd desire to hear from somewhere far below the kwahk, kwahk from a roofless mouth and the deep rumbling of Javitt's voice saying, 'We are hairless, you and I,' shaking his beard at him, 'so's the hippopotamus and the elephant and the dugong – you wouldn't know, I suppose, what a dugong is. We survive the longest, the hairless ones.'

But, of course, he could hear nothing except the emptiness you hear when a telephone rings in an empty house. Something tickled his ear, and he almost hoped to find a sequin which had survived the years under the grass, but it was only an ant staggering with a load towards its tunnel.

Wilditch got to his feet. As he levered himself upright, his hand was scraped by the sharp rim of some metal object in the earth. He kicked the object free and found it was an old tin chamber-pot. It had lost all colour in the ground except that inside the handle there adhered a few flakes of yellow paint.

[3]

How long he had been sitting there with the pot between his knees he could not tell; the house was out of sight: he was as small now as he had been then – he couldn't see over the tops of the bushes, and he was back in Javitt's time. He turned the pot over and over; it was certainly not a golden po, but that proved nothing either way; a child might have mistaken it for one when it was newly painted. Had he then really dropped this in his flight – which meant that somewhere underneath him now Javitt sat on his lavatory-seat and Maria quacked beside the calor-gas . . . ? There was no certainty; perhaps years ago, when the paint was fresh, he had discovered the pot, just as he had done this day, and founded a whole afternoon-legend around it. Then why had W.W. omitted it from his story?

Wilditch shook the loose earth out of the po, and it rang on a pebble just as it had rung against the tag of his shoelace fifty years ago. He had a sense that there was a decision he had to make all over again. Curiosity was growing inside him like the cancer. Across the pond the bell rang for breakfast and he thought, 'Poor mother – she had reason to fear,' turning the tin chamber-pot on his lap.

Some other books published by Penguin
are described on the following pages.

Graham Greene

Brighton Rock

Pinkie, a boy gangster in the prewar Brighton
underworld, is a Catholic dedicated to evil and
damnation. In a dark setting of double-crossing
and razor slashes, his ambitions and hatreds
are horribly fulfilled . . . until Ida determines
to convict him of murder. But Pinkie, on the
run from her pursuing fury, becomes even
more dangerous. . . . 'A superlatively enter-
taining fictional presentation . . . there is not
one character that can, by any chance, be forgotten nor one that could be set aside as untrue
to life' – *The New York Times*. 'This is by all
means a book to read for sheer breathless excitement; but much more, it is a book to read
for its resolution about the "appalling strangeness of the mercy of God" ' – *Saturday Review*.

Graham Greene

The Power and the Glory

In one of the southern states of Mexico, during an anticlerical purge, the last priest, like a hunted hare, is on the run. Too human for heroism, too humble for martyrdom, the little worldly 'whisky priest' is nevertheless impelled toward his squalid Calvary as much by his own compassion for humanity as by the efforts of his pursuers. A baleful vulture of doom hovers over this modern crucifixion story, but above the vulture soars an eagle – the inevitability of the Church's triumph. 'A most remarkable novel, and Mr Greene proves by it that he is the finest English novelist of his generation. . . . His narrative gift is as good as Somerset Maugham's' – Sir Hugh Walpole. 'There is no better storyteller in English today, and he is one of the two or three living novelists who really count' – V. S. Pritchett.

Graham Greene

A Burnt-Out Case

Querry, a world-famous architect, is the victim
of a terrible attack of indifference; he no longer
finds meaning in art or pleasure in life. Arriving
anonymously at a Congo leper village, he is
diagnosed as the mental equivalent of a 'burnt-
out case,' a leper who has gone through a stage
of mutilation. As Querry loses himself in work
for the lepers, however, his disease of mind
slowly approaches a cure. Then the white com-
munity finds out who Querry is. . . . 'The most
bizarre of Graham Greene's works and one of
the most memorable . . . *A Burnt-Out Case* is
an absorbing book and a curiously affecting
one. The spells of a major novelist take possession of the reader' – *The Atlantic Monthly*.
'Graham Greene has written another of his
serious, searching novels . . . perhaps the finest
ever to come from his pen. . . . It examines,
brilliantly and unflinchingly, a fundamental
problem which, whether we care to admit it or
not, confronts every thinking person' – John
Barkham, *Saturday Review* Syndicate.

Graham Greene

The Quiet American

A study of New World hope and innocence, this novel is set in an old world of violence. The scene is Saigon in the violent recent years when the French were desperately trying to hold their footing in the Far East. The principal characters are a skeptical British journalist, his attractive Vietnamese mistress, and an eager young American sent out by Washington on a mysterious mission. 'He is . . . conceded to be . . . one of the great men of modern English literature, a grave and extraordinary artist, surely one of the most compelling novelists of the time. . . . Greene is a superb storyteller. He evokes the most actual streets, the most vivid skies, and individuals who can have a lacerating reality as they search the labyrinth of their lives' – *Newsweek*. 'Once rated as a spinner of superior thrillers . . . he is now seriously discussed as possibly "the finest writer of his generation." No other writer in England enjoys Greene's combination of popular and critical success' – *Time*.

Graham Greene

The Comedians

Like one of its predecessors, *The Quiet American*, *The Comedians* is a story about the committed and the uncommitted. The Negro, Doctor Magiot, is committed. His last letter to Brown, who tells the story, is a statement and an appeal by the committed – by a man who has by his nature to share the terrible events of his time. But the Comedians have opted out. They play their parts – respectable or shady – in the foreground; they experience love affairs rather than love; they have enthusiasms – like Mr Smith for his vegetarian centre – but not a faith; and if they die, they die, like Jones, by accident.

OTHER GRAHAM GREENE TITLES
AVAILABLE FROM PENGUIN BOOKS

The End of the Affair
The Heart of the Matter
It's a Battlefield
Journey without Maps
Lord Rochester's Monkey
Our Man in Havana
The Portable Graham Greene
Travels with My Aunt